The Housewife

The Housewife

Alex Kane

hera

First published in the United Kingdom in 2021 by

Hera Books
28b Cricketfield Road
London, E5 8NS
United Kingdom

A CIP catalogue record for this book is available from the British Library.

Print ISBN 978 1 80032 514 2
Ebook ISBN 978 1 912973 36 1

Look for more great books at www.herabooks.com

Printed and bound in Great Britain by Clays Ltd, Elcograf S.p.A.

I

For my Grampa, who never got to see me become a writer. He'd have read every word if he was here, and I'd have been blushing in the corner ☺

For my Dad. This book is released on your 65th birthday. Happy birthday ☺

Prologue

The ground was cold. The soil wet. The hole deep. Scrambling, she managed to get to her feet and she ran faster than she thought her legs could carry her. But now she was on the ground, a blunt force shunting her forward. He spun her around and she was facing upwards.

Her sight was blurry, her head throbbing, but she could see the sky by peering through the tops of the trees as she was pulled by the feet back towards her own grave. She'd almost got away, almost made it to safety but he was too quick for her. He was determined to make her pay.

She was falling now, into a black hole. Soil and thick clumps of dirt were beginning to pile on top of her. Blinking away tears and dirt that scratched her eyes, the woman tried to open her mouth to speak, to plead with her killer not to do this.

As the dirt piled on heavy, weighing her down, the darkness began to creep in.

One

He questioned how he would do it. A knife to the throat?
A bullet through the skull? Those were the two methods
he preferred and the way the hard men of Glasgow put
their rivals in the ground. But which would be the best
and most *enjoyable* way to kill Frankie Conway?

Terry Reid, Glasgow's most notorious gangster asked
himself that very question on the morning he chose the
second option and shot Frankie Conway, his drug dealing
rival. But drugs weren't the reason Terry put a bullet
through Frankie's skull. Of course he'd been thinking
about ending the fucker for a long time, but he'd been
presented with evidence that had given him the perfect
excuse to finally go through with it.

Richie Jackson, Terry's right hand man and business
partner, had been in the driving seat of the car, waiting
for Terry to give the go ahead. Once they'd finally tracked
Frankie down, it was game on.

The sun shone and the air was particularly warm in
Glasgow that early spring Sunday morning. Frankie had
been walking past the park in Govanhill when Richie
drew up. But Frankie wasn't alone, he was with one
of his so-called bodyguards. A man like Frankie needed
a babysitter. He was one for pissing off too many of
Glasgow's businessmen and it was only a matter of time
before someone took him out.

Turning in response to the approaching car, Frankie Conway had looked Terry Reid in the eye as he shot him three times in the head. He'd gone down fast, landing in a pool of his own blood, before Terry turned the gun on Frankie's guard and shot him too. It was nothing personal against the guy, just business. He had to take out the witness. It was then that Richie sped off. It was early enough that no one else was around. Even if they were, Frankie Conway was the type of lowlife people wouldn't miss in the area. And Terry Reid was the type that no one would speak against, so he was confident that there would be no connection.

'The bastard deserved everything he got,' Richie said as he drove through the Clyde Tunnel, back on to their side of Glasgow. Their own home territory. 'The shit he got away with over the years. I heard a guy owed him money for a bit of coke and he couldn't pay, so he smashed him over the head with a bat and removed his eye. The guy was found days later on the disused railway with his eye in his jacket pocket. And that's just a recent story. Frankie Conway was a *fucking* nut job.'

'Aye well he's paid the price now, I wasn't having him going around telling stories about Kora and making me look like a fucking idiot.'

'Ha,' Richie laughed. 'What the fuck was Kora thinking being anywhere near him?'

'No idea, mate.' Terry said, wondering the same thing. He'd seen the camera footage of the night in question. How she thought she would get away with it was ridiculous. What is it they say? Never shit on your own doorstep? That was what Kora had done, getting involved with Conway on Terry's property when he was out of the country.

3

Terry was quiet now, thinking about how he was going to approach the subject with Kora. It had been rumours initially, and that was bad enough. But now that Terry had hard evidence that Frankie and Kora had been at it behind his back, there was only one outcome.

'What you going to say to her?' Richie asked as he pulled into Terry's drive.

'I dunno, mate.'

'Just... Just stay calm, eh? I know what you can get like.'

Terry raised a brow. He hadn't told Richie about the club CCTV images, or the fact that the staff on the night were quick to tell Terry what they'd seen. He knew what Kora was like and given that she was married when Terry had met her, he shouldn't have been surprised when he saw his missus pressed up against a wall in his club with Frankie at her back. If anything, he was impressed by the sheer audacity and blatant disregard for the fact that they would get caught eventually.

'I'll see you later on, eh?' Terry said as he got out the car.

'Terry, just don't do anything stupid, eh? I don't want a trip to that pig farm doon Helensburgh way, we've enough to deal with.' Richie smiled sarcastically at him before Terry closed the door.

Govanhill would be swarming with police now, Terry thought as he walked through the front door of his home, and into the path of his fiancée, Kora Anderson. As she laid a kiss on his mouth like she always did when he arrived home, it was all he could do not to knock her head off her shoulders. But that wouldn't get him answers. Not that he expected Kora to tell the truth. It seemed she wasn't capable. Terry remembered when he was the other man and how complicated things had become when Kora left her husband. Normally, Terry couldn't be bothered with baggage, but he had fallen hard and fast for Kora. It had always been his way. Always.

Kora Anderson had it all with Terry. A fancy big house with a pool. All the designer bags and shoes a woman could hope for. No need to go out and be a slave to the monthly wage like she had with her previous husband. He wished Richie had been right. Why would Kora go near someone like Conway when she had Terry at home? But she had. And it was killing Terry to think of Kora like that.

'You seem tense. Can I do anything to help?' Kora suggested, allowing her silk dressing gown to slip off her shoulders, baring smooth, tanned skin. He allowed her lips to run over his neck. She knew what she was doing, keeping him on side. But it felt good. That was what Kora was good at, making men feel good about themselves. Shame she felt the need to be that way with Frankie.

As she kissed him and ran her hand down to his crotch, Terry reached for the whisky bottle on the counter and opened it. Kora didn't seem to notice.

Terry gulped back two large mouthfuls before tucking his finger under her chin, lifting Kora's face to meet his.

'I never asked you how your girls' night out went. A good night, was it?' he said, his lips millimetres from hers. He could taste her, feel her heart beating against him. He loved her. He hated her, the betrayal she committed on the edge of his tongue.

'Yeah, it was a laugh. Nothing like being at home with you though,' she replied, unzipping his trousers. Terry closed his eyes and wanted to let go, wanted to forget what he saw on that footage. The last time she was this intimate with someone, it was Frankie.

'Is that right?' He looked deep into her eyes and could see his reflection in them. He wanted her, but not like this. He wasn't the idiot she thought he was and she certainly couldn't fool him into bed so he would believe that she was an innocent, well-behaved little fiancée. He knew fine well she was the very opposite of that.

'Yes, and you know I was thinking we could go out and start looking at wedding venues next week? There's this beautiful place in...' Her words trailed off as Terry took hold of her wrists just as her hand reached inside his trousers. 'Ouch, Terry what the hell are you doing?' she cried out as she tried to pull away.

'What, you don't like it rough? Surely you must if you were able to open your legs for that bastard Conway.' Terry's voice boomed, bouncing off the walls surrounding them.

Kora's eyes filled with terror as they bored into Terry's. 'What the fuck is that supposed to mean?'

Letting go of her wrist, Terry turned his back to her and gulped from the bottle again. The hairs on the back of his neck stood on end as he thought about what Richie had told him just a week earlier.

I've heard around that Kora slept with Frankie Conway. He's been boasting about it around the clubs, has said that she mustn't be getting a lot from big Tezza or she wouldn't have opened her legs to him. He needs bringing down a peg or two, Terry. He's saying it happened in one of your clubs.

'It means, Frankie has had a lot to say about you and I want to hear it from your end, Kora. And don't fucking bullshit me, I'm not in the mood to be lied to.'

Kora straightened her back and her expression turned cold. From the look he saw on her face, Terry didn't know what was going to come out of her mouth next.

'Right, I didn't want to tell you because I knew you'd go off your nut. But I was out with the girls a few weeks ago. It was a Thursday to Sunday session, you know how it is. You were down south securing that deal for Reid Construction. It's not like I didn't tell you I was out when you phoned.' Kora stopped, as if expecting Terry to have something to say. When he didn't say anything, she continued.

'We went to a couple of your clubs. We were drinking, had a couple of lines. You know what it's like when us girls get going. Then Frankie appeared out of nowhere. He was trying it on with me but I kept knocking him back. He was trying it on with all of us, buying rounds of drinks and that.'

It was amazing how good a liar Kora was, but then he couldn't expect anything less of her considering how they got together themselves. They'd met in a bar in the city centre. She'd been on a night out with the girls. Kora had fluttered her eyes at him from across the room and Terry felt a stir within that he'd never felt for anyone before. He saw the wedding band on her finger but bought her a drink anyway. By the end of the night she was back at his and they'd had sex in almost every room. It wasn't long after that she left her husband. Kora was like a drug to Terry, something he couldn't live without. But like most drugs, the high wears off and soon becomes a bad habit. He should have known she would do this. Slamming his hand on the counter, Terry stared deeply at Kora. She didn't blink, held his gaze. He'd had enough.

'Kora.' Terry took a steadying breath. 'Why was Frankie Conway going around telling people he shagged you in one of my clubs?' Terry bellowed and Kora jumped. 'Don't stand there and fucking *lie* to me. You think I haven't seen the camera footage of you? Skirt up your arse, tits hanging out?'

Kora shook her head and sneered. 'Don't you bloody dare insinuate that I wanted him to be all over me.'

'I don't have to insinuate anything Kora, it's there in black and fucking white. You shagged him, didn't you? In my club. He had you up against the wall at the door next to the stock room and you were fucking loving it!'

Kora turned her back on Terry and for a moment he felt like he couldn't breathe. How could she do this? Why would she think Frankie Conway was a better option? He was a nobody, a street boy who wanted to play with the gangsters. Thanks to Kora, he'd ended up with a bullet in his head.

'Terry,' Kora started, her voice meek. 'You're never here.'

'How stupid are you, Kora? To do that on my property. It's like you wanted to get fucking caught,' Terry said, gripping the edge of the sink until his knuckles were white. 'Or is that how you like it? The thrill of knowing that I would find out at some point. Is that what it was like at the start with us? Did you want your husband to catch us? Do you get off on that?'

Kora didn't respond. What else was there for her to say? Terry knew right away that she had ruined everything that he'd had to offer her.

A few moments of silence passed before Kora said, 'I don't know what I was thinking.'

A white-hot blinding light fell across Terry's vision as he pushed himself off the sink and flew at Kora. Gripping her by the throat, he crushed so hard he thought his fingers might pierce her skin. Her eyes bulged from her head as she tried to fight him.

Kora pulled at Terry's fingers as she fought for breath. He couldn't look at her, not while he was squeezing every breath out of her body. She deserved this as much as Frankie did. They could both rot in hell for all Terry cared. He wasn't one to be made a fool of. Not a chance.

'You did this, Kora. Not me, you.'

A few seconds later, Terry let go and Kora dropped to the floor. Stepping away from her, he pulled out his phone and called Richie but just as the phone rang at the end of the line, Richie stepped into the hallway and stared down at Kora's body.

'Jesus, Terry. What the fuck?'

'Mate, I need you to take care of something for me,' Terry said.

'I thought I told you not to do anything stupid?' Richie said, glaring up at Terry.

'Aye well, things didn't quite pan out like that. I need you to get rid of her. Can you do that?'

Blowing air out from his mouth, Richie ran a hand over the top of his head. 'Consider it done,' Richie replied, placing a hand on Terry's shoulder. 'But did it really have to come to this?'

'I don't want your opinion. Just do this for me, please.'

Terry stepped over Kora's body and headed straight for his club. He needed to get away. It was one thing to kill his fiancée. It was another to dispose of her. That was why he had a team.

Slouched on the office chair in his casino and club, Terry Reid replayed the footage of Kora and Frankie over and over. It had happened right outside the stock room and it made him feel sick to think that not only had Kora done this to him, but that Frankie Conway had laughed about it with his street player mates.

Swigging back on the whisky bottle, and having had enough of watching the betrayal committed by his fiancée, he hit the delete button on the system. There was no way he was going to allow anyone to say he'd had motive for what happened to Kora. None at all.

The door to the office opened and Richie Jackson appeared, concern etched in his expression. 'You a'right?'

'Fucking dandy, mate,' Terry replied, taking another drink. 'Job done?'

'Aye, she's well and truly hidden. You've nothing to worry about, mate. It's all sorted. I'm surprised to see you here though.'

Terry readjusted his position on the chair, almost losing his balance as it spun under his weight. 'Didn't know where else to go. I mean, where do you go after you've murdered your cheating bitch of a fiancée? And I was deleting that fucking shit.' He nodded at the screen.

'You've actually watched it?' Richie asked, entering the office and perching himself on the edge of the desk.

'Aye, not without difficulty. It's one thing to know your missus slept with one of your rivals, but to have it on tape and actually see it happen is something else entirely,' Terry replied, slamming the bottle of malt on the desk as he got to his feet.

'When you asked her, before… you know, what did she say?'

'She admitted it but put the blame on me, saying I was never home.'

'Fuck.' Richie exhaled. 'I didn't think you'd do what you did, mate. Was killing that scumbag Frankie not enough?'

Terry moved towards the door, hovered there for a moment. Richie Jackson had been his best mate for years, even when they were just street players themselves from the old Mainhill Estate. But he didn't like being questioned on decisions he made or what he'd done, even by Richie. He thought about how he'd wrapped his fingers around Kora's neck and strangled her; seeing the light leave her eyes was bad enough, but having his best mate dig him up about it made it worse.

'You're supposed to be on my side,' Terry sneered.

'Of course I'm on your side, that's why I'm asking. We don't want a higher body count than necessary, that's all.'

Terry shook his head. 'Then she shouldn't have wronged me, Richie. Fuck me over and you pay for it. You know who I am and how I work. If you don't like it…'

'I didn't say I didn't like it. I'm just thinking what's best for you. You don't tend to get stressed and I don't want this to affect your head.' Richie's concerned expression grew.

Terry knew his mate meant well, of course he did. He'd gotten rid of the body, sorted Frankie out with him. He helped run the organisation with him. There wasn't a bad or negative bone in Richie's body in relation to Terry or the work he did, the decisions he made.

'I know you don't. And it won't. Kora was dead to me the moment I found out what she'd been up to. Now she really is and I can get on with things. Speaking of getting on with things, I'm going to head home. It's been a bit of a shitty day. Need to get my head down.'

'Need me to drive you home?' Richie asked. Terry could tell by the look on his face that he was worried. But he needn't be. Terry had committed far worse crimes over the years than kill his fiancée for shagging someone else. He was Terry *fucking* Reid and it would take a lot more than a slag like Kora Anderson to bring him down.

Two

Glancing down at the little stick she held in her hand, Maisie Whitelaw held in her sobs as it confirmed what she'd dreaded. She was pregnant. She'd just turned sixteen the previous day and Maisie knew that her life was over. Not that it had ever begun. No one had a life if they were brought up in Mainhill Estate. The place was like hell on earth. If you were born into it, there was no getting out.

Wrapping the stick in some tissue, Maisie flushed the toilet and shoved the test into the pocket of her jeans. What was she going to do now? She couldn't tell her mum for two reasons. One, she'd probably slap her but only if she was sober. She was a callous, cold bitch was Rosie Whitelaw. Or two, she'd be too off her face to even comprehend that Maisie was standing in front of her.

And she couldn't very well tell the dad. He wouldn't be interested. All he'd wanted from Maisie was sex. He'd made that clear from the beginning, six months earlier. He was older than her by four years and a friend of her brother, Freddie's. How would Freddie react to the news when he didn't even know she'd been sleeping with Galzo in the first place?

Taking a deep breath, Maisie Whitelaw stepped out of the bathroom and into the hallway. The house she shared with her parents and two brothers was disgusting. She'd hated it from the moment she could understand it. Dark, damp and dingy. All Rosie and Maisie's dad, Cammy, cared about was where the next bag or can was coming from. Not that Maisie was any better. She'd dabbled in all sorts as soon as she'd started seeing Galzo six months ago. She would have done anything to keep him close, and she did. She slept with him just days into meeting him. *Silly little girl*, she thought. *Now look what's happened.*

She'd started off smoking a bit of weed. She'd even done that when she was younger, before she'd met Galzo. It wasn't hard to get hold of the stuff when it was lying around the house all the time. Then she'd gone on to smoking it all the time, along with normal cigarettes.

Then one night at a party in one of the flats on the estate, she and Galzo had been in one of the bedrooms and he'd offered her a pill. He'd made it sound exciting, like it would be the best ride of her life. Maisie didn't even know what it was and didn't bother to ask. All she cared about was the fact that Galzo was spending time on her. So she'd taken it. The trip was horrible, she felt like she was constantly falling from a great height and the paranoia she'd been left with the next day was awful.

It was five months ago that she'd tried heroin for the first time. She'd loved it, it was far better than the pill she'd taken. And now, she was on the methadone program because her brother Lee had pretty much dragged her to the GP to get her help. Maisie was shocked at how quickly she'd become addicted.

Lee Whitelaw had grilled her on who had given her the drugs, but she'd refused to tell him. All she'd said was it had been a guy she was seeing but there was no way she would tell Lee it was Galzo. He'd kill him if he knew.

Thankfully, he'd backed off. But Lee had been keeping an eye on her ever since. Now, she was pregnant and trying to stay clean. What kind of life would that be for a baby to be born into? No, she'd have to get rid of it. There was no other choice, but the thought of going through that process terrified her more than the prospect of becoming a mother at sixteen.

'You a'right there, Maze? You look like shit,' her dad said as she passed him on her way to the front door.

'Aye, cheers for that one Da.'

Slamming the door behind her, Maisie walked down the stairs and over to the centre of the estate. And there he was, the love of her life. With his arm around another girl, one of her so called mates, Galzo glanced across at her. She went to smile but before she could, he turned away from Maisie and planted a kiss on the girl's lips right in front of her. Maisie's heart lurched in her chest. There was no way she could keep this baby. Looking down at it every day would remind her of her shitty relationship with Galzo, if she could even call it a relationship. He'd never been the type of guy to stick to one girl and Maisie had been stupid enough to believe that she could be the one to change him.

Maisie made her way along the street, away from the display of affection between Galzo and her so called mate and she bit down on her lip as she tried not to cry. The growing lump in her throat ached and when she saw her big brother Lee walking towards her, the tears came in waves.

'What's wrong?' Lee said as she almost collapsed into his arms.

Lee, her older brother by six years, was the one who'd cared for her the most when she'd been little, because Rosie and Cammy were too busy taking drugs and drinking their way through her childhood. She trusted him the most out of everyone in her life.

Lee would know what to do in this situation. He was the only smart one of the family, the one who had managed to keep them all fed and with a roof over their heads.

'I'm pregnant.'

The look on his face made her feel shame and disgust at her own actions. How could she have been so stupid? Lee was angry with her but that wouldn't last forever. He'd want to break the legs of the guy who'd got her into this situation in the first place.

'Maisie, how could you be so bloody stupid?'

She let out a sob and Lee sighed as he pulled her close. 'I'm sorry, I didn't mean that. Do you know who the dad is?'

'Of course I do. What the hell do you take me for, Lee? I might be stupid but I'm no slapper.'

'You need to tell me who the dad is, Maze. He needs to know, he has a responsibility.'

Pulling away from her brother, Maisie looked back at where Galzo had been standing. If she told Lee, she'd be responsible for ultimately causing Galzo's death, because Lee would kill him when he found out. Shaking her head, she faced her brother.

'If I tell you, you have to promise to stay calm, and keep this to yourself. Because it could cause a war if it got out.'

Lee stared down at Maisie and suddenly she felt sick. As she explained everything, she hoped that he wouldn't betray her trust and expose Galzo. The truth of the matter was, she was underage when she'd started seeing him. No one liked that kind of thing around Mainhill. But it had

16

been her choice. She'd loved him from that first night and her feelings had only grown stronger.

'If you lose your shit, Lee, you'll only be hurting me,' Maisie said at the end.

'You were fifteen when you started seeing him. That makes him a fucking pervert, Maze. And he's taking the piss because he's mates with Freddie. How the hell did you manage to get involved with someone like him?'

'Lee, I ask myself that every day. But I love him.'

'You love him but you don't want him to know you're carrying his baby? Sounds like a perfect relationship to me.'

Maisie wiped at the tears that were dripping from her nose. 'Don't be angry with me,' she said. 'I didn't plan for this. I was concentrating on getting better. The meth program was working. I had no idea I was even pregnant.'

Maisie knew that wasn't strictly true. She'd missed three periods in a row but she was too terrified to take a test. It wasn't until she'd noticed how she was struggling to do up her jeans that she'd decided to find out for sure. No one in the house had seemed to notice. And why would they when they were on another planet half the time?

'What are you going to do?' Lee asked.

'I've no idea,' Maisie replied.

It was true. She knew keeping the baby wasn't a good solution. But now that she knew Galzo's baby was growing inside her, it meant that she would always have a piece of him. Glancing back down the street, Maisie blinked away tears as she watched Galzo get into his truck and drive out of the estate.

Three

Six months later

Lee and Freddie Whitelaw stepped into the shop with caution and glanced over at the man behind the counter. It seemed there was no one else inside. Just the three of them. Lee almost felt guilty. Almost. But Freddie had fucked up and they needed quick cash. The blade up Lee Whitelaw's sleeve was cool against his arm. Beads of sweat formed on his brow and the back of his neck. He watched as Freddie pulled his balaclava down over his face and moved towards the counter.

Lee waited, as planned. If Freddie couldn't get what he needed, that was when Lee would step in. He didn't want to use a blade, didn't even want to threaten the man with it. He wasn't like Freddie. He wasn't as scummy as the rest of the family. Or the rest of the people on the estate. But he wasn't going to stand back and watch his brother make an arse of the situation if he didn't have to.

'Right, open the till and give me what's inside,' Lee heard Freddie say. He sounded surprisingly calm but it didn't last long when the man resisted.

'I said open the till, you fucking idiot, or I'll fucking cut you.' The words threw Lee into action and he too pulled his own balaclava over his face and moved towards the counter.

As he approached, he saw terror in the man's eyes. Lee couldn't help but wonder why he would ever choose to do a shift in a shop in the middle of Mainhill on his own, knowing what the place and the people were like.

'Do as he said,' Lee warned, allowing the blade to slide out from its hiding place. Holding it outright at the shop-keeper, Lee felt nausea setting in. He kept hoping for the man to spring into action and hand over the money in the till. He didn't want to have to slice the man open, it would bring more aggravation than they needed right now. It was bad enough the situation they were in. Murder or attempted murder was not on the cards.

The man calmly pressed a button to release the till drawer and then stood back. 'Help yourselves.'

Lee frowned under his balaclava as Freddie leapt across the counter and started filling the bag with the cash from inside.

Lee kept the blade up, pointed at the shopkeeper. 'Hurry the fuck up, would you?'

'Got it,' Freddie replied, sliding himself back across and onto the shop floor. As they made their way out quickly, Freddie pulled down one of the stands and a selection of sweets and newspapers fell on to the floor.

'Ha, fuck you, ya bastard!' Freddie shouted as he waved the bag of stolen cash in the air. Lee pulled him onto the street and they ran down the hill towards the centre of the estate where they lived.

Lee still had the blade in his hand as they rushed along the pavement, then weaved in and out of the derelict garages which stood behind the row of council flats. A group of drunk teenagers cheered them on, waving bottles of Buckfast in the air and jumping around excitedly.

Lee ignored them and kept moving towards the centre of the estate, the most notorious part of Mainhill. Freddie on the other hand, swung the bag of cash above his head and laughed along with them. If Lee wanted to plug anyone right now, it would be his brother. It was as if Freddie wanted them to get caught. He wasn't thinking of the bigger picture at all and that was dangerous for not just Lee and Freddie, but for the whole family.

Approaching the stairs which led to the council house they shared with the rest of the Whitelaws, Lee and Freddie took them two at a time. Freddie was inside first, hunched over and sucking in great lungfuls of air and laughing at the same time.

'Quick, shut the fucking door,' Freddie hissed at Lee, pulling off the balaclava and revealing his acne-scarred face.

'Do you think we're good?' Lee said as he locked the door, trying not to show his frustration.

Freddie peered out of the side window and down the stairs towards the street, his chest heaving as he gulped in air.

'Aye, we're good. D'ya think anyone would be stupid enough to come after us knowing you had a blade on you?' Freddie moved away from the window and leaned over, placing his hands on his knees as he tried to catch his breath. Lee stared at Freddie before sliding down the wall. He sat down on the floor behind the front door and removed his own balaclava before wiping the back of his hand over his forehead. Beads of sweat trickled down his face as he too tried to catch his breath.

'Are you no' right in the heed or something?' Lee said, jabbing a finger at Freddie, still holding the blade in his other hand. 'What the fuck was that all about, swinging the bag at those wee fuckers down on the street? Do you want us to get fucking caught?'

'Oi, we live in Mainhill. It's no' like they'll grass on us, is it? That group down there want to be like us, Lee. Stop yer bloody whinging,' Freddie mocked.

Lee removed his balaclava, took another breath and considered what Freddie had said. He was right, as much as it annoyed Lee. Those boys down there would eventually grow into becoming just like Lee and Freddie. A vicious circle of living in Mainhill.

'How much did we manage to get?' Lee asked.

'I dunno, Lee. I didn't exactly stop to fucking count while you held a blade up to him,' Freddie replied, as he dropped the bag to the floor and opened it. 'Bastard thought he was getting sliced open, did ye see his face? Priceless.'

Lee Whitelaw hid his disgust at how much Freddie enjoyed other people's misery. That was where they differed considerably. He leaned forward as Freddie emptied the contents of the bag on to the floor. They'd managed to pull the entire contents of the shop till in their heist. Lee's eyes widened as Freddie counted out the cash.

'Three hundred and seventy-two quid,' Freddie smiled. 'That should keep us going for a while, eh bro?' He nudged Lee with his shoulder and a grin spread across his face.

'Nah, that's going straight to the debt we owe,' Lee replied. As much as Lee liked a smoke and a line every now and then, he was nowhere near as bad as his brother. If Freddie wasn't careful, he'd be on the heavier shit soon enough. No matter how bad things got, Lee always promised himself he'd stay clear of that stuff. Once was enough to get you hooked.

'Fuck the debt, Lee,' Freddie sneered as he began to shove the cash back into the bag.

Lee shook his head and got to his feet along with Freddie, and they moved through the hall towards the kitchen where their mum was standing at the counter with a mug in her hand, looking a little worse for wear. *Barely* standing, Lee thought as he stared at the woman who called herself a mum. She was half swaying, half leaning against the worktop.

The kitchen was dark and dingy. Nicotine-stained wallpaper hung off the walls in tears and strips, and the blind on the window barely held on with one screw. A cloud of smoke floated above their heads, clinging to the pulley dangling above their head. Not that there was clean laundry hanging on it. There were never clean clothes, or bed sheets. They were lucky to have both of those things at all, never mind clean ones. That wasn't one of Rosie's priorities. Heroin, booze and cigarettes were the things that drove her, and even then she could barely get out of bed to source those things. That was a job for Lee and Freddie.

'A'right boys?' Rosie Whitelaw slurred, her eyes almost rolling to the back of her head.

Lee Whitelaw shook his head. He knew her claims of getting clean were bullshit. He'd heard it his whole life and had stopped hoping a long time ago. 'Nice to see you sober for once, Maw.'

Freddie shot Lee a look. He didn't want Rosie to clock the bag of cash they had on them, she would only spend it all on herself.

'What you doing?' she asked, her eyes now almost completely shut. Her speech was slow, barely audible. She hadn't even heard Lee's dig.

'Nothing, Maw,' Freddie replied.

Rosie Whitelaw would have been a looker back in her day if she hadn't allowed the drugs to get a grip of her. Lee knew that Freddie would eventually become the same thing. Nothing but a junkie. That was exactly what Lee didn't want to become. Having grown up around that kind of lifestyle and seeing what it had done to his parents had made him determined to get away from Mainhill and live some kind of normality.

Freddie gestured towards the hallway and Lee made a move upstairs. Freddie was right to want the money out of Rosie's way. But they would have to be careful. Their old man was upstairs and if he saw the money, he too would likely nick it and spend it on himself. Drugs of course, just like Rosie. It was a wonder they weren't dead already. In fact, Lee often wondered if it wasn't the drugs that were keeping them alive. Without them, they'd probably die from withdrawal.

Freddie went inside his bedroom and Lee followed. This was the only room in the house which possessed carpet. Not that it was luxurious by any means. It didn't even fit the space properly and was littered with stains from over the years. Taking socks and shoes off wasn't an option. The rest of the floors in the council house were covered in flattened cardboard boxes.

Growing up in the Mainhill estate, Freddie and Lee had come to learn that most of the families who lived there were the same as them. Druggies for parents (although the Whitelaws seemed to be the only family left with a full set), cardboard boxes acting as carpets; boarded up windows and overgrown grass surrounding the council houses and flats were the defining features of the Mainhill estate. It wasn't unusual to see kids aged around ten smoking and drinking in the street now that Freddie and Lee were older. It seemed as time went on, Mainhill got worse. And if you didn't live in Mainhill, you didn't venture in. Except for the dealers who made a living off other people's misery and addictions.

Just as Lee was about to close the bedroom door, he stopped and listened. Cammy Whitelaw was snoring like a bull.

'Don't wake Da,' Freddie whispered. Lee closed the door quietly and slid the bolt across to secure it. 'He'll only pocket the cash when our back is turned.'

Turning, Freddie was already emptying the bag onto the bed again. Three hundred and seventy-two quid was a lot of money for people like the Whitelaws. It would mean some food and most of all, drugs. But Lee knew that this money had to go to debt. Without question.

A mobile phone started ringing in Freddie's pocket and he pulled it out. By the look on his face, Lee knew who was calling his brother.

'It's them.' Freddie glared at the phone and then at Lee.

Lee held out his hand and Freddie gave him the phone. 'Let me deal with this, Fred. No offence but you're not the brightest of sparks. You'll end up in deeper shit if you try to fix this.'

'Don't answer it,' Freddie said.

'Freddie, Terry Reid isn't fucking stupid. He knows where you live. If we keep ignoring him, he'll just send some of his heavies round. D'ya wanna end up at the bottom of the fucking canal, mate? Coz you know that's what will happen if you don't pay up.'

Freddie sighed heavily. 'We owe them three hundred. That won't leave nearly enough for what we need. Yer as well giving them the fucking lot.'

'First of all, *we* don't owe him anything. This is all down to you. But I'm not going to let you get killed for a couple hundred quid,' Lee said. His thumb hovered over the answer button and he hit it before even he changed his mind.

'Hello?'

Freddie stared at Lee with bundles of notes between his fingers.

'Aye, Richie, nae bother mate. Got it ready and waiting… Aye, right. We'll meet you outside in half an hour.'

Lee knew it was bad when Richie Jackson had said he was coming to get the money himself. He and Terry weren't ones for coming into Mainhill themselves unless they absolutely had to. Lee worried that this could mean the worst.

'Shit!' Freddie exclaimed. 'Well *fucking* done, bro. You've just lost us a good few gram of coke right there.'

Shoving Freddie's phone into his pocket, he ignored his brother and reached for the cash. Counting out the amount they owed to the Reids, Lee opened the bedroom door and headed for the front door. This day was going from bad to worse.

'Oi, Lee ya fucking prick,' Freddie called after Lee, who was ignoring him as he reached the front door.

'What the fuck's all the racket?' Cammy Whitelaw shouted from the bedroom upstairs.

Lee was outside and moved down the concrete steps to the street. He eyed the kids across the street, playing loudly outside the council flats. Women stood in their verandas, smoking and chatting to one another and the group of young teenagers who Freddie had shown off to still stood on the corner of the circle where the Whitelaws lived, drinking bottles of cheap cider.

Lee knew that as soon as Terry Reid's men drew up, everyone would either scarper or the estate would fall silent.

Standing at the bottom of the stairs, Lee waited. It was ridiculous of Freddie to think they would get away with not paying Terry what they owed him. Terry wasn't a one-man show, and he ran the entire city. It would be unlikely that Terry himself would turn up with Richie, but if Lee and Freddie didn't pay up now, then it was a possibility. He *could* walk into the estate and shoot them dead in front of everyone and not one person would say a word when the police came knocking. If the police came at all. It was the kind of place that if the police could avoid it, they would. Mainhill practically ran itself.

'Oi,' Freddie shouted from the top of the stairs. 'Are you fucking deaf?'

'Nah,' Lee replied without turning to face his brother. 'But you're a fucking idiot.'

'Mate, we could hang off for a bit longer. We could double the money we've got in that bag and then pay off our debt.'

Lee turned to Freddie who was now standing by his side looking flustered. 'And how are you going to double the money?'

'I dunno. Casino and that?'

Lee burst into laughter in Freddie's face. 'Like they'd let the likes of us into a casino,' Lee scoffed. 'And have you forgotten who owns the casinos in the city? Aye, Terry Reid. Like I said, you're a fucking idiot. Look Freddie, just leave me to sort this eh? The Reids are already gunning for you for trying to deal a bit of coke you bought off them. Yer lucky I caught that Richie lad in a good mood or you'll have ended up with two broken legs. Just fuck off now, eh? We'll sort out some more cash once I've dealt with this.'

Freddie opened his mouth to reply but thought better of it and disappeared back up the stairs towards the house.

Lee turned to face the street again when Maisie Whitelaw emerged from one of the flats. His pregnant sister was almost ready to drop and had moved into her own place just the previous day. He couldn't believe six months had passed by since she'd told him about the pregnancy. He recalled the conversation they'd had when she found out about the baby. She was certain she wasn't keeping it. But then she'd been for a scan and when she heard the baby's heart, that had done it. Maisie had sobbed, said she didn't want to go through with the termination. So, she didn't.

'How's things, sis?' Lee asked.

'Place is a fucking palace compared to that shithole up there,' Maisie said. 'But it's still a dump. Need to get some cash together and at least give it a lick of paint.'

The closer Maisie approached, the more Lee could smell weed. It didn't seem to matter that she was growing a child in her belly, it still didn't stop her. Although he had to be grateful she was at least off the heroin. Lee gave her a tight-lipped smile.

'Maybe you should be asking that prick for some cash to help you set that place up for when the baby comes,' Lee sneered, although the emotion wasn't directed at his sister.

'What you doing out here?' she asked, ignoring his jibe.

It annoyed Lee that Maisie hadn't bothered to fight Galzo on the fact that she was having his child. He'd shown zero interest in her or the pregnancy. If it hadn't been for Maisie practically pleading with Lee not to, he'd have done him in by now.

'Waiting on someone,' Lee replied, pushing Galzo's face out of his mind.

'The Reids?' she pressed. 'Freddie still owes them money?'

Lee nodded. 'Aye, so you best do one. Don't want you here when they turn up. Bad enough I'm having to involve myself because Fred couldn't finish something he started, I don't want you around when they get here.'

Maisie barely acknowledged the concern in her brother's tone, instead she continued walking and headed up to the house. 'Maw and Da in?'

'Aye, although you'll not get much sense oot Maw, she's off her face again.'

Maisie sighed. 'Granny of the fucking year award, coming up.'

Lee closed his eyes and shifted his stance from one foot to the other, patting the lump of cash in his back pocket. The nerves were making his stomach lurch.

The blade he'd used to threaten the shopkeeper earlier was still up his sleeve, so at least he had some way of defending himself if things got ugly. Lee hoped it wouldn't come to that. That was the last thing the Whitelaws needed, Lee slashing a bloody gangster.

Around twenty minutes had passed when Lee heard the sound of a car turning into Mainhill. It didn't sound like the rickety pieces of shite he was used to hearing in the estate. There was a softer purr to the engine. A newer machine.

28

Looking up, Lee saw the pristine Range Rover. Brand new. Tinted windows, blinding shine. The vehicle's approach made Lee feel sick…

The Range pulled up next to Lee and the back, driver-side door opened. 'Where's Freddie?' Richie Jackson asked. Lee stared into the car and felt his stomach drop at the sight of Terry Reid.

'He's away for a few days,' Lee lied. 'I said I'd take care of his debt.'

'Oh did you now? That wasn't your call to make,' Terry replied from inside without making eye contact with Lee.

'Get in,' Richie said.

Trying not to tremble with fear, Lee felt the blade of the knife up his sleeve nip his flesh as he climbed into the back of the car.

Terry wasn't driving. He was in the passenger seat. Richie took them out of Mainhill, through the centre of town and out to the town's substation grounds. Lee knew this wasn't a good thing. Terry Reid was clearly angry that payment was late.

'How ye doing, young Lee? Things going well?' Terry said, sounding abnormally cheerful.

'Erm, aye. Good Terry.'

The Range stopped in the staff carpark outside the substation. It was empty. Lee knew he was in trouble.

Terry turned to face Lee as Richie got out of the car. 'Good, ye say? Word has it you just knocked the till from your local newsagent's. One of our properties. A lot of takings, were there?'

Shit, shit, shit. Freddie and his bright fucking ideas.

'Got anything to say about that, Lee?'

'Terry…'

'Mr Reid, please.'

'Mr Reid, I have your money right here. Three hundred. I'm sorry it's late but—'

'So you're paying me with dirty money?' Terry said just as Richie opened Lee's passenger door. 'I don't take dirty money, Lee. You should know that by now.'

Lee looked at Richie who was gesturing for him to step out of the car. Lee did what he was told without words and Terry got out of the car too.

'Mr Reid, Freddie's skint. He didn't have a choice,' Lee replied, trying to keep the desperation from his voice. 'We just wanted to pay you back.'

Terry glanced at Richie. 'You know what, Richie? The Whitelaws have absolutely scunnered me over the last few months with their excuses.'

'Aye, me too mate.'

'And now, Lee,' Terry's eyes fell upon Lee. 'Can you take a guess at what is going to happen when I take that money off you?'

Lee was silent, his eyes darting between the men in front of him. *This is it*, he thought. *I'm dead because of my brother.* Terry continued.

'I'll have to go back to Mr Stewart's shop and hand this money back to him, and give him the additional seventy-two quid that you've left at home. That shop is his livelihood, and you and your thieving rat of a brother thought you'd be able to just take what you needed. Ever heard the expression "robbing Peter to pay Paul?"'

'Mr Reid—' Lee started, but Richie is already in his face.

'Oi, shut your mouth and fucking listen.'

The blade of the knife shifted inside Lee's sleeve. He could take it out, brandish it at them as a warning. But it would be stupid of him to do that. He was in the middle of nowhere, in a substation carpark, face to face with Glasgow's biggest gangsters. He'd be dead within a second. And even if he did somehow manage to get away with doing something so stupid, he'd be on the run for the rest of his life.

No wonder the shopkeeper had been so bloody calm, Lee thought. He'd have known fine well that the Reids would sort this out.

'Once you give the money back, you're going to apologise on behalf of you and that rat you call a brother. Then you've got three days to find three hundred quid, plus seventy per cent as a late payment charge.'

Lee felt the bottom of his stomach almost fall out his arse. How the fuck was he supposed to find that amount of money? He didn't even know what seventy per cent of three hundred was off the top of his head, but he knew it was a lot more on top of what he already owed. *He?*. Freddie was to blame for this. Lee had tried to tell Freddie to pay the money back straight away but Freddie thought he was fucking invincible these days.

They'll no' come looking for me, bro. They've got bigger things to be getting on with.

Aye, killing folk like you who haven't bothered to pay what they owe, Lee had thought.

'Oi, dream boy? Is there anyone in there?' Richie shouted, knocking on Lee's head. 'Do you get where we're coming from, Lee?'

'Aye, aye I get it.'

The knife slipped down towards Lee's hand but he didn't allow the blade to reveal itself from under the sleeve of his jumper.

'Good, because I don't want to have to shoot you or that family of yours. Young Maisie, she's due her baby soon, is she not?' Terry said. Lee saw a glint in his eye and knew not to push his luck.

'I'll get your money, Terry. With the interest,' Lee replied, desperate to distract Terry from thoughts of his pregnant sister. Maisie was only sixteen. It wasn't her fault Freddie fucked up. And Lee was only doing what any brother would do for his family and trying to take control of the situation.

'In three days, mind,' Richie said.

'Aye, in three days,' Terry repeated.

Terry and Richie fell silent and Lee wondered if this was it. They were just playing a sick game with him, making him think that they were going to give him another chance to get the money.

Lee followed Terry's hands with his eyes as they moved inside his jacket. His heart banged against the wall of his chest and Lee wanted to close his eyes. He took a deep breath as Terry produced a handgun and a surge of adrenaline like electricity forced its way through Lee's body. Terry moved closer and held the gun to Lee's forehead, pressing hard into his skin.

Shit, shit, shit!

Lee stood perfectly still, like a frozen statue in the middle of the substation carpark. He felt the vibration of the electricity humming in the cables above him.

'I don't normally conduct my business like this, Lee. I don't often come out to the streets to sort out the likes of you and your family, I've got dealers for that. But I've had enough of you lot taking the fucking piss. I don't take kindly to people thinking I'll just sit back while they try to fleece me. Luckily for you, Lee, I'm in a good mood and I've got something else I need to deal with. So three days or I blow you apart, blow all of you apart. Got it?'

Lee nodded as Terry pulled the gun away and pushed it back inside his jacket. Terry and Richie backed away, an evil smile slithering across Richie's face. They got into the car and drove off, leaving him alone. The bastard gangsters.

The fear weighing in Lee's belly dispersed along with the sound of the Range in the distance. He looked out to the main road which led back to Mainhill and began walking. It would take around an hour if Lee walked at a good pace. But that was fine, because he was alive and he hadn't expected to be at this point.

'I'll fucking kill Freddie for this.'

Four

Glasgow was almost silent, illuminated by city lights and the full moon above them. As he stared up at the sky, he realised that tonight was the first night in three months that he had been able to think of Kora without picturing her with Frankie Conway. Six months without Kora. It had felt more like six years. Glancing down at his hands, remembering the last time he'd touched her, his stomach clenched as he recalled that night. How her eyes bulged from their sockets. How he squeezed so hard he thought he might break her neck as life left her body.

They'd been together for two years, engaged not long before that night. He'd thought she was the one. She had left her husband for him after all. Terry remembered wondering if he should have gotten involved with her knowing that she was married but Kora had a way about her. It was almost as though she'd cast a spell on him. Her name on his lips, her face in his mind, caused a stir inside he'd never felt before. Their relationship, the fact that he'd proposed had clearly meant nothing to her, considering what she'd done. Terry felt like an idiot. Kora had treated him the way she'd treated her previous husband. Maybe she was only interested in his money, his business. Knowing that when she married him, half would belong to her. What if he'd married her before finding out what a cheating little bitch she was? The casino and nightclub, the construction company, she would have fleeced him for half. And that would be just the start. He would have lost fifty per cent of everything he owned because he was blinded by his love for her. What an idiot he would have looked in front of Richie and his associates. Kora got everything she deserved.

The construction company was progressing quickly. Terry Reid's properties were beginning to pop up all over the place. Luxury apartments in Glasgow, town houses and business complexes were being snapped up quicker than he could have imagined and the money was coming through so fast, Terry was having to move a lot of it offshore to avoid massive tax bills. Terry had invested a lot of his money in land, with his construction company building holiday complexes around the UK and with more people doing the whole 'staycation' thing nowadays, he was raking it in from that venture too. The casino club had been his beginner business and it was his baby. He rarely had to be there to keep the place going, it ran itself. Then there were the smaller businesses, the security firms, the drug and gun running operations. No wonder Kora showed an interest so quickly. She knew fine well what she was doing, getting her hands on him meant getting her hands on his money.

Blinking away his thoughts, Terry Reid was distracted by sounds of shallow breath coming from behind. Looking in the rear-view mirror at the young lad sat in the back seat, he pushed Kora to the back of his mind.

The boy's eyes darted back and forth between Terry and Terry's right hand man, Richie Jackson, fear shining out of them. Good, Terry thought. He should be bricking it. Terry had had his fill of young lads taking the piss out of him whether it be clients or dealers. Who did they

35

think they were? He'd already let one off with a payment extension, when really he should have just done what he would normally and put him out his misery. But too many bodies were never good for business. They just gave him a headache. Being in around Mainhill and seeing it with his own eyes reminded him of how far he'd come since being a boy and living on the estate himself. The fact that it was a distraction from Kora was a bonus.

'Right, young Angus. Tell me again what happened,' Terry said, turning his focus to the river Clyde in front of them. The moon shone down and glistened on the surface of the murky water.

Angus swallowed hard; Terry heard it and shook his head.

'I don't know, I swear Terry.'

'Hmm,' Terry sighed, his brow furrowed.

'Right,' Richie said. 'So you're telling us that five grand worth of our supply just disappeared into thin air? What are you, a magician now?'

Terry glared back at Angus in the mirror. He was staring at Richie, obviously terrified by the prospect of what his future might hold after lying to his bosses.

'Now, Angus. I think we all know that's bullshit. For a start off, I don't even believe in magic, do you Richie?'

'As much as I believe in fucking Santa Claus, Terry,' Richie sneered.

'I'll give you a few scenarios as to what I think has been happening, and then you can tell me which one sound plausible? Sound good? Great. Right, scenario one.' Terry paused, cracked his knuckles and then lit a cigarette before opening the window a little. Exhaling, he said, 'You got the taste of the good life, saw the amount of money you were making and then thought to yourself that you could sell some on the side, make a few extra quid. Basically you decided to fuck me over. Bad scenario.'

'Fucked up scenario, Angus,' Richie added.

'Two. Your little girlfriend, the blonde one with the skirt up her arse, got the taste for the good life and you decided that you wanted to impress her even more, stole five grand worth of my stock over the last few months to spend more money on her just to keep your dick wet. Bad choice.'

'*Desperate* and fucked up, Angus.' Richie gave a breathy laugh.

'Three. You've been taking five grand of my stock in small doses, hoping we wouldn't notice and dishing it out to your mates at the pub and telling them, "It's a'right, the boss is sound, he'll no' fun oot."' Terry impersonated Angus's voice and Richie laughed loudly.

'Or four. All of the above rolled into one. Because all of those sound plausible to me, Angus. Don't you agree?'

Terry kept his eyes on Angus whose eyes glistened against the moonlight. Just like the river, Terry thought.

'I... I...,' Angus started.

'Got yourself a stutter, Angus?' Richie said.

Terry gestured for Richie to make his move and at that, Terry got out of the car. Inside, he watched as Richie shoved a rag inside Angus's mouth and forced him out and on to the ground.

'Thought you'd get away with it, wee lad? Thought you'd be able to make the money back through the bookies and I'd be none the fucking wiser. I'm actually pretty surprised that you didn't gamble in my casino to make your money back. It's quite clear you didn't know I had eyes on you, Angus. Which in itself is a pain in the pisser, because it seems you underestimated who you work for. But let me assure you,' Terry looked down at Angus whose eyes were now wide and filled with tears and terror. 'You've fucked me over for long enough and you will *not* get to do that to me again.'

A nod in Richie's direction led Angus to an almost standing position. The lad couldn't bear weight on his right leg since Richie had stamped on his knee upon arrival at his front door.

Terry followed as Richie dragged Angus to the edge of the dock overlooking the derelict shipyard, the lad's hands bound behind his back. He didn't fight against his fate. There would be no point. He knew what he'd done, who he'd fucked over. Too little too late, Terry thought.

'You see my problem, Angus, is I trust people too quickly. I'm a take them at their word type of fella. And for the most part I'm normally proven right. But with you, well… I don't like to be proven wrong, as you can tell.'

Richie let go of Angus and allowed him to stand at the edge, looking out at the far away lights. Traffic sounded lightly in the distance. It was almost peaceful.

Lifting the gun, Richie held it against the back of Angus's skull and a feeling of euphoria flooded Terry's veins when Angus whimpered.

Terry stepped forward and patted Richie gently on the shoulder before turning his back and heading to the car. The sound of the single gunshot muffled against the silencer, followed by Angus hitting the water below made Terry smile inside, but he kept his expression neutral as he climbed back into the driver seat of his Range. Switching on the sound system, the car was filled with the music of Khachaturian, Masquerade Suite's Nocturne. He sat back, resting his head on the back of the seat and watched as Richie slid his gun inside his coat and moved towards the car.

Richie climbed in and shut the door before turning to Terry with a raised brow. 'Really?'

'What?'

'Do we have to listen to this shit?'

'Oi, its quality music that stuff. Chills me right out after coming across a wee prick like Angus McDade.' Terry took a deep breath as he remembered switching this particular piece on after what had happened with Kora. It was the one thing that kept him calm.

Richie laughed and pulled the seatbelt around him as Terry pulled out of the dock.

'The lads down there waiting?' Terry asked.

'Aye. Body disposal team at your service, big man.' Richie rubbed his hands together.

Terry nodded as a smile crept onto his face before turning the volume up as Nocturnes faded out and Mazurka began. Richie shook his head with a smile as the Range pulled onto the main road.

Being a legit and not so legit businessman gave Terry a buzz. He would shake hands with the big wigs at the council when a sale went through on a land purchase. Planning permission was always fast tracked when Terry applied to build luxury apartment complexes because between those handshakes were big notes. No one in a suit ever said no to him and he loved that feeling.

He equally enjoyed the power that came with being the boss of little rats like Angus who sold his drugs to the everyday lad on the street. It wasn't often that his employees fucked up, but when they did that was when Terry put his power into play. You don't get away with trying to screw over the boss-man. Yes, Terry Reid was a strong and powerful businessman. His weakness however was when he opened up to someone he was falling for. When he fell, he fell hard. And when he landed, he usually took someone with him. In this instance, Kora had borne the brunt of that fall and now he was doing anything he could to keep her out of his mind. He wouldn't let his business suffer from it.

Five

The Balness Inn was packed this Friday night. Not unusual, but certainly fuller than normal. The local looked everything a rural village pub should look like. Old beer barrels for seats, wooden bar, wooden tables. Antlers mounted on the walls, black and white images of The Balness Inn from the Sixties took pride of place behind the bar. The warm glow from the cast iron chandeliers hung above the tables giving the place that Game of Thrones feel. Mostly familiar but also with some unfamiliar faces crammed inside, ready to take on the weekend and of course, everyone was pissed.

Leah Martin was stood at the bar among a long line of women, all mums from her son's class at school. Mums' night out, a monthly occurrence in the village. It was something Leah always looked forward to, something that kept her going each month.

'Right, ready?' Leah called out to the already tipsy group of women all holding their hands out, a strip of salt coated on the backs. A shot glass and a slice of lime sat on the bar top in front of each woman, including Leah. The music pumped from the speakers mounted in each corner of the wall, one of those lads from One Direction singing about watermelons. Leah could feel herself beginning to sway to the music. As much as she was old enough to be Harry Styles' mother, she thought he was handsome.

'Three, two, one, go!'

Quickly, each woman licked the salt off the back of their hand before knocking back their shot of tequila. Leah gulped it down as quickly as she could and raised the lime to her teeth, biting down as hard as she could and attempting to stop the tequila coming back on her.

'That's fucking awful,' one of the women called out as she slammed her shot glass on the bar. Funny how a couple of gins and a shot could loosen the tongues of the mostly classy women of Balness village. 'I'm going to throw up.'

'You know the rules, Kim. You chuck it up and you have to do a dare,' Leah called out, hoping that she herself wouldn't vomit all over the bar. Why did they insist on doing this every time? It never ended well.

'I need more lime,' Kim laughed back, eyes watering from the shot. 'Leah, how can you do that without your face screwing up?'

Leah laughed and lifted up her gin glass. 'Coz I'm a Glasgow burd.'

The women cheered and whooped and began dancing along to Harry Styles, singing along even though they didn't know the words and they sounded like a cat's choir.

Swaying on the spot with her glass in hand, Leah took a long drink and closed her eyes, taking in the sounds and smells around her. The sound of her friends laughing and chatting settled gently inside her and this was the thing that kept her going all month: knowing that she would be able to let her hair down at the end of the month and have a blowout.

Leah danced her way over to the table and sat down, with some of the other mums joining her. Ashley, Charlotte and Debs sipped on their drinks as Kim sat down next to Leah. All of these women had sons and daughters in Samuel's class at school, Leah's son. Mums' night out had been a thing since primary one and now the kids were all in primary six. They'd been having these nights for six years and still they were able to get drunk, have a laugh and be the talk of the village for a few days.

'Right,' Kim said. 'Since no one threw up their tequila, why don't we have a game of never have I ever?'

Leah raised a brow. 'A game of dares would be much funnier.'

'No, never have I ever. You get to find out people's darkest secrets with that game,' Ashley giggled.

Leah swallowed hard. 'Alright, Kim, you go first.'

Kim cleared her throat and gave a mischievous grin. 'Okay, drink if you have done it...' She took a breath and thought. 'Never have I ever had sex in a public place.'

Ashley and Charlotte raised their glasses to their lips, as did Leah and they all took a drink, laughing loudly as they did.

'Debs, you're such a goody two shoes,' Kim grinned. '*Everyone* has done that, surely.'

'Just because I haven't shagged someone outside doesn't make me a goody two shoes,' Debs winced.

'Right then, you come up with something,' Kim replied. Leah remained silent, ready for the next revelation.

'Never have I ever slept with someone I shouldn't,' Debs said.

'Och come on, that's shite. We've all done that,' Leah replied as everyone took a drink. The women erupted into a fit of giggles and Leah felt her head begin to swim from the shot. This was the kind of night she needed. A night with the girls on the piss. Something to take her mind off the relentless packed lunch prep, football kit prep and PTA meetings. Although secretly she loved all that because it kept her busy, kept her on the go. She needed that, to be on the go all the time.

'Okay then, Miss *I've done everything*, you think of one. Or are you such a wee dirty that you can't come up with anything you haven't done?' Debs grinned widely.

'Shut it you cheeky cow. And why does this game always have to be about sex? Fine, you want a new one, how's this?' Leah started, lifting her glass from the table. The girls all leaned in, straining to hear her over the music. Now they were being subjected to some awful one hit wonder from the nineties.

'Never have I ever taken drugs.'

No one drank. Except Leah. The girl's eyes were all wide and their mouths fell open.

'No way you've taken drugs,' Debs said. Kim raised a brow at Leah and shook her head.

'And you're trying to tell me you haven't dabbled? Come on Debs, let's not pretend we didn't have a life before we became parents.'

The girls went quiet, all with a hint of a smile on their faces. No one wanted to admit it but Leah was the only one with balls to actually say it out loud. As much as Leah loved being a mum, she did miss her single, more exciting albeit dangerous life sometimes.

'Okay then, what kind of drugs? When? What was it like?' Charlotte piped up.

Leah shook her head and wagged a finger at them. 'Just a bit of speed here and there. No big deal. It was obviously before I had Samuel. And *long* before I met Tom. He's not into that kind of thing. But my ex, well he was a different story.'

Charlotte and the rest of the girls laughed and Leah sat back in her seat. It wasn't often she allowed herself to think about her old life or her ex. He'd been exciting, dangerous. Everything that Tom, bless him, wasn't. Of course she loved him with everything she had, and she'd worked hard to earn the life she was living now. But every so often, she'd feel herself drift off to another time. It was like watching someone else on screen when she replayed it all in her mind.

A cackle of laughter from the girls brought Leah back. She blinked away the memories and listened as the girls opened up a little more about their lives before kids. When they were their own person without responsibilities. Leah couldn't remember what that felt like, but nights like tonight, in the pub drinking shots of tequila and laughing until it hurt, brought the old girl in her back to life.

A sudden urge to look over her shoulder gripped her then. She felt eyes on her from across the crowded pub. But then she was drunk and the place was full, so it would be hard not to find someone looking in your direction. She scanned the space around her, looking for the reason why she was feeling so watched. She hated this sensation but then she was used to it. Had been for a long time now.

'I've got another one.' Leah sat forward again and the girls' ears pricked up. It was as though they had nothing else going on in their lives other than their kids and these nights out every month. They always loved it when she led the games. But tonight, Leah was feeling a little too cocky.

'Never have I ever stolen something.' Leah drinks.

The girls laugh and they all drink. They don't get it, Leah thought. There's no way they would have stolen the amount of cash that Leah had.

'I stole a microwave from Asda once. Put it in that bit under the trolley when I first had Alana and forgot to get it scanned. The alarm never went off and I didn't realise until I got to the car. I thought, fuck it. I'm not going back in,' Debs laughed. 'Baby brain at its finest.'

'Oh my god I did that with a box of nappies once when Evie was little,' Charlotte admitted through giggles.

'No, I meant stolen something big. Like money,' Leah said, leaning in.

'Who did you steal money from?' Kim asked, sounding more intrigued as she sipped on her gin.

'It doesn't matter who. But I did. And it wasn't just a tenner. I stole twenty grand.'

The girls at the table fell silent and the music pumped around them. Turning to the left, Leah saw a face through the crowded pub. Eyes on her, narrow as though they were trying to see her properly. The alcohol was really settling now, she was feeling more pissed by the second.

'Are you serious?' Kim asked, her voice turning to a whisper. 'Why? Did you ever get caught?'

'Deadly serious.' She drank again. The face in the crowd disappeared, leaving a feeling of unease. Turning back to face the girls, she could see a look of uncertainty on their faces, like they didn't believe her. And why would they? She was just a suburban mum who was head of the PTA. The woman who organised the weekly football kit wash, the woman who had the perfect suburban life with her perfect husband and her beautiful son in their stunning home. But none of them knew her. Not the real Leah. No one did. Not even her husband Tom. 'Do you think I'd be sitting here if I did get caught?'

Leah was screaming at herself inside that she should shut her mouth but for some reason she felt compelled to share this information. She wasn't just Leah Martin, wife and mum. She was her own person and she had a past. A past that was dying to be let out because the alcohol was loosening her lips and her inhibitions.

'You'd be in prison, Leah,' Debs replied with a raised brow.

'Worse than that,' Leah drank the last of the gin from the glass. 'I'd be fucking dead because the person I stole it from would have killed me by now.'

'You've had too much tequila, Leah,' Kim laughed. But her eyes remained suspicious. Did she believe Leah? It was hard to tell.

'I might be drunk but I'm *not* a liar.'

An awkward silence fell over the group and Leah took a deep breath. Getting to her feet, she stumbled a little and made her way to the bar. Her vision blurred a little and she kicked herself for not eating enough before coming out tonight. She ordered another gin from the bar and her eyes fell upon the corner from which she felt like she was being watched. The small booth was empty. She glanced around the pub and that's when she saw him. The man was there by the exit, watching her again. Leah tried to focus on him properly, but she was too drunk. The tequila was making its way into her blood quicker than usual.

Turning on her heel, Leah made her way through the crowd of Friday night drinkers, attempting to keep her eye on the man who was staring at her. For a moment, she didn't think he was going to move, that when she approached him, he'd tell her that she'd got it all wrong and that he was actually waiting for someone.

As she passed by the girls, they called out to her but she ignored them, headed straight for the man. She thought she recognised him. A far away memory in a corner of her mind. A place she didn't often visit.

'Oi, wait,' Leah shouted across the pub as the man disappeared through the door. She followed him out, the heel of her right shoe collapsing under the force as she tried to speed up.

'Excuse me?' Leah called out. The man was halfway along the main street of the village of Balness and about to climb into a car. 'Oi, I'm talking to you.' Her words slurred and the fresh air hit her like a freight train. Before she could stop herself, she was going down. The car pulled away from her and disappeared into the night. The red lights became tiny dots in the distance.

'Leah, what the hell are you doing out here?' Charlotte's voice filtered into Leah's consciousness before she could fathom what has happened.

Charlotte helped Leah to her feet, albeit still wobbling on her heels. 'I think I knew that man.'

'What man?'

'The one who was... watching me in the pub,' she slurred.

'Right, you need chips and a can of coke,' Charlotte laughed, letting go of Leah as they headed back inside the pub. 'There was no man watching you. We'd have seen him.'

Maybe Charlotte was right. Leah was exceptionally pissed and had been drinking on virtually an empty stomach for a few hours now. Something that she always said she would never do because the hangover was always a bitch the next day.

'Yeah,' she replied.

'Come on, we never finished our game. I'll get you a coke and you go and sit down with the rest of them,' Charlotte smiled.

'Okay,' Leah nodded warily. 'Charlotte?'

'Yeah?'

'Do you believe me?'

Charlotte's brows furrowed at the question. 'About the man outside?'

'No. About the money.' Leah's eyes were becoming heavier. 'When I said never have I ever... stolen money?'

Leah watches as her friend's eyes narrowed at the question. But Charlotte didn't say anything. Instead, she smiled at Leah and it put her in mind of the look you gave when listening to someone talking absolute crap. Charlotte *still* didn't believe her, but she was telling the truth.

'Right, come on you,' Charlotte said, trying to encourage Leah to go back in with her.

'I'm not just a mum, you know. I'm not just the person who heads the school events or makes packed lunches and drinks tequila at the weekend. I used to have a life before I had Samuel.'

Charlotte's smile quickly turned to concern. 'We all had a life before we had our kids, Leah. But becoming a mum changes you. You know that. Sometimes reminiscing about the past, before you had to dedicate every waking second to a tiny person, you remember things differently. Almost as if things were better than they actually were.'

Leah wobbled again on her heels before sighing. 'Yeah, I suppose you're right.'

49

Allowing Charlotte to lead her into the pub, Leah wondered if her friend was right. Was she remembering things more fondly because of the normal life she was leading now? But how could she? Things had gone bad very quickly. She'd had to take that money. There was no other way around it.

Twenty grand was a lot of money. And the owner of that money would be looking for her. They wouldn't stop until they found her.

Six

Leah Martin peeled her eyes open and waited for the impending doom of the tequila and gin hangover. Why did she always have to overdo it? She could never just have one or two drinks. More like one or two bottles.

It hit her then, the sensation that her mouth and throat were coated in sand from the Sahara. Temples pounding and heart racing. Nausea crept over her, slowly at first but soon she was rushing to the bathroom, her head over the toilet as she retched. As soon as she was sick once, she'd feel better. This was always the way of it. Then she would be able to get on with her day as normal.

'Morning,' Tom called, gently tapping on the bathroom door. 'There's a coffee waiting for you in the kitchen if you can stomach it.'

Pulling on the flusher, Leah steadied herself as she stood up. 'Thanks,' she called out to him. Checking herself in the mirror, she was surprised to see that she'd actually taken her makeup off before going to bed. She couldn't remember doing that. In fact, now that she thought about it, she couldn't remember much from 'mum's night out' and knew that the only way she would know what happened was to check the WhatsApp group. But first, coffee.

Leah made her way downstairs and sat down at the kitchen table. A mug of coffee as promised sat in front of her and she took a sip. She could hear Tom and Samuel outside in the garden. Samuel was kicking a football around as per usual and Tom was painting the garden fence, ready for the summer. In actual fact, Leah had asked him to do it prior to Samuel's tenth birthday party. She didn't want the neighbours thinking the garden looked shabby.

Leah picked up her phone from where she seemingly left it on the table the previous night. Not that she could remember putting it there. She couldn't even remember leaving the pub or getting home. The screen was filled with WhatsApp notifications from the 'Boozed Up Mums' group and Leah feared what was being said. There were always one or two pictures of her acting like a drunken idiot on these nights, but they always made her laugh.

> **Debs:** I'll bet no one's hangover is worse than mine. Why do we always have to do tequila? I blame Leah.

> **Kim:** I feel okay. But my hangover always comes in the evening. So it'll be Chinese takeaway for dinner and I will die quietly ☺

> **Charlotte:** I blame Leah for the tequila too. Does anyone remember getting home last night? I woke up fully dressed on the bathroom floor at six this morning
> #badmum

Leah laughed and took another sip of coffee. She began tapping out her reply.

> **Leah:** Hair of the dog, anyone? ☺ I think you'll find I've already vomited this morning. So yes, I blame me too but you girls didn't do anything I didn't do myself. Tom made me a coffee and I'm already starting to feel less fuzzy, thankfully, because I need to head into town to do some party shopping for Samuel. I don't remember getting home but I did wake up in my own bed. Can't stop laughing at the thought of Charlotte passed out on the bathroom floor. You're worse than all of us put together. Great night girls, well what I can remember of it. Any pics? Speak soon.
> X

'Good night then?' Tom appeared in the doorway and smiled at Leah.

'I have no idea. But the good thing is the hangover isn't so bad.'

Tom kissed Leah on the cheek and sat down next to her. She was incredibly lucky to have found Tom. He'd come along at the right time. She'd been working in a café in Stirling when they'd met. Struggling as a single mum, Leah was working all the hours she could to pay her rent and nanny fees for Samuel. That had been at a time in her life where she was trying to figure out who she was and what she wanted from life. A hard task when you're a single mother with a two-year-old. She'd had savings, quite a substantial amount but she didn't want to fritter the money away. It would be something that she was intending on keeping for Samuel for when he was old enough to go to university.

'What's your plan for the day then? Town?' Tom asked. He had that fresh out the shower smell that she loved about him. It reminded her of when they first got together. Then she realised she must stink of stale alcohol. Not attractive at all.

'Yeah. I want to get in before midday and get as much as I can. You know what Sam's like, he'll want everything perfect.'

'Just like his mother then,' Tom kissed her again and Leah drank in his scent.

Leah smiled, a feeling of sadness washing over her. They'd been trying for a baby for three years now and it just wasn't happening. Leah wondered if it was the universe trying to punish her for what she'd done. She was lucky enough to have one son. She didn't deserve another.

'Have you forgotten what day it is next week?' Tom asked. Leah shook her head. Of course she hadn't. How could she forget the day she met him. He'd changed her and Samuel's lives for the better.

'Never in a million years, Tom.'

'Good. I want to take you out. I want you to let loose and forget about all your responsibilities for once. I want to celebrate us.'

If Leah didn't stink of stale alcohol, she would have jumped on him there and then. Instead, she went for a shower and got ready for a day of shopping for her son's birthday party. The sun was already warm and she decided on a little summer dress with denim jacket and sandals. Tom took Samuel to football training and that meant that

Leah would have peace to get things done. No time to think about anything else. Because when she stopped, that was when the memories began to creep in. They were too awful to face, hence the busy schedule.

–

The city of Glasgow was heaving with shoppers. Her Saturday morning venture into the high street to buy what she needed for Samuel's tenth birthday party had quickly turned into a Saturday afternoon. She fought through the crowds of people as she headed for the car which she'd parked at the St Enoch centre. The hangover had subsided now, although with the amount consumed she wasn't sure how. In fact, Leah wondered if she should have driven the car at all after a night on the tequila. The sound of drums and bagpipes filled the air, and as she got closer to the carpark, she watched as crowds gathered around several men, wearing just kilts and sporting long hair. A woman moved along the edge of the crowd and from what Leah could see, she was selling CDs. Glancing down at the sign, she saw that the group were called Clanadonia and were available for functions.

She stopped and listened. The music gave her goose bumps and she watched as people, seemingly strangers, linked arms and danced around the open space. Smiling, she felt her foot begin to tap and the music that surrounded her also kept the bad memories at bay. She could stay here forever, listening to the beat of the drum and watching the people dance. This was what she loved about Glasgow, its ability to catch you at the moment you needed most.

After a few minutes, reality kicked in. Tom and Samuel would be wondering what was taking her so long, and the drive back to the village of Balness would only add to the amount of time she'd been out of the house.

Backing away from the cheering crowd, she started back on Argyle Street towards the car. Clutching her shopping bags and hoping that the car key was at the top of her handbag so she didn't have to search for it, she heard her phone pinging like crazy. The girls were chatting among themselves about their night out. Lifting it from her bag, she had to stop herself from laughing out loud at the images coming through from the girls. Boomerangs and videos along with images of them taking shots, dancing and singing reminded her of how lucky she was to have friends like them. Although, they didn't know her. Not really. She had created a version of herself in her little suburban life in the village of Balness. But her past was the polar opposite to what she was now. She preferred this version of herself. It was safe, secure and normal. If no one else knew about what she was before, what she'd done, then didn't it mean that none of it was real? She liked to think so.

She sent a reply to the girls with the laughing emoji and tucked her phone back into her bag. But then something caught her eye. Someone. A distant sensation of déjà vu. The face was familiar, yet unfamiliar. She thought she knew who he was, yet didn't. Her heart rate climbed and her stomach flipped, yet she had no idea why. Who was this person coming towards her? The feeling was strong, so strong that it scared her because in her mind, the face could not be matched with a name, a place or a date.

So many faces surrounded her in that moment, yet this one stood out. The brown hair, the clear yet older complexion. It seemed so familiar and yet out of reach.

He looked dead into her eyes for a split-second, so short that if Leah had blinked she'd have missed it.

The man approached her, was close enough that she could reach out and touch him. But why would she do that with a complete stranger? But he wasn't a complete stranger. She knew him.

Her phone pinged again and the sound jolted her. In the time it took her to reach into her bag and notice a message from Tom – he was going to make fajitas for dinner – the familiar yet unfamiliar face was gone. And that was when the nausea crept in, the flashes of memory from the night before taunting her. Something happened last night. She'd done something or said something she shouldn't have.

Never have I ever stolen money.

Shit, shit, shit. Had Leah revealed her darkest secret to the girls last night? Looking in the direction in which the man she saw had disappeared, another hazy thought entered her mind. She'd felt watched last night. In the pub. Charlotte had picked her up from the pavement. She'd been chasing the man she thought had been watching her. Was it the same man she'd seen now?

Jesus Christ, Leah thought. *Never have I ever stolen money.* What the fuck was she thinking saying something like that? It was the tequila. It always loosened her tongue.

Leah reached the car, piled her party supplies into the boot and headed home to Balness, in the hope that the girls didn't remember the game. She couldn't remember much else, so she could have said more. Anyone could have been listening, creating the terrifying but very real possibility that he could find her. The man she'd run from would want his money back and he would do anything he needed to get it.

Seven

'A'right bro, where the fuck you been?' Freddie asked. He lay slumped on the grubby sofa in the living room behind a cloud of smoke, a joint between his fingers. 'You've been gone ages.'

Rosie and Cammy were sat on the other sofa, avoiding the spring that protruded from the centre of the cushion between them. They too were almost hidden by a smoke cloud. Lee's eyes began to sting.

'Son, you look a bit worse for wear, what's up?' Rosie Whitelaw slurred, barely able to lift her head or open her eyes. She was clearly still off her face. Cammy Whitelaw said nothing as he lifted a can of super lager from the coffee table and slurped loudly.

Lee didn't respond to anyone, instead he launched himself at Freddie and pulled him off the sofa, fistfuls of T-shirt and threw him to the floor.

'Oi, what the fuck you doing?' Freddie attempted to get to his feet but Lee reached down and landed a punch on his jaw.

'What the fuck are you awe aboot, Lee?' Cammy shouted and got to his feet, attempting to pull Lee from Freddie.

'This fucker right here has only gone and got us a death sentence and left me to deal with it,' Lee shouted as he shook Cammy off. 'Da, you need to get a grip of him.

He's got the biggest fucking gangsters in the city telling me that if I don't get him his money in three days, I'll be dead. And it's all thanks to Billy big bollocks here.'

Freddie glared up at Lee and got to his feet. He swung a punch but missed and fell back to the cardboard strewn floor again. 'What are you on about, you fucking head-case? You had the money. You gave it to them?'

'Naw, I didn't. Because he wouldn't take it. He said that I had to give the cash back to the fucking shop we stole it from because believe it or not, Terry Reid *owns* that fucking shop. I've just had to go in and hand it back to the guy we fucking stole it from and apologise.'

Freddie grinned widely and started to laugh.

'You think this is funny? How stupid are you, Freddie? He's given us three days plus seventy per cent as a late payment fee. You had the fucking money *weeks* ago and you pissed it up against a wall.'

Freddie's expression turned sour then as he pulled himself up to the sofa and leaned back, growling loudly. 'Fuck.'

'Right, calm down, Lee. We can sort this,' Cammy said. 'How much do we owe now?'

'Three hundred plus seventy per cent.' Lee shook his head, feeling broken.

'That's a total of over five hundred quid, Freddie.' Cammy shot his son a look.

'Aye, and we cannae even pay the fucking rent on time so how the fuck are we going to manage this?' Lee shouted.

'We'll manage,' Cammy replied, taking another gulp from the super lager can.

'How? Are you gonnae go round selling fucking Avon?' Lee turned and headed for the door.

His family were bottom of the barrel scum and he knew he was part of that. If Maisie had any sense she'd apply for a flat out of Mainhill and get as far away from the place as possible. But she didn't know any different, having been brought up by junkies. Lee wasn't sure how he'd managed to stay away from that crap having been around it his whole life. He could have fallen victim to the cycle of living in the estate, allowing coke and speed to get a grip of him. Thankfully he hadn't and that was best for all of them right now because he was the only one thinking straight about how they were going to pay off the debt. If he could, he might have a chance of getting away from Mainhill himself.

'Where are you going?' Freddie called after him.

'To figure out how to get us out of the mess you got us into in the first place. You should do the same,' Lee called back before slamming the door.

Taking the stairs two at a time, Lee reached the bottom and stood on the street. He saw Maisie at the window of her new flat, hanging out of it smoking a joint.

No one in this estate had a chance in life, especially if they were brought up by parents like Cammy and Rosie. It was a vicious circle, he thought. And Lee didn't want to be part of it. As soon as he could work out a way of paying off the debt to Terry Reid, he would make a better life for himself, away from the shithole of Mainhill.

Eight

Terry Reid sat at the end of the bar in the pub that he owned in the east end of Glasgow and sipped on the pint he'd just ordered. Free of course, perks of being the boss. The new girl behind the bar stood with her back against the till and she smiled at him invitingly. Narrowing his eyes, Terry held her gaze for a few seconds before looking back down at his newspaper. It was clear to him that she had no idea who he was, otherwise she wouldn't be looking at him like that. He was flattered, of course. But she was too young for him. He liked his women a little more mature than a blatant flirt across a bar.

'Terry. You got a minute? I need a word?' Richie appeared by his side.

He took a sip from his pint and then lifted his eyes to meet Richie. 'This had better be good, Richie. I was just about to pick my horse.'

'The deal, it's going to be delayed,' Richie said. His eyes were ablaze and Terry knew something was up.

'The Collins deal?'

Richie nodded and Terry sighed heavily. The Collins deal had already been delayed once before because one of the brothers had only gone and got himself banged up for drunk driving on the weekend the handover was due to take place.

'For fuck sake, what did the stupid bastard do this time?' Terry asked, lifting his pint and closing the paper.

'Skelped a polis during a search of his club. He's a fucking idiot, doesn't know the meaning of the word subtle.'

Terry nodded. Richie was right, Neil Collins was an idiot and now, Terry might have to find another buyer to supply that side of the city. Not only that, he had far too much gear sitting doing nothing that could be making money and he was already down a dealer in Mainhill, after the stunt Angus pulled.

'Any thoughts?' Terry asked.

'Well, we know he can cough up the cash and it's not as if he doesn't want the deal to go through. He's just not reliable. So, we either wait until we know things are sorted with him, or we find another buyer. Either scenario has a long timeline.'

Terry patted Richie on the shoulder. 'Leave it with me, I'll have a think and get back to you.'

Richie nodded and sat on the bar stool next to his boss.

The Collins deal didn't worry Terry. It was just a pain in the neck he didn't want to deal with. He opened his paper again and read through some of the horses that were due to race in the Grand National that coming weekend.

'Oi, who's the new bird?' Richie nudged Terry and smiled.

'I don't know her name. Hayley deals with recruitment for this place.'

'Aye, well she's got her eye on you.'

Terry glanced up at the new barmaid who was still smiling at him. He couldn't have been less interested in her if he'd tried. 'Am auld enough to be her da, Richie. Get a grip.'

'Ha,' Richie laughed. 'Well I'm not.'

'Knock yourself out mate,' Terry rolled his eyes and then asked Hayley for a bag of nuts from behind the bar.

'He better no' break her heart like he did the last one, Terry,' Hayley said as she handed him the bag. 'Stupid girls can't face coming in here after he's shagged then dumped them.'

Terry swallowed the laughter and opened the bag of nuts as the young barmaid turned her attention to Richie. 'Och leave him, he's in the prime of his life.'

Hayley shook her head and instructed the young barmaid to go through the back to do some stock checks. Hayley had been right for the job as bar manager when Terry had first met her. She didn't take any shit. Ballsy and straight to the point was the kind of person he'd needed to get the place running like clockwork, and that was exactly what she'd done.

'How you doing anyway, Terry? Things going okay?' Hayley asked.

Terry glanced up from his paper and narrowed his eyes. 'Aye, fine thanks, Hayley.'

'I take it you've not heard from her then? Kora?'

Terry took a breath before answering. He didn't like it when Kora was brought up in conversation, he still wasn't out of that dark place. 'No, I haven't Hayley.'

That last night with Kora would always stay with him. He still couldn't get his head around her choosing Frankie over him. He'd wanted Kora to be by his side through life, to share all his success with him. He'd even imagined kids in their future. Then she'd gone and messed it all up, causing him to lose control and put an end to things completely. The situation could have gone a different way. He could have tried to sort things out with her but the image of her and Frankie had sent him into a murderous rage.

Nodding and clearly understanding the shortness of his reply, Hayley turned her attention to wiping down the bar.

He had too much to do, too much to focus on with the organisation. His relationship with Kora had got in the way of that, knocked him out of sync with what was really important. Having grown up in Mainhill Estate himself, he knew what it had been like as a kid. His mum had left when he was too young to remember and his dad was a drunk. Terry had gone day to day as a child, not knowing when his next meal was coming. His clothes were never clean and he lived a life of misery until he was twelve. That was when he'd started working as a van boy. Selling drugs from the ice-cream van around the estate was making him more money than if he had several paper rounds going at once. By the time he was fifteen he was earning five hundred quid a week. That was when he'd left the estate and moved to the town centre into a studio flat. Terry didn't even bother to tell his dad that he was moving out. Not that the man would have shown an interest. If he'd known how much money his son was making he'd have tried to take it to fund his own habit.

At aged fifteen, Terry was beginning to make a name for himself around the estate. He was fast becoming the main dealer for Mainhill and he was making a shit ton of money from the resident's habits. By the time he was eighteen, Terry had recruited his own van boys and was head of the dealers in the estate. Giving them a cut and keeping the rest for himself made him feel like he was finally in control of his life. When he found out that his dad died from a drink and drug overdose, he was numb to any grief. In a way, he'd finally been set free from being a victim of his dad's addiction and lifestyle. And he didn't feel guilty from what he was doing. Being part of Mainhill Estate meant there were only two ways in life. You either became the addict or the dealer. Terry had gone one step ahead of that and now; he was the most successful businessman in the country as the owner of Reid Constructions which included the holiday complexes, housing and business complexes, as well as the casino club, various small properties which included newsagents and small pubs, not to mention the security firms and drug and gun running operations. Going back into the estate to deal with people who owed him money didn't bring back terrible memories as a child. It reminded him of how hard he'd worked to get to where he was now. He was responsible for his own wealth and no one could take that away from him. He supposed in a way that was why he'd lost control with Kora. She'd let him down, made a fool out of him. She was the reason they'd lost what they had. Not him.

Terry's one downfall was that he trusted to quickly, and with Kora he'd fallen too fast. It had been his one true weakness. But he couldn't help himself. He'd always wanted that woman by his side, the one he could share everything with. Not that he'd ever said that out loud to anyone. It wasn't very gangster of him, didn't fit his profile.

Returning his gaze to the paper, he picked up his pen and circled the horse he wanted. Blazing Ember. He liked the sound of it. Fiery, determined. A lot like himself and the people he surrounded himself with.

Lifting his head when the door to the pub opened, Terry watched a redheaded woman step across the threshold. Suddenly, he couldn't blink. He watched as she approached the bar and smiled; the universe was telling him he'd picked the right horse.

'Double vodka,' she said to Hayley. 'No ice.'

Hayley caught Terry's eye and then turned back to the redhead. 'And a mixer?'

'On its own. Gets into the blood quicker.'

Hayley nodded and fetched the drink and Terry laughed. 'A woman after my own heart.'

'Aye, needs must,' she said without turning to meet his gaze.

'Bad day?' Terry asked.

'Try a bad year.'

Hayley placed the double vodka in front of the girl and the redhead handed over a note. Terry held his hand up and said, 'On the house.'

The redhead finally turned to face him and raised a brow. 'Aren't bar staff meant to be on the other side of the bar?'

Captivated by how her eyes matched her hair, Terry reminded himself to respond. 'I own the place, so I like to sit at the end and give out free drinks to the people I think need them.'

'And *you* think I need a free double vodka?' Redhead's mouth lifted at the corner and she smiled slightly.

'Hey,' Terry lifted his hands in mock defeat. 'You're the one who said drinking it straight helps get it into the blood quicker. If that's not a need rather than a want then I apologise for getting it wrong.'

Redhead smiled widely this time before wrapping her fingers around the glass. 'Well, thanks.'

At that, she raised the glass in thanks and took a seat at the end of the opposite end of the bar. Terry's eyes followed her for a moment and then Richie came into view, smiling like a clown. The young barmaid was back and practically lying across the bar listening to Richie's patter, clearly having lost interest in Terry.

'Richie, do me a favour?' Terry said.

'What's that, boss man?' Richie teased.

'Stop trying to shag my bar staff and let them get on with their work.'

The girl's face fell and she stepped back from Richie and bowed her head. Terry laughed gently before the redhead caught his eye again. She was watching him, smiling. He found himself smiling back.

Nine

Annie Wicks sat down at the table in the corner of the bar and resisted the urge to knock the vodka back in one go. A single shot wouldn't be enough to delete the images circulating inside her head, but at least this one was free. She glanced up at the guy sitting at the end of the bar. He'd said she looked like she needed it. Could he see right through her? Was she that transparent? At the age of thirty-two, she hoped she had a little more mystery about her.

Resting the glass on her lips, Annie did what she was trying to resist and practically threw the vodka down her throat. It burned on the way down and she suppressed a gag. Getting to her feet, Annie moved to the bar and stopped in front of the woman standing behind it.

'Another?' She asked.

Annie nodded, 'Please.'

The woman didn't falter and certainly didn't judge. That's what a barmaid was supposed to do, serve the drinks and ask no questions.

'Special occasion?'

Annie turned to face the man who claimed to own the pub. As she watched him hovering over his paper with a pen in hand and a pint by his side, Annie wondered if he had as many thoughts in his head as she did her own.

'Celebrating,' she replied.

'Oh?' He raised a brow. 'Something exciting, I hope?'

'Celebrating freedom.'

Nodding, he closed the paper in front of him as the barmaid handed Annie the glass. He raised his pint and said, 'Well then, here's to freedom.'

If he was curious about her, he wasn't showing it. Annie clinked her glass against his. They both drank, this time Annie drank a little slower.

'I'm Terry, by the way.'

'Annie.' She avoided wincing at the burn travelling down her throat.

Taking a closer look at him, she realised how attractive he was. His presence alone piqued her curiosity and that was enough to allow her to step out of her own life and into his.

'So, you own this place?'

Terry nodded. 'I do. It was my local and about to close. The guy before me couldn't afford to keep it open so I bought it, paid him off and here I am, five years down the line and the place is running like a dream.'

Without admitting it, Annie was a little impressed by this guy. Yes, she'd only just met him, but perhaps he was the distraction she needed from her own life. After everything that had happened, could she really face going back to that?

'Can I get you another?' Terry asked, glancing down at Annie's empty vodka glass. She looked down at it herself. When she'd woken up that morning, her plan had been to drink enough vodka so that she would pass out and then she would be able to forget. Now that she was standing here in front of Terry, she had another way of forgetting. And this way would mean she wouldn't feel like a piece of shit the next day.

'Thank you,' she replied. 'But I'll have a beer.'

Terry nodded at the barmaid before pulling the stool out next to his. Annie sat down next to him and felt a little flutter of excitement in her chest. She hadn't experienced that sensation in a long time.

'I'll bet this is a daily occurrence for you, picking up women with your "I own this place" line.' Annie grinned at Terry and he laughed. So, he had a sense of humour.

'Actually, the girl from last night is still asleep upstairs right now,' he winked.

Annie didn't care if that was true, although she knew it wasn't. Conversation with a complete stranger, about absolutely nothing would take her far away from what she'd had to deal with. As the thoughts began to creep in from the corners of her mind, the image of what happened tried to cling to her. Annie took a deep breath and ordered a beer from the barmaid.

Terry chatted and Annie kept her eyes on him. Aimless, meaningless discussion about absolutely nothing. That was perfect.

–

Eight hours of drinking and eating had passed and Annie had wiped her mind of all the darkness from the past two months. As the day had gone on, Annie had been surprised by how many people had come into the pub on a Tuesday, then she realised they were all friends and acquaintances of Terry. She'd learned a little bit about him. He was a businessman and a successful one at that. He hadn't gone into too much detail and frankly at the moment, Annie didn't care. All she cared about was that Terry was a laugh and that they'd seemed to hit it off almost immediately. She liked him and she could tell he liked her too. His friends were okay from what she could gather. Mostly men her age. It didn't bother her that there were no women aside from the two behind the bar. The younger girl was still flirting with Richie, Terry's best mate. He was a laugh too, albeit he thought a lot of himself but seemed harmless.

It hadn't been her plan to go out and find a man but sometimes these things just fell into your lap when you least expected it. And Terry had come along at the right time.

'So,' he said. 'Since you're celebrating freedom, do you fancy carrying on with the night?'

'What do you suggest?'

'You could come back to mine? I've got the night off.'

Annie glanced down at his left hand. No ring. Good sign. Terry noticed and smiled.

'I live alone. I don't need to celebrate freedom, I've always had it.'

Sometimes, Annie wished she could say the same. Laughing, she said, 'You're not one for commitment then?'

'Well, no I wouldn't go that far. It wouldn't just be us though, some of the lads are coming back after closing.' Terry eyed Richie, his right-hand man by all accounts and the girl he'd been chatting up. 'You might not be the only female to join us.'

Annie followed Terry's gaze and laughed then turned back to face him. 'Aye, that sounds good to me. The more drink the merrier, eh?' *The more I drink, the easier it will be to forget.*

They were quiet for a moment and Annie slid along the seat so she was just inches away from Terry. This

71

moment couldn't end. She had to make it last because it was working, keeping reality at bay with a mixture of alcohol and new lust. Leaning in, she hovered in front of him, waiting to see if he would respond. And he did.

He kissed her gently and it created a spark in Annie's belly. This was what she needed. Complete and utter distraction from… everything.

'So,' she said, pulling away. 'Where is your place?'

Ten

Tom took the bags from Leah as she entered the house. Carrying them through to the kitchen, Leah kicked off her sandals and looked at her phone. The WhatsApp group was still going mad but thankfully, no one had asked about what she'd said. Bloody idiot that she was.

'You get everything for the party?' Tom asked, re-appearing in the hallway. He kissed her on the cheek and slid an arm around her waist.

'Yeah,' she yawned. 'And I thought my hangover had gone but it's back with a vengeance.'

Tom laughed. 'Well, there's a bath up there all ready for you. I'll cook tonight. Samuel is staying at a friend's house so we have the place to ourselves.'

As much as Leah loved her son, she could have kissed Tom's feet for arranging that. She needed a night without PlayStation, football and tenth birthday party chat. Her head was beginning to throb and the fear from the night before had well and truly set in. How could she have been stupid enough to think it would be a laugh to tell the girls she'd stolen twenty grand off someone? How often did that happen to people? She wasn't sure, but if that information got out then she was in deep trouble.

'Thank you, Tom. Not having Sam for the night will be...' She tried to think of the word.

'Quiet?' Tom laughed.

'Yes, that. But also good for us. We've not had a night just the two of us in a long time.'

Leah climbed the stairs and soon, she was slipping into the bath to relax. The hangover fear had her thinking all sorts of crap, but the lavender scent was beginning to work its magic.

Lying back and closing her eyes, she couldn't stop her mind wandering back to that time when she was in a bad place in her head as well as her life. She'd needed cash, and she'd needed it quick. The person she'd taken it from was dangerous and there was always that fear in the back of her mind that told her she'd be found eventually. But for now, things were good. Samuel was doing well at school and excelling in his football. Leah's online business of selling handmade jewellery and bath salts seemed to be gaining momentum. Of course, it wasn't going to push her over the tax threshold but it was enough to keep her busy while Samuel was at school and Tom was at work. She was a long way away from being that single mum working in a café and Tom had continually told her she didn't need to work, he earned enough for them all to live comfortably. But she needed something that was just for her. She didn't want to be just a mum, a wife, head of PTA. Having something that was just hers was like keeping a piece of herself that couldn't be contaminated by other parts, other people.

Feeling herself dozing off, Leah's eyes shot open at the sound of the doorbell ringing. Tom's footsteps padded across the hallway floor before he opened it. Leah strained to hear, but there was nothing. Tom called out to her.

'Leah, there's a letter here for you.'

Tom's footsteps grew closer and he opened the bathroom door after gently knocking. He peered around the door, smiling.

'Who's it from?' Leah asked, sitting up.

'I don't know. Whoever it was, was gone by the time I got to the door. They left it on the mat.' Tom said. He wasn't holding said letter in his hand. 'I wondered if you fancied a bottle of wine with dinner. Or are you still too hungover?'

Leah shook her head, allowing a smile to creep onto her face. 'I'm sure a glass or two won't kill me. That would be lovely.'

'I'll head down to the Co-op now and grab a bottle,' Tom said before closing the bathroom door.

Was it just a coincidence that she'd been spooked by a face in the crowd last night at the pub? And today in town, she'd seen him again. Now a letter had shown up at this time of the day, no one at the door after they'd rung the bell. Tom didn't seem too bothered by the fact that someone had left a letter for Leah and not shown their face. Paranoia seemed to be one of the lasting effects of the tequila and gin hangover. But her curiosity would get the better of her. Hearing Tom leave to go and get the wine, Leah got out of the bath, wrapped a robe around her and went downstairs to see who it was from.

Lifting the letter from the side table in the hallway, she saw her name was written across the front. There was no address, no stamp. Whoever sent it had hand delivered it. She didn't recognise the writing.

Turning over the envelope, she pulled at the flap and ripped along the edge with her finger, her heart pounding hard in her chest.

Pulling out the paper, her eyes fell upon an image. It was a picture of herself, from before she had Samuel. In the image, she stared down the lens of the camera, or rather at the person behind it, smiling widely. She remembered how happy she was at that time in her life and it was all because of the man behind the camera. Her hair was longer, her dress reminded her of how she'd changed over the years and how she'd never get away with wearing something like that now. Nausea took over then, sending hot flashes across her skin and up from her stomach to her throat. Flipping the image over, six words screamed back at her. Black, bold capital lettering pierced her eyes and at that moment, Leah thought she was going to pass out.

I WANT MY MONEY, BITCH!

Eleven

The party was in full swing and Richie had brought the young barmaid back to the house with him, as Terry had suspected he would. She wouldn't last long with Richie, they never did. He wasn't one for keeping them around for long. Get in and out as quickly as you can was what Richie would say.

'This place is…' Annie glanced around the room.

'Nice?' Terry suggested, looking down at her as she admired the space around them. Terry was proud of his home. The piano in the corner had once belonged to his grandad. Terry never knew how to play but was happy for it to sit there looking the part.

'A little over the top for a guy who lives on his own,' she replied. Her grin widened.

'Oi, I like it.'

'Needs a woman's touch,' she said, sipping from her beer bottle.

'Oh does it now?'

'Aye,' she paused. 'Maybe you could get a cleaner?'

Terry laughed loudly. He liked Annie. There was something mysterious about her he hadn't seen in any other woman before, not even Kora. He wasn't going to tell her about his ex, not yet anyway. The party had spilled out from the kitchen and into the main hallway of the house. If Annie was at all impressed by the place, she wasn't showing it. Instead, she stood next to the piano and listened as people chatted. She didn't seem at all bothered by the fact that there were people snorting coke off the table in the kitchen, or that there was a debate going on between Richie and some of the others about whether Rangers of Celtic were going to win the league.

Terry moved away from her a little to see if she would follow him. When she didn't, it intrigued him as to why not. She didn't know anyone else here, yet she seemed comfortable to be on her own. Moving across the floor towards Richie, he pulled him from the football debate and into the lounge.

'What's up?' Richie asked.

'I want you to chase up the Collins deal tomorrow morning, first thing.' Terry said.

Richie eyed him suspiciously. 'I was already going to do that but you said you would look into it.'

'Aye, well I want you to do it.'

Terry hovered for a moment and as he went to walk out of the room, Richie placed a hand on his shoulder and pulled him back.

'What did you really want to say to me?'

'What do you think of Annie?' Terry asked. 'I mean she comes out here with a bunch of strangers without so much as blinking. She doesn't care that folk are taking drugs, drunk and quite frankly almost fighting about football.'

'You fancy this bird or what?'

'She's a belter, I'll admit. But what I mean is, she reminds me of me.'

Richie shook his head. 'Look Tez, I'm not a relationship doctor. If you fancy her, get her into bed and get it out your system. Just don't do what you did with Kora and move her in after the first shag. I mean, look how that turned out.'

Richie left the room and headed back to his position within the football debate. Terry was a little annoyed at that last comment his friend had made. Though he had a point. How was he meant to trust anyone after Kora?

There was something about Annie that made him want to know more about her but he couldn't put his finger on what that something was. Was he just pining for Kora, or at least what Kora had represented? A normal life, marriage and kids. He thought about both women and how different Annie seemed in comparison. Unlike Kora, she didn't seem impressed by the grandness of it all. The wealth or the size of the house. That in itself was a turn on, almost like she was playing hard to get.

Twelve

Maisie Whitelaw opened the door of her new council flat in Mainhill to her brother Lee. He looked like he'd been hit by a truck.

'Jesus, what the hell's up with you?'

'Freddie screwed us over,' Lee answered as he stepped inside. 'The bastard has gone and got us a death sentence with the fucking Reids.'

Maisie closed the door and followed her brother into the living room. Lee was her favourite out of the whole family. Her parents were nothing but junkies, let downs. And Freddie, well Lee said it all.

'What do you mean?' she said, slumping down on the armchair and laying a hand on her enormous pregnant belly.

'We owe Terry Reid five hundred quid and I've got three days to find it. And that's with interest. Freddie had the money weeks ago but instead of paying off the debt, he decided to fucking drink it, snort it and smoke it.' Lee dropped on to the other armchair on the opposite side of the room and exhaled loudly.

'He's an absolute bellend at times. Lee, how the hell are you going to get hold of that kind of money in three days?' Maisie asked, rubbing at her huge bump and feeling genuine concern for her brother.

'I have no idea, Maisie.'

Reaching down the side of the chair, Maisie wrapped her fingers around the bottle of vodka her mate Nicole had left behind the previous night. 'Here, there's only two out of it. You look like you need it.'

Lee got up and took the bottle from Maisie. 'Cheers sis.' She watched as he opened it and took a few swigs, grimacing as he swallowed. 'I could kill Freddie for this.'

Maisie shook her head. How could Freddie do something so stupid? He knew the Reids weren't to be messed with. Maisie was only a young girl with her own problems and even she knew that. He had put them all in danger, including her. Although she couldn't say she was at all surprised. Their dad, Cammy, had acted much the same way when they were younger. She'd lost count of the amount of times they'd had the door kicked in over the years because Cammy owed folk drug money. Maisie had a clear memory of him having his leg broken by a couple of guys when she was just five years old. That memory alone was enough to make her realise that she had to move into her own place for the sake of her baby. That kind of thing wouldn't stop now, the habit was too hard to break and Cammy probably didn't want to stop. The only difference now was that Freddie was buying in drugs for everyone, although at times he was keeping most for himself.

Maisie had wanted to get out of Mainhill, but with no money or prospects of a brighter future, she'd settled for the flat. It wasn't perfect, but it was hers. Hopefully with her own space away from her wasters for parents, she could be a better mum than her own.

'Look, Lee you're the clever one out of you and Freddie. You'll think of something. You have to, for the sake of all of us.'

Lee took another swig and stood up, screwed the cap back on and placed the bottle on the floor. 'Maisie, I might be less of an idiot when compared to our brother, but I'm not magic. I can't exactly click my fingers and hope the money will just turn up.'

Maisie sighed. He was right. 'Look, why don't you stay here tonight? I'm worried you might actually kill Freddie if you go back up to the house.'

'Aye, cheers Maisie. I've got just enough here for a packet of fags but cannae go up the shop. The icey due?'

'Aye, any minute now actually.'

Bang on the dot, Lee heard the chimes of the ice-cream van and headed down to the street to get himself a packet of cigarettes. He joined the back of a queue of eight people. Two kids at the front bought a few single cigarettes and some ice-cream cones. Lee remembered when that used to be him and Freddie.

Staring down at the ground, hands in his pockets, Lee felt defeated. It was an impossible task to find a tenner in this estate never mind five hundred quid.

'A'right mate, how's the motor coming on?' A lad older than Lee approached another man standing two ahead in the queue from Lee.

'Aye, no' bad mate,' the man replied. 'She's coming on well. Just had a respray, she's looking pristine.'

'Yer missus said yer wheels arrived?'

Lee's ears pricked up then and he listened carefully as the queue moved a little more.

'Aye, eight hundred quid but they're crackers. Got them in the garage until I can get them fitted tomorrow,' the man replied, rubbing his hands together.

'Aye, she's a cracker alright,' the lad turned and stared at a Subaru Impreza estate sitting in one of only four drives in the street. A brick garage sat behind it, the door up and exposing the inside to the street.

'Cost me enough.'

Lee turned and looked at the car and in the corner of the garage he saw the wheels. Brand new. Eight hundred quid. Lightbulb moment, as Maisie would have said.

The man and the younger lad moved onto another topic of conversation and Lee tried not to look too suspicious. The man said he was having the wheels fitted tomorrow. That only gave him a short window. Even if he was successful in getting the wheels out of that garage and into a safe place, he still had the task of trying to sell them.

Lee moved his way to the front of the queue and purchased his cigarettes before heading back to Maisie's flat. He had to call Freddie. As much as he thought his brother was an idiot, Lee knew that Freddie would be able to get those wheels sold quicker than it would take to steal them. He knew people, dodgy people.

Pulling out his phone as he stood at the entrance to Maisie's building, he called his brother.

'Meet me at Maisie's, I've got an idea of how to get us out of this mess but I'll need your help.'

Thirteen

Climbing the stairs and leaving the party behind, Annie followed Terry into a room at the end of the hallway.

Switching on the light, Annie was mesmerised by what she saw. An old record player sat in the centre on an oak table and the walls were lined with vinyl sleeves. She took a breath at the beauty of them.

'So, you're not into Spotify then?' She smiled at Terry as he stood by the record player.

'The world is too dependent on convenience these days. I like a physical copy I can hold in my hands, you know?'

Annie moved along the wall, pulling out some of the sleeves and looking. He was a big fan of the classical music, she came to see. Unusual for a guy you'd meet in an east end pub.

She glanced over at Terry and noticed a stack of books on a slim bookshelf. A reader too?

'Did you just bring me up here to impress me?' She raised a brow.

'Are you impressed?' He asked, lifting a beer bottle to his lips.

'Surprised, not impressed. I'm not into classical stuff. Or reading books for that matter. I'd much rather lose myself in other ways.' She smiled.

'Oh yeah?' Terry mused. 'Care to expand on that?'

Annie didn't know how to answer him. She didn't know how she wanted to lose herself, had never truly tried. But she knew that Terry would be a good start. He was handsome, charming and by looking around her, had a fair few bob in the bank. She wasn't stupid, though. The men downstairs weren't what she would class as true mates. Acquaintances, employees perhaps. She could tell Terry was the top man of whatever business it was he owned and she wasn't just thinking of the pub. A pub alone wouldn't buy a house like the one she was standing in now.

'So, how long did you say you've owned the pub?' she diverted.

'Around five years. It was going down the shitter and I bought it off the owner for a fraction of what it was worth. Guy just wanted out and to fuck off with his cash and start a new life abroad.'

'Sounds like his life was going down the shitter too,' Annie surmised.

'Aye, he was a gambler. Well, recovering addict. Owning a pub next door to the bookies wasn't exactly good therapy for him. Plus he couldn't afford the business rates and… why am I telling you this?'

'I don't know. But it's better than listening to some of the crap on these shelves.' Annie teased and sat down on the sofa next to the window.

'Oi, you just don't know how to appreciate fine musical art.'

Terry sat next to her and they sipped their drinks quietly. She glanced at the picture on the side table next to her. An image of Terry, recent by the looks of it, standing next to Richie. Behind them was a boat, a yacht rather.

Without wanting to admit it, now she was impressed. Just a little.

'You sail?' she asked.

'Aye,' Terry replied, glancing over at the picture. 'When we get a rare day off me and Richie like to go out to Loch Lomond and fish.'

'You go fishing on a yacht like that? Very luxurious, you definitely don't slum it like the average fisherman, do you?'

Terry laughed. 'Nothing like doing it in style, eh?'

'You ever catch anything?'

'Richie does. I don't fish, I usually just take a disposable barbeque and a few cans.'

Annie nodded and looked at her own beer. The bottle was empty. She placed it on the table next to her and Terry got to his feet.

'Same again?'

'Thanks,' Annie said, rising from the seat.

'No, no. You wait here. I'll be back in two minutes.'

Terry disappeared out of the room and Annie moved towards the table in the centre of the room which held the antique record player. Running her hands along the smooth wood, she sat down on the seat in front of it. There were two drawers, one on either side. Out of curiosity and the need to fill her head with other things, Annie pulled the drawer to the left open. It was empty, aside from a diary and a few pens. She pulled the right drawer open and stared inside. Neither was she impressed or surprised to see a handgun sat in the centre, surrounded by pieces of paper, pens and a few mobile phones.

She closed the drawer quickly and moved back to the sofa and sat down. Annie didn't feel frightened that she was in the presence of someone who possessed such a weapon. Nor was she concerned that he may have used it to hurt someone, or was planning to. This was exactly what she needed to rid her head of the thoughts, the guilt that had consumed her.

The door opened and Terry entered, carrying two bottles. 'Here,' he said, offering one to her.

She took it from him and smiled. Should she ask him about the gun? Would he get angry that she'd snooped in the drawers when he wasn't looking?

'Like what you saw?' he asked. 'Did it scare you?'

Annie stared up at him as he stood in front of her. His expression was neutral.

'The gun, you saw it? I've got cameras in every room.'

Annie took a deep and steadying breath. Fuck, she hadn't banked on security cameras in the house. Outside, yes. 'I saw it.'

'And?'

'And what? You want me to say I'm terrified?'

'I could tell by the look on your face that you weren't bothered by it at all. Which is strange to me. Most women I've had in here have found it and done a runner.'

'So you've had a lot of women in here?' Annie asked. Terry laughed.

'You've just found a gun in a house belonging to a guy you've only just met and you're concerned about the amount of women I've had in here?'

Annie laughed along with him but still couldn't gauge how he felt about her snooping. 'And for your information, I'm not most women. The shit I've been through, I couldn't give a shit if I'd found a severed hand in that drawer.' She took a large mouthful of beer and swallowed back the emotional outburst that threatened. She didn't want that to happen, not here in front of Terry. He'd think she was unstable.

No longer neutral, Terry's expression changed to surprised. 'Jesus.'

'And *he* can take a fuck to himself.'

'Okay, how's this? *Shit?*' A smile raised the corner of Terry's mouth and instantly, the emotion that gripped at Annie's throat disappeared.

'That's better.'

Terry tore his eyes away from Annie, as if he knew that whatever was in her head, she didn't want to talk about it. And she was thankful for that. She supposed that was what she was owed from him, considering she didn't ask any questions about why he might possess a gun. He sat down next to her.

'So, what do you do?' he asked.

'Nothing.' Annie replied.

'You don't do anything? No job, no partner? Kids?'

What did he take her for? 'Are we really going to do this?' she asked, turning her body and lifting her feet off the floor as she rests her knees on the sofa.

'Do what?' Terry asked, his eyes fixed on hers.

'Pretend we're interested in each other in any other way except physically.'

Terry looked surprised and then he laughed. 'I suppose not.'

Annie climbed on to Terry's lap and pulled at the buttons of his shirt. She couldn't cope with questions or conversation. Annie needed to do whatever it took to get her disastrous life as far from her thoughts as humanly possible.

Flashes of memories and faces appeared in front of her as she kissed Terry. Squeezing her eyes shut, she pushed them out of her head and focused on the moment.

Fourteen

'Hi,' Leah said when Charlotte picked up the phone. 'Do you have a minute to talk?'

Leah paced the floor, phone in one hand and picture in the other, the words on the back of the image swimming around in her mind. This was her own stupid fault. If she'd just kept her mouth shut about the money, instead of getting cocky because she'd had a few drinks then this might not have happened.

'Yeah, the kids are in the garden playing. What's up?' Charlotte asked, sounding as though she hadn't sensed the panic in Leah's voice. How could she not have? The feeling of terror was coming in waves now, making her voice shake.

'Did you put something through my door just now?' Leah asked, hoping that having told Charlotte about the twenty grand, her friend had a truly fucked up sense of humour that she didn't know about and thought it would be funny to wind her up about the money.

'What? No, why?' Charlotte replied, her voice laced with confusion.

Shit, Leah thought. Of course Charlotte wasn't the one to have dropped that image through the door. Why would she? And it was a photograph from before they'd met, so where would she have even got it from?

'Fuck,' Leah hissed down the phone. 'Sorry.'

'Leah, what's wrong? Are you in some sort of trouble?'

'No, nothing like that,' Leah lied. 'Listen, can you do me a favour. Can you forget what I said last night? I was way too drunk. It was the tequila talking.'

Charlotte laughed gently on the other side of the line. 'What's new? That stuff always does the talking for us.'

It was though Charlotte didn't have to forget what Leah had said, it seemed like she hadn't remembered at all.

Leah fell quiet and she heard Charlotte take a breath before she said, 'Are you okay? You were acting really strange at the pub last night. Not your usual self, you know what I mean?'

Yeah, Leah thought. She did know what she meant but she couldn't very well tell her friend what was going on, she'd already said too much.

'Leah? Do you want to meet? Just the two of us? You know you can trust me with your life. Anything you tell me wouldn't go further.'

Leah couldn't be more thankful to have a friend like Charlotte and that was why she felt guilty, because Charlotte didn't really know Leah at all. No one did.

'Honestly, I'm okay. I just don't want anyone thinking I'm a loony once I've had a drink, that's all. Do you remember much from last night?'

'No,' Charlotte replied. 'Although I do remember playing never have I ever? Did I make an arse of myself?'

Leah sighed with relief. If Charlotte did remember, then she wasn't letting on. 'No, not that I recall. What happens at tequila night stays at tequila night, eh?'

'Ha, god yeah. If anything comes back to me I'll let you know.'

'Look Charlotte I have to go, that's Tom back in with the wine. I'll see you Monday morning at the school gates.

Maybe we could grab a coffee once we've dropped the kids off?'

Leah ended the call quickly. She couldn't bring herself to lie to Charlotte anymore. Raising her hand, she glared back at the image of herself. The girl in that picture had committed a crime against someone who would punish her much harder than the law would. And it would seem that this person had found her.

It wasn't just Leah that was in danger, it was her entire family. She would have to come clean to Tom, tell him what she'd done. But would he understand after all this time? She hoped so.

Flipping the picture over once more, she read the words on the back.

I WANT MY MONEY, BITCH!

Leah knew what the absence of that money meant to the person it belonged to, and what it meant for her. If she didn't give it back, she would be dead before the end of the week. Because they knew where she lived now and they wouldn't hesitate to get in touch again. She was sure of that.

Fifteen

Lee watched as his brother Freddie appeared at the top of the stairs. Freddie hadn't said anything to Lee about the punch he'd taken for his stupidity towards Terry Reid. As much as Freddie grated on Lee, he was still his brother and he wouldn't have anyone else by his side while trying to sort this shit out.

'How's it going, Mike Tyson?' Freddie said, his hands shoved deep in the pockets of his jeans and his head bent low. Lee sensed Freddie was remorseful for what he'd done, but knew it wouldn't last.

'Aye, very good Freddie. Look, I'm sorry about earlier. But you've got to understand that what you did could have got me fucking done in back there. And you just didn't seem to give a shit. I've pulled you out of a hole so many times Freddie and now I'm the one having to deal with your mess.'

'Look,' Freddie said, removing his hands from his pockets. 'I'm sorry. I fucked up. I didn't mean for you to get taken away by them. I don't know what I was thinking. You know what it's like Lee, when you get your hands on some cash, it's just too tempting not to spend it on the things you need.'

'The things you need? What you *needed* was to pay the Reid's the money you owed them for the drugs they gave to you on tap. What are you even doing getting them on tap anyway?' Lee shook his head as he stared at his younger brother.

'Give it a rest with the lecture, Lee.'

'You're an idiot Freddie. Have you learned nothing from Dad? Or has your drug-addled brain wiped the memories of him having his legs broken when we were kids?'

Lee remembered the beatings Cammy took when he was younger, how Rosie used to usher them into the back bedroom and shut the door while the latest dealer their dad had pissed off came round to knock seven bells out of him. Lee didn't want that for him or Freddie.

'So, what's this plan all about then?' Freddie said, dodging the question about Cammy. It was a sore point for Freddie because he looked up to their dad so much. Lee couldn't understand why.

'Not here,' Lee replied as he headed for Maisie's flat. It was the only place they would get any privacy and he certainly didn't want Rosie or Cammy to hear things. They'd either play down the situation or make things worse. They always found a way to make things worse.

As they climbed the stairs, Freddie and Lee were silent. Freddie was likely thinking ahead of time, about who he could rob to get money. Lee wasn't that far ahead. If his plan worked, he wanted to fuck off away from Mainhill. The place was a shithole, junkie-ville. Nothing but bad memories came from the estate and Lee was sick of living a life with no prospects.

Maisie opened the door and Lee stepped inside. Freddie followed. The place wasn't very appealing to the eye, but then none of the council houses or flats in the estate were. And the handful of houses in the estate that were privately owned looked out of place, especially when the exteriors had been painted or the grass had been cut. It was a rare occasion that the council arrived to cut the communal grass. Lee often wondered what the privately owned houses looked like inside – or in fact, what any house other than his own and Maisie's looked like inside. He wondered what it would be like to walk on floor that wasn't covered in broken down cardboard or an actual carpet that wasn't worn down and stained by alcohol from years of abuse.

'You boys want a drink?' Maisie asked. Immediately, Freddie eyed the vodka bottle Lee had left on the floor earlier and headed straight for it.

'No chance, Freddie. I need your head clear tonight,' Lee said, swiping the bottle from Freddie's grasp and handing it to his sister. 'Get rid of this for now, eh Maisie.'

Maisie disappeared into the kitchen and Freddie flopped down onto the armchair.

'Right,' Lee began. 'The brick garage that sits next to the house at the end of the flats here?'

Freddie raised his eyes and got out of his seat to look out the window at where Lee was looking. 'Aye, what aboot it?'

'There are a brand new set of wheels in there worth eight hundred quid. I heard a guy talking earlier, said he was getting them fitted tomorrow. But we need those wheels to sell, Freddie. So, we're going to break in and then you're going to get rid of them.'

Freddie started laughing almost instantly. 'Are you fucking kidding? The guy that lives in that house has a fucking Rottweiler. I don't want to lose my baws for the sake of a few wheels.'

'Well, it's either you take the risk and hope you don't, or Terry Reid gets a hold of us in three days and we lose a lot more than our fucking baws. I'm telling you, that Terry is a fucking nut, held a gun to my head. You're doing this. You got us into this so you'll get us out of it. Or how's this? I turn you over to Terry myself, let you deal with him face to face? Is that what you want? Because I could do that and walk away from this shit right now. Like I said, this is all your doing.'

'Awe, for fuck sake, Lee,' Freddie moaned. Lee knew this was a sign indicating he wasn't happy about it but he would do what he had to.

Lee and Freddie sat down on the armchairs in Maisie's lounge and discussed how and when they were going to attempt to take the wheels from the garage. It was a simple plan. Wait until the estate was in darkness and the place was silent before they made their move.

'Once we've got them, we need to get them sold pronto,' Lee said.

'Aye, no worries there. I know a guy who will take them off our hands,' Freddie replied. 'Ma old mucker Galzo. He's made a mint punting car parts.'

Lee knew Galzo was a dodgy sort but could get the job done. Even with everything that had happened, Lee knew he could trust Freddie with this. But could he trust Galzo? He'd already ruined Maisie's life and the idea of working with the guy killed Lee and Maisie might question Lee's loyalty.

'I'll give him a bell just now, let him know there might be a punt heading his way,' Freddie said, lifting his phone from his pocket. 'I'd rather tell him about the possibility first, rather than us bumping those wheels and then I cannae get a hold of him, ye know?'

Lee nodded. Freddie made sense, for once.

'Galzo, ma man, how's it going?' Freddie said, overly loud. Maisie appeared in the living room with a confused look on her face. Lee got up and left the living room, and Maisie followed him into the kitchen.

'What the hell is he doing phoning that idiot?' Maisie hissed.

Lee frowned at the hardened expression on his sister's face. 'I know, I'm sorry, As much as I hate him, me and Freddie need him to help us with a job…'

'I hate him, Lee. He's left me in the shit. He's a right bellend.'

Lee smiled. He liked how his sister told it like it was. 'You don't have to have anything to do with this Maisie. This is a life or death situation so if Galzo can turn up for us then I'll take that.'

Maisie shook her head and turned her back to Lee. He understood there was history between her and Galzo, but at this moment in time Lee had to put that to one side. Freddie didn't know about Galzo being the dad of his sister's baby and Lee had to make sure it stayed that way until the job was done at least.

'Right, he said if we can get a hold of the wheels he can punt them for what they're worth, but he wants a cut,' Freddie said as he entered the kitchen, shoving the phone in his pocket.

'Whatever, Freddie. So long as we've got the money for Terry then I couldn't give a shit.'

'Right then,' Freddie rubbed his hands together. 'A wee voddy while we wait?'

'No chance, Freddie,' Lee shook his head. 'You need to be stone cold for this otherwise it won't work.'

Freddie sighed loudly and disappeared back into the living room. Lee glanced at Maisie, who was biting her thumbnail nervously. He knew that look. It was the one she'd had just before she told Lee she was pregnant. Something was troubling her.

'Maisie, what's up?'

'Nothing.'

'Liar.'

Maisie sighed, rolled her eyes and dropped her hand to her side. Her eyes began to dart back and forth, unable to meet Lee's eye.

'Maisie, just tell me what's wrong.'

'It's Galzo. I told him about the baby.'

'And what did he have to say for himself?'

'He told me I must have got it wrong, and that the baby must be someone else's. I assured him it was his but he was having none of it. Told me to fuck off.'

Lee felt the blood drain from his face. How could Maisie have got involved with someone like Galzo? He was a small-time stolen goods dealer, as well as dealing a bit of coke on the estate, which to Lee was insane considering it was Reid territory, but he was also a bastard when it came to women. Freddie thought the sun shone out of Galzo's arse and Maisie had begged Lee not to tell Freddie about her relationship with him. It had taken all his strength not to say anything.

The anger in Lee's stomach rose to his chest. If he didn't need Galzo's help to punt those wheels he'd have it out with him.

'Please, don't tell Freddie.'

'I won't, not yet. But once this shit is sorted with Terry Reid, I'll fucking have him, Maisie.'

Sixteen

Terry kept his eyes on Annie as she pulled her top over her head. He took a draw of his cigarette. Her slender back was hidden by long auburn hair, her skin milky white. She turned and smiled at him. He lifted his hand and placed it on her hip, next to a small tattoo he was unable to make out before she pulled her shirt over and covered it.

'You're leaving?' Terry asked.

'Come on,' Annie started. 'You and I both know you're not the type of guy who keeps a one-night stand going until the next day.'

'Do we now?' He took another draw on the cigarette. 'Annie, you don't know anything about me, so how could you possibly know that I would want you to leave?'

Annie got to her feet and moved across the room towards the oak table. She placed her hand on the drawer and met Terry's eye but didn't move.

'If anything, I would want to keep you close by. Keep an eye and ear on you. You've already seen too much.'

They were both silent for a few seconds before they burst into laughter. Annie removed her hand from the drawer and walked back to the sofa, sat down and began to put on her shoes.

'Listen, last night was fun,' Annie said as she slipped her feet into her ankle boots. 'And if it's meant to continue then it will.'

Terry inched closer and trailed his hand down Annie's spine. 'It's meant to continue. Trust me.'

She turned, nose inches from his. She smelled sweet, her hair falling around her face.

'Stay, at least for breakfast.' Terry got up and moved across the room to the door.

'What about your party guests?'

'Ah, they'll have fucked off hours ago. Come on,' he said, holding out a hand.

Annie got up and allowed him to lead her to the kitchen. The house was empty aside from evidence of a party the night before. Empty bottles sat on tables and kitchen counters and Terry silently cursed the place. He felt embarrassed that this gorgeous girl who was younger than he was, was seeing the place in such a state.

'What do you fancy?' he asked.

'Just coffee, black. No sugar,' Annie replied.

He pulled two mugs out of the cupboard, made up two coffees and sat at the table with Annie. They drank in silence and he noticed how pretty she still looked after a night on the sauce.

'So, you still think I want you to leave?'

She smiled.

'Do you want to leave?'

Annie shook her head.

'Good. I don't want you to leave either.'

For the first time in a long time, Terry felt an excitement stir in his stomach. His one-night stands usually consisted of going back to the girl's place, a quick shag and then he would never see her again. He'd liked it that way, before Kora of course. But with Annie, something different had happened. There was something about her that he didn't want to let go of. She was private. Whatever it was that she wasn't telling him about herself showed him that perhaps she valued the art of silence. It made him want her more. And he instantly trusted her, which had surprised him because of what had happened with Kora. He'd invited Annie into his home, let her see his sanctuary. That had to mean something.

'So what is this, then? I mean, I don't want to leave and you want me to stay. We've known each other for what,' she glanced at the digital oven clock, 'almost twenty-four hours. Not long at all. I've seen what you have in that desk upstairs, you know I've seen it yet you're not fazed by it. Neither am I. So what are we doing?'

'Does it have to have a label?' Terry asked.

Annie hesitated then said, 'No, I don't suppose it does.'

Terry moved around to the side where Annie sat at the table and pulled her onto his lap. 'And you're right, if you'd been bothered by that gun you'd have done the off before I'd come back in with that beer. I think it excites you.' He kissed the corner of her mouth. 'And I think that it would excite you even more if you saw the kind of man I really am.'

Annie held his gaze and smiled slightly.

'Am I wrong?'

'We'll have to wait and see, I suppose.' She pushed her lips close to his. 'Maybe we're exactly what the other needs right now.'

Terry breathed her in. He was curious about her. But she was right. Annie *was* exactly what he needed right now.

Seventeen

It was dangerous to be alone, Annie thought. Terry was in the shower and she was sitting in the study. Surrounded by classical music, books and leather sofas, Annie wondered how she got here. Just a short time ago, she was living an entirely different life. Had experienced hell. She couldn't stop thinking of what she'd done when she was alone. How could she have let things happen the way they did? She could have stopped it. Surely there would have been a way to stop what had happened? But she didn't. Couldn't. She would have to live the rest of her life racked with guilt.

Now, Annie sat in what she could only describe as a mansion you'd see on *Selling Sunset*, owned by a man who possessed a gun and did god knew what as a business.

The thought of knowing that she was riding on the edge of a knife between guilt and excitement made her stomach roll. The whole experience could go one of two ways.

Opening the drawer, she pulled the gun out and held it in her hand. The steel was cold against her skin. A buzz of power and excitement washed over her as she lifted the gun and pointed it towards the far wall. Finger poised over the trigger, Annie felt herself go into a trance-like state. Then she heard the sound of the shower stop and Terry stepping out.

Lowering the gun, she sat down on the chair at the table but kept it in her hand. She wanted Terry to teach her how to shoot. She wanted to know what it would feel like to eject a bullet into the air. She wanted to eject all thoughts from her head in the same way, at the same speed.

As her mind wandered, Annie noticed something else in the drawer. Realising it was a photograph, she reached in and pulled it out. Staring down at it, she wondered who the girl clinging to Terry in the image was. She placed it back in and kept her focus on the gun, feeling powerful as it weighed heavy in her hand.

Terry appeared in the space between the hall and the room where Annie sat and noticed immediately that she was holding the gun.

'What the fuck are you up to?' he said with a smile as he walked towards her with only a towel wrapped around his waist.

'What does it look like I'm doing?' she replied, waving the gun at him.

'It's not loaded, you know. I'm not that stupid.' He approached her and peeled the gun from her hand. She liked the look on his face. The fact that he didn't know what she was thinking only added to the excitement.

'I want you to teach me how to shoot that thing.'

'Why, planning on killing someone?' Terry asked as he slid the gun back into the drawer. His hair was still wet, dripping down his neck and onto his chest. Annie took a deep breath at the sight of him. *No*, she thought. *I've already done that.*

'No. I've just never shot a gun before. Let's just say it's on my bucket list.'

Terry's eyes narrowed at that and it made Annie laugh. 'What exactly do you need a gun for anyway?'

Moving out of the room, Annie followed him along the hall and into a bedroom and suddenly wondered why they had spent the night on a leather sofa and not the super king size bed in the centre of the floor.

Terry let the towel drop to the floor and stepped into his clothes. A suit. She regarded him, wondering why a pub landlord needs to wear a black suit to work.

'What, are you a funeral director now? Oh I know, you shoot them dead to get the business?' She laughed and Terry shook his head.

'You're a lippy one, aren't you?' he said as he did his tie. Annie stepped closer and gripped the knot in her hand.

'I'll just go then, shall I?'

Terry wrapped his hand around hers and stared deeply into her eyes. She knew he didn't want her to leave and she wasn't planning on going anywhere.

'You really want to know what it is I do for a living?'

'Besides the pub, yes.'

'Then get yourself sorted and I'll meet you at the pub in an hour.'

Annie nodded, kissed him and left the house. Terry had a driver out the front, waiting for her. Still not impressed nor surprised, Annie climbed into a Mercedes and the driver took her home. Back to the flat that she couldn't stand to be in.

Twenty minutes later, she was standing in the bedroom as she tried to focus on why she was there. An ice-cold shiver trailed up her spine as she pulled a black and red fitted dress from the wardrobe and hung it on the back of the door. It was her favourite.

Pushing the thought from her mind, she went to the bathroom and stepped into the shower. The hot water ran over her and Annie scrubbed at her hair and her skin, vigorously and with speed. She wanted to look her best but didn't want to be late to meet Terry. The need to know what his life was all about was overwhelming and purely there to help her forget about her own.

Within twenty minutes, she'd showered, dressed and put on some makeup. Lining her lips red and running the straightener over the ends of her hair, she stepped into a pair of heels and glanced at herself in the mirror.

A steadying breath and a moment later she was back in the car with Terry's driver and they were on their way to the pub.

The driver glanced at her in the mirror but before she had a chance to smile, he pulled his eyes away and back onto the road. He said nothing the entire journey and she sensed he'd been told to keep quiet. He was just a driver.

What kind of businessmen had drivers? The kind who kept a gun in their desk drawer, she thought. Laughing inwardly, Annie shook her head. Maybe he wasn't a driver. Maybe he was Terry's security guard?

They pulled up outside the pub and just as she was about to step out of the car, Terry appeared by the door and climbed in.

'Good afternoon Mr Reid. Where to?'

'Alright Gerry? Mr Collins's place. Richie is meeting us there so no need to bypass his place.'

The driver gave a nod and pulled back out on to the road. Annie glanced at Terry in his pristine suit and smiled.

'You look very professional,' he said.

'Is that the look I was supposed to be going for?'

Terry smiled and shrugged. 'I told you to get yourself sorted. You wanted to know what I do and you've dressed for the occasion. It would seem you already have a fair idea.'

Terry lifted his suit coat, revealing the gun that normally lived in the drawer and Annie's stomach flipped. He let go and faced forward before placing a hand on her knee.

Annie's breath quickened, her heart pounding in her chest. For the first time in a month, this feeling wasn't one of dread. It was excitement.

Eighteen

Darkness had fallen over Mainhill estate. Lee and Freddie Whitelaw stood outside Maisie's flat, smoking a cigarette and waiting for the remainder of the teenagers to finally move on from the corner of the street where they had been loitering most of the evening.

Lee exhaled and a plume of blue smoke swirled above him into the night air. No words were exchanged between him and his brother. All Lee could think about was Galzo and how he'd taken the piss out of Maisie. He'd taken the piss out of all of them and thought he'd got away with it.

A sudden rush of footsteps caught Lee's attention and he turned to see the teenagers scarper, before two police officers on foot took chase. Good, Lee thought. That meant the already thin resources were taken up elsewhere, allowing Lee and Freddie more uninterrupted time to get into the garage and out before anyone would notice. Hopefully.

'Keep an eye on that house, Freddie. I'm going for a slash,' Lee said, dropping his cigarette to the ground.

Freddie nodded in response and Lee went up to Maisie's flat. Once inside, he heard a faint sound coming from the bedroom, a breathy, distressed sound which made him stop. 'Maisie?'

Nothing.

Shit.

Moving into the bedroom, he saw Maisie hunched over the bed, sweat pouring off her as she sucks in deep lungfuls of air.

'Maisie, what the fuck?'

She looked up at Lee, terror in her eyes. 'It's the baby, Lee. It's coming.'

'But you're not due for another month,' he panicked.

'Aye, well it's coming now,' she said through gritted teeth.

Throwing his hands up and resting them on top of his head, Lee felt the panic creeping up from his chest and into his throat. 'What do I do?'

'Nothing,' Maisie said. 'I've already phoned an ambulance. I'll be fine.'

'Jesus, Maisie you can't do this yourself,' Lee moved closer as his sister's knees buckled from under her. She gripped the bed covers with her hands and her knuckles turned white.

'Lee, if you don't do this tonight you won't get another chance. I'll have doctors and nurses to help me.' Maisie cried out in pain and Lee went to her.

'Let me get Mum.'

'Nah, I don't want that junkie near me. I got clean when I found out I was pregnant. Being around her will only make me want to use if she's off her face once the baby is out.'

The guilt that rippled through Lee was beginning to cloud his vision, but he knew Maisie was right. Now was the only time he would have any chance of paying Terry Reid off.

'I'm so sorry Maisie,' he said, kissing his sister on the head.

'It's fine,' she hissed through the pain. 'Just go. Come to the hospital as soon as you can.'

Lee moved away from his sister and back out to the street. He could hear sirens in the distance and he knew the ambulance was coming. Its blue flashing lights and sirens could fuck up his plan.

'What the hell is happening?' Freddie asked as Lee approached.

'Dunno,' Lee lied, trying to distract himself from abandoning the plan to be with his sister instead. He also didn't want Freddie to know about Galzo being the dad to Maisie's baby otherwise the plan would be scuppered. It was easier to lie. 'Come on, let's move out of sight.'

Freddie didn't argue or ask any more questions. So much was going on in Lee's head right now, but the most important thing was getting Terry's money. He had to push Maisie and Galzo to the back of his head for now.

Lee led Freddie to the back of the houses to the play park, where there was a hole in the fence which led into the garden they needed to access in order to get to the garage. It was a lot further down the street and away from ambulances and prying eyes. The house was in darkness and seemed still. Either the owners were in bed or out. Lee didn't know which option would be better.

'Is that the polis?' Freddie asked as they stopped in the park behind the house.

'Maybe, they'll be after those kids earlier.'

They fell silent again, watching the house. After another twenty minutes or so, the estate was in silence again. The sirens had stopped and the flashing blue lights no longer illuminated the gaps between the houses and flats. Lee thought about Maisie. She would be in the ambulance by now, on her way to the hospital. In safe hands. He and Freddie would have to make it through the night, through the job if either of them ever wanted to see their sister again, meet their nephew.

'Right,' Lee said. 'Let's do this.'

Nineteen

'Samuel, if you don't get up now I'm going to cancel your birthday party and I'm not kidding. You've got thirty seconds.' Leah Martin stood at her son's bedroom door and projected her voice to an annoying level that she knew would work. It worked most mornings and today was no different, although having the added bonus of using an empty yet at the same time fully loaded threat like cancelling his birthday helped even more.

'Right,' Samuel groaned, throwing the covers off himself and getting up. He stamped across the bedroom floor in his batman pyjamas and Leah ruffled his hair.

'Good lad. Your breakfast is waiting for you in the kitchen. You've got fifteen minutes before we need to be ready to leave. The threat of me cancelling your party still stands if you're not by the front door, dressed and ready by half past eight.'

Samuel didn't reply as he made his way downstairs and Leah began to make the bed.

Busy, she thought. Just keep busy. That was the key to keeping the images of what was coming at bay. She hadn't mustered up enough courage on Saturday evening to tell Tom about the envelope. She'd lied that it was something to do with the end of term school fair and Tom had accepted her lie so easily. Sunday came and went and she couldn't bring herself to talk about it with him then either, especially when Samuel had arrived home from his sleepover.

Glancing up at the clock, she saw that it read eight twenty. Leah dressed herself quickly and made herself look presentable enough with minimal makeup, a little bronzer, lip gloss and some mascara. That would have to do until she could get home and sort herself properly.

Ten minutes later, Samuel was at the front door waiting for her with his school bag on his back and that look of defiance and frustration ten-year-old boys tend to have when they don't get their own way.

'What's up with you this morning?' Leah asked him, reaching across and unbolting the door.

'Nothing. I tried to shout on you but you didn't hear me. You just missed the man at the door. He said he was a friend of yours and that he left you a message at the weekend and that he would be back later to pick up the thing you borrowed from him.'

It took Leah every muscle in her body to keep herself upright. This was bound to happen; she hadn't fooled herself into thinking that it wouldn't come up behind her one day, but she hadn't expected it to happen like this, with her son in the middle of it.

'Did he say anything else?'

'No. I said that he could come in and wait for you but he said that he could see that I was just about to go to school and he would come back later.'

The terror and fear of the words coming from Samuel began to claw their way up from the pit of her stomach, threatening to escape her lips. Leah saw her own horror in the eyes of her son. *Calm*, she thought. *Stay calm.*

Leah looked down to see that her son was holding a small, red jewellery box. 'He also said that I was to give you this.'

Leah took the box from Samuel and stared at it before peering out of the window again. The street was beginning to fill up with parents walking their children along the road to school. Nothing seemed to be out of the ordinary. The man she was hiding from wasn't going to come after her in broad daylight. He would be waiting in the shadows for her. The best thing she could do right now was get Samuel to school. He'd be safe there, away from her.

'Thanks honey,' she said, slipping the box into the pocket of her jeans. Whatever it was that was in there, she didn't want to open it in front of Samuel. 'Right, time for school.'

Leah opened the door and looked out into the street before merging with the crowds of parents and children walking in the same direction. It took less than five minutes before they arrived at the school gates, where Samuel took off in the direction of his friends who were already kicking a football around the playground.

'Hey you,' Charlotte called from across the road.

Leah watched until Samuel was safely through the gate before she headed towards her friend. The rest of the girls were there too, all smiling and waving at her. She wanted so desperately to run away from here. She wanted to make herself safe. But he'd found her and if she disappeared now then she would be putting her entire family and potentially all of her friends in danger. She had to face what she'd done.

'You okay? You look like you've not slept off the hangover,' Charlotte smiled while waving off her two kids to school.

It was at that point that Leah realised she wanted to blurt everything out there and then; she couldn't hold it in.

'Charlotte, I'm in trouble.'

Charlotte turned to face Leah and that was when the tears that had been threatening since she and Samuel had left the house began to spill over. Her hands trembled as she felt for the red box she'd shoved into her pocket.

'Hey Leah, I've got some ideas for the summer fair that I want to run by you,' Kim said, suddenly standing by Leah's side. Upon seeing tears in her eyes, Kim said, 'Oh shit. What's up?'

Leah quickly wiped at her eyes and shook her head. She didn't want to talk about this with everyone. She didn't want anyone to know, but she'd opened her big mouth when she was drunk and Charlotte might be the only one she could talk to about what was going on.

'Nothing,' Leah said and plastered on her best smile. 'Just chuck your ideas on a bit of paper and stick it through the door. I've got loads to do in the run up to the fair as it is and I've got a few jewellery orders still to get through.'

'Okay great,' Kim replied, concern plastered across her face. It quickly faded and turned to a beaming smile. 'Right ladies, I'll catch you all later. Simon is taking me for a fancy day at a spa while the kids are in school.'

Leah watched as Kim climbed into the car and drove off before the school bell had even rung. That was Kim all over; as soon as she could get rid of her kids, she was off living a life of luxury until she absolutely had to be a mum again.

Debs smiled at Leah and Charlotte but kept her distance. It was as if she knew there was something going on that Leah didn't want to talk about. Good, Leah thought to herself. She really didn't.

Charlotte slipped her arm through Leah's as her hand rested on her hip, and stood silently. A moment later, the school bell rang and all of the children disappeared inside the school building. The silence rang out louder than the bell itself. The parents in their fancy cars dissipated and Leah felt the tears begin to roll down her cheeks.

'Right. Why don't we go back to yours and you can tell me what's going on?' Charlotte suggested.

Taking a deep breath, Leah tried to compose herself. 'No. We can't go back to mine. I mean, you can't come to my house. It's not safe.'

Charlotte turned, and a look of confusion swept across her face. 'What do you mean it's not safe? What kind of trouble are you in, Leah?'

'Not here. Can we go somewhere busy?'

'Okay,' Charlotte's eyes widened. 'Now you're scaring me. Is this about what you said on the phone the other day about the message that came through the door?'

'Yes, and believe me, you're not the only one who's scared.'

Leah and Charlotte got into Charlotte's car and they drove out of the village, around four miles south towards the small shopping complex on the Loch side. When they arrived, Charlotte parked the car and they went into the Oak Tree café. Leah ordered a strong black coffee and prepared herself to open up. But she couldn't tell Charlotte everything. Not before she told Tom. She just needed to offload first. And she couldn't go home, not after the picture and the note. Not after Samuel said the man had come to the house. Then she remembered the box in her pocket.

Charlotte stood by the counter, waiting for the coffees. Leah was alone at the table. Standing up, she took the red jewellery box out of her pocket and sat back down. Closing her eyes, Leah opened the lid and took a breath before looking down.

'Oh my god, Leah,' Charlotte said. Leah's eyes snapped open as she looked up at her friend. She'd appeared at the table with the coffees without Leah noticing. 'Is that what I think it is?'

Leah followed her friend's wide open gaze down to the box in her hand. What was inside chilled her to the very core.

'It's a bullet,' Leah whispered, her voice caught up in the fear of what was happening. Lifting it carefully between her finger and thumb, she took a closer look at it.

It was engraved with a name. Her *own* name.

–

Clutching the bullet in the palm of her hand, Leah sat back in the car as Charlotte drove them back to Balness.

'You have to go to the police, Leah.'

Leah hadn't given Charlotte the full details of the person behind the bullet, or of her involvement with them. The fact that she'd told her about the money was dangerous enough in itself. She couldn't put Charlotte at risk by telling her anything else.

'I've already told you, Charlotte. I can't do that. It's just too complicated. And how would that look at the school for Samuel? You know what this village is like, full of little gossip groups who would love nothing more than to hear a bit of drama, especially from me. You know what some of the mums are like, the ones who wanted to head up PTA and didn't get picked. They behave as though I pissed on their kids, for Christ's sake.'

'Don't try to make me laugh Leah,' Charlotte said with a light smile perched on her lips. 'And it's not drama. What you're holding in your hand there is a death threat. This person wants you to know that he's still around. How could you not have told Tom about this?'

Leah shook her head. This was all far too messed up. The lies had gone on long enough, Charlotte was right.

'If you're not going to go to the police, at least promise me you'll tell Tom. He'll want to protect you. This lunatic showed up at your house, Leah. You've got Samuel to think about.'

'I know. But I know what this guy's capable of. He won't do anything that will risk him going to prison. I know this sounds silly but I don't feel unsafe.'

Charlotte let out a sarcastic laugh. 'You're holding a bullet with your name on it, Leah. What are you going to do, wear it on a chain around your neck.'

An involuntary smile crept across Leah's face then. She couldn't help but laugh at the image. But the situation wasn't funny at all. The bullet was a stark warning that he was coming for her.

Charlotte pulled up outside Leah and Tom's house and as Leah was about to get out of the car, she grabbed hold of Leah's hand.

'Leah, I'm worried about you.'

'Och don't, I'll be fine,' Leah feigned confidence. 'I promise I'll sort this. But thank you for this morning. I appreciate your support.'

Leah got out the car, bullet in hand and keys in the other. Opening the door, she waved Charlotte off before closing herself inside and putting on the bolt. The named bullet glared up at her from the palm of her hand and she felt herself sliding down the door, her chest constricting as she tried to suck air into her lungs.

Then her phone rang. Pulling it from her pocket, she looked down at the screen to see a number withheld notification. She knew it would be him. Who else?

'Hello?'

A breathy silence hung on the other end of the line. Then came the words she'd been dreading.

'You've got a week to get my money, or there'll be another bullet with your name on it.'

The sound of the voice took her back to the last time she'd heard it and nausea crept in.

'Only this time it'll go into the back of your skull. But not before I make you watch your family suffer. And don't think I won't do it. Your boy will be first, then that husband of yours. I know where you live, where your son goes to school. I know that you run your own business from home and that you're having a birthday party for that kid of yours. Don't underestimate me. I mean it. One week and if I don't have my money and a fucking explanation, you're done. You're all done.'

The line went dead and Leah dropped the phone before everything went black.

Twenty

The car stopped and the driver put on the handbrake. Terry stepped out of the car and moved around to the other side and opened the door for Annie. As she placed her right foot on the pavement and rose to stand next to him, she smiled widely at him.

Terry didn't say anything but led her to a door in the centre of a block of luxury flats. She peered up at the large balconies at the top and imagined how hot it must get up there when the sun was at its highest.

'Terry,' Richie said as he opened the door and stepped out of the building. He eyed Annie and Terry narrowed his eyes. He didn't want to answer any questions about Annie right now.

'Richie. Hungover?' Terry asked.

'Naw. Hair of the dog and all that.'

Richie and Annie locked eyes and he nodded politely. 'It's Annie, isn't it?'

Annie nodded back and Terry slipped his hand around her waist. 'Nice to meet you again, Richie.'

Terry could see the look of concern etched on Richie's face and he excused himself from Annie for a moment. Richie followed him, a few steps and they were by Richie's BMW.

'Why have you brought her here?' Richie hissed. 'You only fucking met her yesterday.'

'Aye a'right. Calm down. Listen, this is my deal and it's my choice who I bring with me,' Terry replied.

'Listen, Terry. I don't mean to sound disrespectful but do you not think you should be splitting business and pleasure? She could be an undercover or anything.'

Terry rolled his eyes. Did Richie really think he was that bloody stupid? 'I've had her checked out. There's not much to tell but she's clean, alright?' Terry assured Richie, lowering his tone. Of course he didn't want Annie knowing that he'd had one of his tech guys do a search on her. It hadn't been hard or taken long to find out about her. She'd been a waitress in various restaurants in the city. She'd worked in a bar in the west end and been a nanny for a short time. There was nothing about her that made Terry suspect she was anything other than normal. The only thing different about her to the other women he'd been with was that she had a fair idea that he could be dangerous and it didn't seem to bother her. Annie hadn't so much as blinked when she saw that gun on him in the car and she'd asked no questions about the job he'd taken her on. Something about her made him tick and although he'd only known her twenty-four hours, he knew he could trust her. That feeling hadn't been there with Kora, not immediately like it was with Annie. She reminded him a little of himself; there was a wild side to her that he wanted to explore and perhaps bringing her closer to things was the way to do that. If she saw him, the full version of Terry and what he was, then maybe she would stick around.

'You thought Kora was clean, then she went and shagged that fucking twat Conway behind your back,' Richie said.

'Don't go there Richie,' Terry warned.

Terry appreciated that Richie wasn't convinced by Annie. But he didn't have to be. Turning to Annie who was standing where Terry had left her, he said, 'Annie, Richie here thinks you're an undercover polis.'

Annie glared at Richie and with a raised brow she said, 'How do you know I'm not?'

Terry laughed and Richie's expression fell. He didn't like being made a fool of, Terry knew that. Especially when they're just about to close a deal that could make them a shit ton of money.

'This deal is important, Terry,' Richie said.

'Aye, I fucking know.'

'And you think, no offence love,' Richie glanced at Annie, 'that bringing your new bit of meat around is a good idea.'

'Oi,' Annie shot Richie a warning glance. It made Terry stir. 'Who do you think you're talking about? I might be a woman but I can handle anything that's thrown at me. And just because I'm female doesn't mean you can talk about me like that, especially when I'm standing right here. So do yourself a favour, eh? Don't be a prick.'

Terry stifled a laugh and there was hesitation from Richie before he broke eye contact and moved back to the front entrance of the building. That was him well and truly told.

As Richie opened the door, Terry approached him and allowed Annie to go inside first. Richie followed behind Terry and they stepped inside the lift to take them to the fifth floor.

Inside, they were surrounded by multiple reflections of themselves.

'You ready for this?' Richie asked Annie, eyeing her in the mirror. 'I hope you realise what you've let yourself in for. If shit hits the fan then you'll need to be ready to—'

'Richie,' Annie held a hand up at his face. 'Has anyone ever told you, you talk too much?'

Terry smirked, but he wondered if Richie was right. Would she be able to handle this? There was only one way to find out if she wanted him for who he was. Patting Richie on the shoulder before the lift came to a halt, they stepped out and on to the landing.

Frustration made the muscles around Richie's mouth twist as he lifted his hand and knocked on the door. Terry waited.

Annie said nothing and Terry searched her eyes but found them difficult to read. Was she excited? Scared? But the biggest question he had to ask himself – was he doing the right thing?

Twenty-One

Annie regarded the man who opened the door. He was around Terry's age, perhaps slightly younger. He wasn't wearing a suit like Terry or Richie. He was a little more casual, black jeans and a white T-shirt. His aftershave almost choked her as he welcomed them inside and she passed him.

'Mr Reid, Richie, good of you to stop by,' he said but his eyes were on Annie.

'Mr Collins,' Terry shook his hand. She watched how Terry held the man's hand firmly. Kept one eye on him.

'Och, come on. Call me Derek.'

Annie followed Terry and Richie into a large dining room where another man, a little younger sat at the end of a table with his feet up. A gun sat on the glass surface and Annie's stomach flipped a little. What the hell was this guy all about?

'Put that away, Kenny,' Derek Collins said. Kenny did as he was told, lifted the gun and slid it into the back of his jeans. 'And this lovely lady must be…?'

'Annie,' Terry said. Derek Collins appeared to hover, awaiting a status as to who she may be or why she was even present. Terry didn't offer it and Derek nodded politely, although Annie could tell he didn't mean it.

Annie saw two types of men within the four that were present. Professional and amateur. She knew nothing of what was about to happen and if she was honest with herself, the prospect of the unknown scared the bloody shit out of her as much as it thrilled her. But just by looking at them, she could see boys and men. Why had Terry brought her here? A distraction? A negotiation? Was he testing her, to see if she really was interested in him? She couldn't tell, he had such a good poker face.

'So, Neil's in the jail, I hear?' Terry said, taking a seat at the table upon Derek's gesture to do so. The rest of the men follow suit and Annie sat down next to Terry.

'He is,' Kenny replied. 'Stupid bastard. Nearly fucked things up again. I'm telling you, he's a liability.'

'Kenny…' Derek said with warning to his tone. 'Watch your mouth. He might act like an idiot at times, but he is your brother and a bloody good businessman.'

Kenny shut his mouth then and lowered his gaze. It would appear that Derek was the boss.

'So where does this leave us? There is a lot of stock sitting in our warehouse and I want it shifted, Derek. The longer it sits there the hotter it gets. You know the fucking drill,' Terry said. 'If you can't uphold the agreement then we shop elsewhere.'

Derek's gaze shifted between Terry and Richie before he rose from his seat and moved to the counter behind him. He lifted a bottle of malt whisky and poured a small amount into four glasses. Clearly Annie wouldn't be part of the whisky drinking gangsters, she thought.

'The deal goes ahead. We can look after things on our end even with Neil in the jail,' Derek said. Annie noticed a smile appear on the other man's face. She glanced at Terry and Richie, wondering what was going to happen next.

'Do you even know what the deal entailed, Derek?' Richie asked.

Derek placed the four glasses of whisky on the table, one in front of each man. He eyed Annie and smiled, silently confirming her thoughts that she wasn't to have one. Fuck him, she thought.

'You don't think I know what deals my brother makes? You think I get kept in the dark? Neil may well be the front man, Terry. But I'm the one holding things together. You got that?'

Richie and Terry were silent. Annie noticed how Terry placed his hand on the side of his jacket. He was getting ready to brandish his gun. Fuck!

Annie wanted to get up and ask to use the bathroom but she was rooted to the spot. Terry wouldn't have brought her here if he didn't want her to be a part of this, to see what life was like in his business. And she felt she had a point to prove, not just to Terry but to Richie in particular. The way he'd spoken to her outside, referring to her as Terry's piece of meat had riled her. She'd been through too much to be branded as some tart who didn't know her arse from her elbow.

'Right then, so you'll know that there's a new pick up point, new date, new time. Your men meet ours, the transfer takes place and then the drugs are dispatched among your dealers. Once they're sold off, we get our cut of seventy per cent,' Terry said.

Derek glanced at Kenny, and Terry glanced at Richie. The building tension made Annie's heart race.

'Neil said the cut was sixty forty,' Derek said.

'Of course he fucking did,' Richie sneered.

Annie couldn't take her eyes off Terry's pocket, praying that this would end well.

'No. The deal was seventy thirty. If you're not happy with that then fine, find your supply elsewhere. But you know the quality won't be anywhere near as good value for money. The demand for a purer product is high, Derek, and you know it. We're the only people who can provide that. The more it's cut, the less revenue. It's your call.'

Derek sighed and nodded silently before he and Terry shook hands.

All four men nodded, got to their feet to stand with Derek and clinked their glasses together.

'Maybe if things go well, we'll do business again?' Derek said as he saw them to the door. 'It would be a shame to see this pretty face just the once.'

Annie smiled at him, imagining his expression as she brought her knee up to his balls and crunched them into his stomach.

Annie, Terry and Richie left the Collinses flat and stood in the lift in silence as it dropped them slowly to the ground floor.

Annie's legs were shaking but she kept her composure. Richie shook Terry's hand before departing to his car. She watched as he pulled out of his space and disappeared down the road.

'You coming?' Terry asked, holding the door open for her. Annie walked to the car and climbed in, followed by Terry on the other side. The driver brought the car out to the main road and Annie was silent, trying to work out in her head what she'd just witnessed and why Terry had wanted her to be a part of it.

'Thoughts?' Terry said. The single word threw her.

'Thoughts? You want my thoughts? Okay.' She tapped her hand on the leather seat twice before turning to face him. 'What the *fuck* is it do you do for a living?'

'I think you know what I do,' Terry replied. 'We weren't exactly talking sherbet lollies up there, Annie.'

'So the stock, the products, all drugs? Knocked off bevy? Guns?'

'Not all for the Collins deal but yes, pretty much.'

Annie had a sharp intake of breath and sniggered. 'You know Richie was right, I *could* be undercover police. And you'd be fucked right now.'

'But you're not undercover police. You're Annie Wicks. Currently running away from something you don't want to share with me.'

Annie stared at him, her mouth open a little wider than she'd wanted. 'How do you know that?'

'Because it's my job to know everything about everyone I surround myself with. Take Gerry, my driver. He's got a wife, Carolyn. Lovely lady. Three grown up girls. One is married and a stay at home mum. One is a nurse and the other is travelling Thailand on a gap year from university. He lives in Clydebank and because of this job he's just paid off his mortgage. Ain't that right Gerry?'

Annie glanced in the mirror at Gerry and he nodded and gave a gentle smile but said nothing.

'Yeah but he works for you. I don't. So why do you know things about me I haven't told you,' Annie asked. The thought that he could know about her past terrified her more than the gun in his pocket and the deal she'd just witnessed up in that flat. That would mean possibly having to explain it. To talk about it. Annie couldn't have that.

'Because Annie, I had to know everything about you if we're going to spend more time together. I don't like to waste my time on someone, especially if later down the line I find out something that means I have to step away from them. And I like what I see with you, but you might not like what you get with me. You can walk away now if you want. I don't expect you to stay. But if you can handle what just went on up there, then there could be longevity in what's going on with us.'

Annie frowned. 'That's verycontrolling.'

'Like I say, you can walk. If you want to.'

They were silent for a moment and Annie didn't know if she should ask about the girl in the photo. But she knew herself well enough to know that curiosity always got the better of her.

'Who's the girl in the photo?'

Terry didn't meet her eye. 'What photo?'

'The one in the drawer next to your gun. I wasn't snooping, honestly. I just found it when I found the gun.' Annie took a breath, wondering if she'd overstepped the mark. 'She's pretty. An ex of yours?'

The car pulled up outside Terry's pub and the engine went dead.

'Yes. Her name was…' He cleared his throat. '*Is* Kora. We were engaged to be married, but we ended on bad terms. I didn't even know that picture was still in there.'

Annie frowned, unsure as to how true that was. If the picture was in the same place he kept his gun, surely he would know it was there.

'What happened between you?'

'She cheated on me,' Terry replied. 'I confronted her, she denied it. I got angry. We argued. I left. I haven't seen her since.'

Turning, Terry leaned over and kissed Annie on the cheek and then he got out of the car. She climbed out too and watched as he stepped inside, leaving her in the street. And it was as simple as that, she thought with sarcasm. The tone in which he said it made it sound as though he was still hurt by what this Kora did to him. But everyone had a past, didn't they? Annie knew that better than anyone.

Gerry stepped out and smiled at her. 'Do you need a lift home?'

Annie returned his smile and shook her head. 'No, thank you Gerry.'

Pushing the door open, Annie went inside and stood next to Terry who was at the same part of the bar that she'd met him just the day before when she was looking for something that would take her out of her horrendous life and into a new one. She didn't think it would happen in the literal sense but it had.

'Drink?' he asked without turning.

'Vodka. Double.'

How could so much have changed inside twenty-four hours? She glanced down at her watch and realised it had been thirty hours since she first laid eyes on Terry Reid.

'If you want me to stick around, Terry, then I want to know what's going on.' She practically throws the vodka down her throat and places the glass on the bar. Terry gestures to Hayley for a refill.

'That was always my intention.'

'Always? You mean since yesterday?'

'Well, spending thirty odd hours intense time with someone is like going on five or six dates, isn't it? So technically we've been dating for a couple weeks at least.' Terry turned to her and smiled as he offered her the glass.

As the vodka settled in her stomach and warmed the blood in her veins, she began to feel the excitement creep back in. This was what she'd wanted. She shouldn't be complaining.

'Look, I don't know what it is about you but you pulled me in the second I laid eyes on you. I know it was possibly a really stupid decision to take you along to the Collins deal today, but I just knew you'd be able to handle it.'

'And you're sure I'm not just some rebound after your missus done the dirty on you?'

That seemed to sting him hard as he drew his eyes away.

'No. I don't do rebounds. If I bring someone in on my life, it's because I trust them. And I trust you. You wouldn't have been part of that today if I didn't.'

They fell silent for a second as Terry's fingers brushed over her hand. Pulses of electricity surged between them and Annie took a breath. Maybe they were both on the rebound, but whatever this was, Annie knew she wanted it. And it would seem Terry wanted it too.

'I'm not sure your mate's a fan of me right enough,' Annie said, sipping at her vodka.

'Richie's one of those guys who likes to keep his cards close to his chest. Once he gets to know you, he'll come around. But you don't have to worry about that.'

Annie smiled, unconvinced about Terry's thoughts that Richie would come round. The way he'd spoken to her, even the way he'd looked at her told Annie all she'd needed to know. He didn't want her around, taking over from him. It was ridiculous that she was even thinking that when she'd only known Terry a day. It was madness, but then hadn't that been what she was looking for?

'Right, Gerry's waiting for us. Let's go back to my place and we'll talk properly. Lay all the cards on the table.' Terry led her outside and Annie wobbles on her heels a little.

Annie was excited to go back to Terry's house, but she didn't want to lay her cards on the table. Well, not *all* of them.

Twenty-Two

Lee and Freddie Whitelaw crossed the park under the cover of darkness and headed for the garage. Lee's stomach was spinning with the nauseating reality of what would be if this didn't go as planned. Freddie didn't seem to understand the full extent of the situation. In a way Lee accepted that this was his doing; he'd always sheltered Freddie from reality when they were kids, but of course Freddie had ended up going down the same route as Rosie and Cammy anyway. Maybe it was a good thing not fully believing that death could be staring you in the face in little under seventy-two hours.

Squeezing through the gap in the fence that led them to the garden, they stood at the back corner, staring down at the brick building. Lee turned to look at his younger brother and wondered what would have been if their parents hadn't been such wasters when they were growing up. Maybe they wouldn't be in this position right now. Of course, Lee understood that it wasn't just Rosie and Cammy's fault. The estate had a lot to answer for. Lee had seen good kids move into Mainhill and slowly but surely, as they became integrated with the young team and hit the drugs and alcohol that was readily available, their lives had dissolved from under them. They'd had good families right enough, but all it took was for one of the parents to lose a job and have to move to the estate. No amount of good upbringing could fight against the everyday truths of what it was like to be a kid and a teenager in Mainhill.

'Right, looks like we're good to go,' Freddie whispered. 'I'll cover the front like you said and you get in and get out as quick as. Galzo will meet us at the end of the estate in his Lanny, he's got the trailer.'

Lee nodded but didn't say anything in response. He thought if he did he might throw up at that moment. Just earlier that day, he'd held a knife up to the local shopkeeper and robbed the place. Now he was about to rob someone else without them knowing. The adrenaline that was coursing through his veins made him put one foot in front of the other as Freddie tiptoed around the side of the garage and out of sight. Getting this right was crucial in order for them both to survive.

Excitement, fear and sheer panic forced Lee towards the side entrance and he pulled his sleeve over his hand before trying the handle on the door. To his amazement and the owner's stupidity, the door opened. Lee peered inside and staring back at him was a brand new set of wheels. All eight hundred quid's worth.

'Jackpot,' Lee whispered as he moved inside. Looking for something to wedge the door open, he saw a tool box in the corner. Creeping quietly over, Lee lifted it and places it in front of the door as silently as possible.

Lee quickly began to pull the first wheel down and rolled it out of the garage and into the garden, around the side of the building and onto the street. Freddie met him at the gate and the calm expression on his face settled Lee's stomach.

Freddie mouthed at Lee to get the rest of the wheels and Lee didn't hesitate. A few heart-wrenching minutes passed and Lee was replacing the tool box in its original place, careful not to leave his prints behind, before closing the door.

Back out on the street, Freddie and Lee began rolling the wheels down the back of the next house which was nestled between the park and a row of council flats. Lee could hear the sound of a car engine and his stomach somersaulted.

'That'll be Galzo,' Freddie said as they entered the park further down the estate. 'He's waiting for us at the other side.'

Lee hadn't anticipated how difficult it would be to roll two wheels down a street, in darkness and in silence. But now that he was doing it, now more than ever he wanted to knock his brother out for how stupid and naive he'd been.

They finally reached the opposite side of the park and moved through the gate to see Galzo leaning against the bonnet of the car and smoking a joint. Lee could almost smell it from the other side of the park.

'A'right boys,' he said, exhaling loudly. 'Got the goods. Nice one.'

'Aye, help us get them in the fucking trailer, Galzo eh?' Freddie said, stopping by the back of the Land Rover.

'Oh, aye nae worries boys.' Galzo kept the joint between his lips as he helped lift the wheels into the trailer. 'Right, let's go get these sold on.'

Lee and Freddie climbed into the back of the Land Rover and Galzo pulled out of the estate and headed for the town centre.

Twenty-Three

Tom Martin zipped up his son's football bag and dropped it at his feet while waiting for kick off. Leah had woken up this morning with a headache and Tom had insisted she stay in bed and that he would do the training duty today.

The whistle sounded for the start of the game and Tom kept his eyes on Samuel. The football coach at the side-line shouted words of encouragement at the team and Tom clapped along with the other parents when the favoured team had possession of the ball.

'They're a good team, eh?' a voice said to Tom's left. Turning, he saw a man around the same age as him.

'Aye, they're definitely better than last season,' Tom replied and the man laughed. 'Your son out there?'

'Aye, he's on the away squad though.'

'Oh, should we be discussing this?' Tom raised a brow as a sarcastic smile spread across his face.

'You're Tom Martin, aren't you?'

Tom felt his brow furrow a little. 'That's me. And you are?'

'Oh god, sorry,' he held out his hand. 'I bought some jewellery for my missus from your wife's online store last month. She loved it and started following her on Instagram.'

Tom's frown turned to a grin. 'Ah, Leah will be delighted to hear that. I'll pass it on.'

The referee's whistle sounded again and the man pulled out his phone, took a picture of his son. 'For the missus, you know. Loves to see the wee man play.'

A commotion was taking place on the pitch and Tom shook his head. Even as kids, the competitive streak was still there. That whole 'it's not about winning it's about taking part' crap never worked on him as a child and kids these days didn't fall for it either.

'Tom,' Charlotte's voice came from behind. 'No Leah today?'

'Nah, she's got a banging headache. She's at home in bed.'

'Did she talk to you yet?' Charlotte asked and Tom pursed his lips.

'Talk to me about what?'

The man beside Tom excused himself and made his way along the side of the pitch and into the crowd of parents from the opposing team.

'Erm,' Charlotte hovered. 'She said she wanted to talk to you about something that was bothering her. It's not really my place to tell you.'

Tom had no clue what she was talking about and shrugged his shoulders, waiting for Charlotte to tell him what she meant.

'She hasn't said anything yet?'

Shaking his head, he kept one eye on the game. Samuel was in possession of the ball and Tom cheered for him.

'Okay, well I think you should talk to her. It's important and kind of urgent.'

'What do you mean, urgent?' he asked, his stomach lurching at Charlotte's revelation. 'Is she in some kind of trouble?'

'Awe, I shouldn't have said anything. I'm sorry. It's really not my place. But please talk to her. I'm worried for her.'

Tom caught the look on Charlotte's face and realised just *how* worried she seemed. What was it that Leah had told her that she had failed to mention to him, her husband?

'Can't you just tell me now, Charlotte? I mean if it's that important?' Tom pressed. But he knew what Charlotte and Leah were like. She would never betray Leah's trust like that. Giving him enough so that he would have to tell Leah that he knew there was a problem would be as far as she'd go.

'Look, Tom, I have to go. I'm sorry, I didn't mean to cause any upset. But Leah is my friend, she's an important person in my life and I'm worried that in not telling you what's going on, she could end up in serious shit.'

Charlotte hesitated before she headed down the pitch and out of the school grounds. An unease settled inside Tom and he pulled out his phone to send Leah a message. But did he really want to ask her about this over a text or WhatsApp message? He couldn't say that he'd noticed any change in Leah recently. She'd been her usual, busy self. Running a small business, heading up school events, being a mum and a wife took up so much time he found it difficult to comprehend anything else in her life that would get her into trouble like Charlotte said.

Glancing down at his phone, he pulled up Leah's number but instead of calling, he typed out a text.

Met Charlotte. You want to tell me what the hell is going on? She was in knots, telling me that she's worried about you. When I get home with Sam, we need to talk.

The crowd around him erupted then and he realised that Samuel had scored the first goal of the game and he'd missed it. Shit.

'Nice one wee man, get in there,' Tom roared across the pitch, attempting to hide the sickening thought that his wife was hiding something from him. Was she having an affair? Was she in debt? Neither of those things made sense to him.

Looking down at the screen as the game played on, Tom watched as two blue ticks appeared on the screen. Leah had seen the message.

But she never replied.

At the end of the match, Samuel stood in with his team, celebrating their win. The man who'd said he'd bought jewellery from Leah's website was heading in Tom's direction with a smile on his face.

'Well done. Your boy did good,' he said. 'I guessed by your reaction he was the one who scored?'

'Aye. He's a cracking wee player. Here, what's your missus name? So I can pass onto Leah about what you said.'

There were a few seconds' silence before the man smiled. 'It's Annie. Her name's Annie.'

Tom nodded. 'Great. Thanks. I'll let her know. Nice to meet you mate.'

'Aye, you too.'

The man turned as Samuel came running towards them, but before Tom could get a chance to ask him what his name was, he'd already gone.

Twenty-Four

Annie pulled her feet up from the floor and under her, repositioning herself on the sofa in Terry's lounge. Having decided to go back to his house with him, she realised she'd been sat on his sofa for over four hours and she'd barely asked a single question about his line of work. They'd had sex as soon as they got back and then lay on the sofa for a few hours. They'd spoken about everything other than his work.

They'd ordered pizza and ice-cream, and Terry carried the boxes into the lounge and placed them on the coffee table in front of them.

'So,' Annie said as she reached for a slice of pepperoni. 'The Collins deal.'

'What about it?' Terry replied before taking a bite of his own slice.

'Is it drugs?'

'Yes.'

'What kind?'

'Class A mostly,' Terry said, pausing mid bite.

Annie knew of various types of drugs but she didn't know what class each belonged to. But of course, Class A would be the harder stuff. She wasn't stupid.

'You ever taken drugs before, Annie?'

'That would be telling.'

Terry nodded, a grin creeping across his face. 'You've never smoked a bit of weed, done a bit of coke?'

'I said that would be telling. All you have to know is I don't do anything like that now as you know me.' Annie smiled. She liked the idea of drip feeding him information about herself. It would keep him interested. 'So, the deal, it's for heroin, coke? That kind of thing?' Annie pushed. As much as she wanted to keep things close to her chest, she also wanted to know what she was getting involved with.

'Aye, and the rest.'

Terry didn't seem too fazed by her questions, or the fact that the drugs he was putting out on the streets could kill people. If Annie was honest with herself, she wasn't either. In fact, Annie wasn't fazed by most things these days. Not after what she'd been through, not after what she'd done.

'And what will those men do with the stock?'

'They'll put them on the streets. They'll have their own distribution team that will supply various parts of the city and the outskirts.'

Annie laughed and Terry stopped mid chew. 'What you laughing at?'

'Distribution team?' She raised a brow.

'Well, what would you want me to call it? It's a team of lads who sell the gear in certain areas.'

Terry nudged Annie and laughed with her. She couldn't believe that she was talking about distributing drugs around the city as though it were something as innocent as newspapers.

'And the Collins deal, there are more like that?'

Terry nodded as he popped the last piece of crust into his mouth. 'Aye, we've got a varied amount of business partners. Some on the east side of the country but mostly Glasgow and surrounding areas.'

She could tell that he wasn't going to give up information unless she asked and she was happy to bombard Terry with questions.

'And what about guns? You supply those too?'

'Richie takes care of that side of things mostly.'

'And you said alcohol too?'

'You know the term, off the back of a lorry?' Terry asked. Annie nodded and decided she didn't care much about the alcohol. The drugs and the guns were what piqued her interest the most.

She wanted to know everything, see everything. Annie wanted to be part of this, something that she could really sink her teeth into.

'Have you ever killed anyone before?' she asked.

Terry gave her a sideward glance before picking up another slice of pizza from the box in front of him. 'Annie, I'm what people would describe as a gangster. A drug lord, a criminal. It would be like asking a tattoo artist if he had any tattoos. It comes with the territory.'

'Who?' Annie asked, a stir in her belly caused her to shift in her seat.

'It doesn't matter who, or how many. All that matters is that I'm willing to do whatever it takes to get to the top in this game. Anyone with ambition would. All you have to do is look at the politicians and the powerful people who run the world. Most of them are sociopaths. They'll put themselves in any position if it leads to success. I've definitely done that. Have you?'

Annie thought about her life before Terry and how quickly things had changed.

She was sat with one of Glasgow's top criminals, faced with the opportunity to be part of something much bigger than her and the life she'd wanted to lead.

'Not in the way you mean.' Annie shook her head and Terry smiled.

'Well, there's a first time for everything, isn't there?'

Terry lifted the pizza box and offered it to Annie. She took a slice and bit into it.

Yes, there was a first time for everything. Up until yesterday, she was a vegetarian who'd never have imagined how much her life would change.

Now, she was eating a pepperoni pizza with a man who'd probably killed a lot of people to get what he wanted. If the last day had shown her anything, then doing things for the first time was certainly enjoyable.

'Right, when are you going to teach me how that gun works?'

Twenty-Five

Standing in the warehouse just outside the town centre, Lee and Freddie shook hands with Galzo after he handed them their cash, taking his own cut beforehand.

'Cheers mate, you've no idea how much this helps us out,' Freddie said.

Lee hadn't realised how much of a kiss arse Freddie was when it came to Galzo. It made him want to knock Galzo's teeth out more than ever, but refrained from doing so. He needed to make sure that the money was in Terry's hands first.

'Pleasure doing business with you boys,' Galzo replied, folding up his cut and sliding the notes into his back pocket. Galzo met Lee's eye and his brow furrowed. 'You a'right Lee?'

Lee gave a tight-lipped smile and nodded. *Keep quiet for now, that's all you have to do*, he thought. 'Aye. Just glad we got the cash for those wheels.'

'Freddie, we'll catch up soon eh? Couple of beers and a few joints. It's been a while,' Galzo suggested and Freddie nodded a little too enthusiastically, Lee thought.

As they watched Galzo depart, Lee decided to tell Freddie that their sister had gone into labour.

'Jesus, we should go to the hospital,' Freddie suggested, only half-heartedly. Lee knew his brother well enough to understand that becoming an uncle didn't excite him. He didn't care about Maisie. Not really. No drug addict and alcoholic from the estate cared about anyone other than themselves. That was why they were in this mess, owing money to a dangerous gangster. It was lucky Lee did care otherwise they'd all be dead by now.

'Nah, they won't let us both in. Why don't you go home and I'll head up to see her. Then I can get Terry to come and meet me so I can pay back the cash we owe and put this shit behind us.'

Freddie agreed, barely mentioning Maisie or the baby again. They got into separate taxis and Lee headed up to the hospital to see his sister. The one in hospital giving birth to Galzo's baby. The baby he had no interest in.

When he got there, he asked at the front desk about Maisie and said that he was her birthing partner but was late back off a job, which in fairness wasn't far from the truth.

Soon enough, he was led through to a ward and a nurse was dressing him in gowns. 'Your sister is being prepped for an emergency C-section. Don't worry, she's okay but the baby will be here soon so you need to get in there and help her.'

Lee felt sick at the idea of his baby sister being cut open. He wanted to strangle Galzo, but pushed the useless twat out of his head as he was shown into the surgery room. Maisie seemed relatively calm, but Lee knew it would be the drugs getting her through.

'Hey,' she said. 'How you doing? All sorted?'

'Never mind that, Maisie. How are you?'

'Well, baby got stuck so they're about to do a C-section. I could really go a fag,' she replied with a smile.

Lee laughed but in truth he was holding back tears. Maisie seemed to be holding her shit together right there at that moment and he admired her for that. Another Whitelaw in the family by the end of the day, how could that be happening? He hoped this one would turn out better than the rest of them, including himself.

Little over half an hour later, a nurse placed Maisie's baby in her arms and this time, Lee allowed his tears to spill over. There was no point holding them in. Staring down at the little face of his new nephew, Lee made a silent promise to him that he would do whatever he could to keep him safe and get him away from the estate as soon as he could. The little guy looked like Maisie when she was just born, just sixteen years earlier. She'd been the cutest thing he'd ever seen, such innocence on her face as he'd held her for the first time. Worry and fear gripped him as he remembered that Maisie was going down the same route as Rosie and Cammy. He'd have to make sure that didn't happen.

'Meet baby Whitelaw,' Maisie said, glancing up at Lee. 'This is your Uncle Lee.'

Lee knew then that if anyone was going to be a father figure to that baby, it would be him. Galzo wouldn't get anywhere near his sister ever again.

'Wow,' Lee said as the nurse took the baby from Maisie and placed him in Lee's arms. 'A baby boy. He's just lovely.'

Looking down at his new nephew, Lee felt the weight of the world crushing down on him. He had to get away from Mainhill, get his sister and the baby out of that life. He couldn't allow things to carry on like this, with Maisie spiralling the same way their mother did, Lee digging them out of every hole Freddie dug for them.

He'd be able to get a job doing something honest, surely? Window cleaner, bin man. Anything to break the cycle of poverty and drug addiction this family had been cursed with. Anything to show this little lad that living a good and honest life was better than growing up in Mainhill.

Swallowing the lump in his throat, he looked at his sister who had tears in her eyes. It was as if she could hear his thoughts.

'I'll look after you both, Maze. I promise.'

–

Standing outside the hospital, Lee took a long, deep draw on the cigarette. It had been a heavy night, over twelve hours since Maisie went into labour. So much had happened inside that time. And now, he was awaiting Terry Reid to pick up his money.

He didn't have long to wait as he looked up and saw the Range Rover pulling up beside him. Lee climbed inside and Richie pulled out of the hospital grounds.

The men were silent as they sat in the front seat and Lee felt his heart hammer against his chest. Once the money had exchanged hands, Lee hoped he would be able to walk away from the mess his brother had created. He could have allowed Freddie to deal with this but knowing his brother only too well, he'd have ended up getting himself killed with the mouth on him.

Richie pulled the Range into a derelict carpark not far from the hospital and killed the engine before Terry turned and looked Lee dead in the eye. All this crap for a measly five hundred quid. It almost didn't seem worth it. But if a gangster was owed money, then it needed paying back regardless of the amount.

'I've got to say Lee, I was surprised you got in touch so soon,' Terry said.

'Aye, me too Mr Reid.'

Lee fumbled in the back seat, trying to pull the notes from his back pocket. Handing the money over, Terry counted it and handed the bundle to Richie who also counted the cash.

'How'd you get this?' Terry asked.

'I sold a set of wheels,' Lee said hesitantly. Would that be another bad decision in Terry's mind? Lee hoped not.

'Resourceful. I like it.'

Lee remained silent, unsure of what would happen next. Richie started up the engine but Terry placed a hand on his right-hand man's arm and the car remained stationary.

'I've had my eye on you over the last few weeks, Lee. I've seen how you conduct yourself. You're ballsy but not cocky. There's an element of pride I don't see in your brother or Cammy,' Terry said, keeping his eyes locked with Lee's.

'You know my auld man?' Lee asked.

'Aye, he's a chancer. Always has been. I can see where Freddie gets it from. But you... you're different.'

Lee sighed. How was he supposed to respond? And more to the point, where was this conversation headed?

'We have a proposition for you, Lee. But you would have to keep it under wraps.'

'Aye, top secret, Lee,' Richie said.

Lee's eyes darted between the gangsters and it wasn't until now that he realised just how broad Terry Reid's shoulders were. Even when the man had been pointing a gun to his head just twenty-four hours previously, Lee hadn't noticed. He'd been too busy hoping he wouldn't die there on the spot.

'A position has opened up within the organisation and I think you'd be perfect to fill the spot. You see, one of my boys had to leave quite suddenly and I need someone to step into the role relatively quickly. You know Mainhill well which is valuable. It doesn't take a genius to work out that you want away from Mainhill, to start a better life for yourself. But without qualifications or any real life or work experience, it's unlikely that you'll get very far on your own.'

'Lee, this could be the new start you've been looking for,' Richie piped in. 'You would have enough money coming in to help your sister kick her drug addiction. You know she's struggled staying off the junk since getting pregnant and we know you're worried about what she'll do once the baby is born. I assume she's had the baby given where we picked you up?'

Lee nodded, astounded by how much Terry and Richie knew about him and his family. It was as though they'd been in the operating theatre with him, listening to his thoughts about reforming and taking his family out of Mainhill.

'You could pay for her to get proper help. None of this quick fix methadone from the chemist crap, I mean proper help in a rehabilitation centre, away from the estate. I'm assuming you want out of Mainhill?' Terry paused.

Lee sighed and slumped in his seat. They were right about everything they'd said. He was worried for Maisie post pregnancy. She wasn't a strong girl, so young and easily influenced. And Lee wanted more than anything to be able to stand on his own two feet without the need to threaten someone with a knife to achieve that.

But he'd seen it before, with people he'd grown up with himself from the estate. You're born there, you become an alcoholic or a druggie, or both, you have kids, they become the same, and they have kids who become the same. It's like the circle of life handed to you by the devil himself.

Lee hated to admit it to himself but Terry and Richie were right. Lee had zero life or work experience, no qualifications, nothing. He hadn't even completed high school, could just about read and write enough to get by. The offer on the table from Terry and Richie could be the only way to get Maisie the life she deserved. Her and the baby. Lee didn't care about what happened to him.

'What's the job?' Lee asked, straightening his back and taking a breath. 'What would I have to do?'

Twenty-Six

Terry Reid had arranged a session at the local shooting range. The Valley Club had been Terry's go-to place whenever the job was too much, causing stress or when he just needed to vent without killing someone that didn't need to be killed.

Annie had wanted to use Terry's own personal gun, but there was no way he was going to let her do that. It made him laugh that she thought they could just go out to the garden and she could shoot at a tree. It would appear Annie was inexperienced, yet excited by the power of holding something in her hand that could end someone's life.

'So, you've been coming here for years?' Annie asked as they got out of the car at the club.

'Since I was a boy. My dad used to bring me here,' Terry said, not wishing to elaborate on his old man.

'Where is your dad now?' Annie asked, not sensing his wish to end the conversation there.

'He's dead.'

'Ah shit, I'm sorry.'

Without hesitation, Terry took Annie's hand and led her through the main door where they were met by the owner. Speaking of his old man and remembering that part of his life before the drugs and alcohol truly got a grip of him was hard to do. Mainhill was closer to Terry than he cared to admit. The place where he and Richie grew up was no different now to what it was back then, except now they were the suppliers. Terry was often referred to as 'The Bossman'.

'Mr Reid, good to see you,' a man said, appearing at the sign in desk at the front entrance. Terry held out his hand and they shook. 'The range has been booked out for you sir.'

'Cheers bud,' Terry said and led Annie through a door.

'I'd have thought that a shooting range would have been a tad louder than this. Is it even open today?'

'That was Gibby, he used to be an old mate of my dad's. Kind of took me under his wing when things went bad. Been running this place for years. Anytime I want a couple hours of shooting, he closes the place to the public.'

'So it's just us?' Annie asked, sensing not to prompt him further on his past. It was as though he and Annie had a mutual understanding about that. Terry nodded as he pushed through another door, leading Annie into the indoor shooting range. He glanced at her and saw that her eyes were scanning the room. She was curious and he knew she wanted to be a part of his world. But why? They'd known each other for a week, yet they'd spent almost every minute together since their first meeting in the pub.

He knew they both had secrets they wanted to hide from each other and so far he was fine with that. His check on her had been satisfactory, he knew she didn't come with a police threat and she wasn't part of any rivalry. She was on her own from what Terry could gather.

'Stand there,' Terry said, leading Annie to the first lane.

'How come you can do this on your own without an instructor?'

'Because I own the place,' Terry replied, lifting a bag from a locked cupboard at the bag end of the range.

Annie's eye widened and she smiled. 'Nice. Seems you've got fingers in all sorts of pies.'

'Need to make a living somehow,' he replied sarcastically. Lifting the bag, Terry placed it on the ledge and instructed Annie to watch him. 'You need to take all of this in, Annie. If there is anything you don't understand then you have to tell me. Otherwise you don't get to do this. Got it?'

Annie nodded and Terry handed her a pair of goggles and ear defenders. 'Put those on.' He watched as she did what she was told and he did the same.

Terry pulled the magazine out from the bottom and checked that it was empty. He pulled the slide back at the top and did the same. 'Always check the gun isn't loaded before you start. Point the gun down range and keep your finger off the trigger until you're ready to shoot.'

Annie watched his hands and then nodded.

Terry then loaded the gun, pushed the magazine back in and unlocked the slide at the top. 'Aim like this and then pull the trigger.'

Annie jumped as the gun went off. Terry hit the target dead in the centre and smiled. He placed the gun down on the ledge, stepped back and guided Annie into position. 'Ready?'

He could feel her tremble a little, but he could tell it was excitement by the look on her face. Adrenaline taking over and rushing through your body would do that.

'Ready,' she said. She pulled the trigger and as the bullet left the gun, Terry watched as it hit the target close to his own shot.

Smiling to himself, Terry realised that this time he'd got it right. Kora was just a practice relationship for the real thing. As quick as his feelings for her had developed, he knew Annie was the one. Watching her with the gun in her hands as she focused hard on her target, he knew he would do anything to keep her in his life. He wasn't letting this one go.

Twenty-Seven

She hadn't needed to buy more things for Samuel's party but seeing that message from Tom, knowing that Charlotte had told him about what had happened had caused a wave of panic to consume her. She'd needed to get out of the house, get away from the inevitable truth she would have to face.

Her phone had pinged, so many messages from Tom.

> Where are you? Why aren't you answering my messages? Are you okay? I'm worried, please come home and tell me what's going on, this is messing with my head.

Now she was sitting in the car hours later and putting off going home. How was she going to explain her past and what she'd done before she met him? It wouldn't just affect Tom, it would be bad for Samuel too. He could lose the closest thing he'd ever had to a dad because she couldn't be honest with Tom in the beginning. But back then, eight years ago when she'd met Tom, things were still too raw. It would have put her and Samuel in danger to tell anyone about where she'd come from and the life she was escaping.

Sighing, Leah knew there was no getting away from telling Tom the truth. Placing her hand on the key, Leah went to start the engine when she heard an enormous bang. So loud, her ears squealed in the aftermath. Then she heard a woman scream. It was blood-curdling and Leah knew she was in the presence of something horrifying.

Frozen, she wondered if she could just pull out of the car parking space, feign ignorance and drive away from the scene. Before she had a chance to make a decision, another bang came. It seemed louder this time. Another scream, followed by another. Longer this time and it sounded painful. The sound of tyres screeching on the concrete followed by a revving engine alerted Leah's attention to the car fast approaching. Two men were inside the black car, both of them sporting balaclavas of the same colour. They looked urgent, guilty.

The car flew down the ramp and skidded before almost stopping in front of her. The person in the passenger seat turned in her direction and looked her dead in the eye. That was all she could see, his eyes. But she could tell a smile was creeping onto his face by the way the skin at the sides of his eyes creased. Raising a hand, he pointed a finger at her. Frozen in fear, Leah knew she was in trouble. A second gone by, a blink and she was staring at a gun pointed straight for her.

'No,' she screamed, throwing herself across the passenger seat. Something exploded. Shards of glass rained down on her as she began to scream. Someone was trying to shoot her. Trying to kill her. The image of the bullet with her name on it came to mind. This *wasn't* a coincidence. It couldn't be. It had to be him.

Tyres screeched in the distance and Leah's heart hammered inside her chest, the sound echoing in her ears. Her right arm felt wet, warm. She was bleeding.

'Oh my god, are you okay?' a voice cried from outside the car. Leah sat up and looked out through the gap where the windscreen used to be. 'Are you hit?'

Leah shook her head, feeling surprisingly calm. 'No. It's not a bullet. It's glass.'

The earlier screaming continued. A female who was clearly hysterical. Leah opened her door and stepped out on to the concrete. Following the sound of the woman's voice, Leah felt the sudden urge to run towards what had occurred. She didn't have far to go, she could already see the top of the woman's head. She was standing by the driver side of the car, hands in her hair and face greyer than Leah had ever seen in a person.

'Help me,' the woman said, glancing down at the car.

Leah looked down into the car and saw someone else. A younger lad, in his twenties. The windows were spattered with blood, or at least what was left of the windows. Taking a step forward, she felt glass crunch beneath her feet.

'Jesus fucking Christ,' Leah said, her hands shaking. Attempting to pull her phone out, she noticed a crowd beginning to gather and the sound of sirens approaching. People were already calling for help.

Moving around the driver side, Leah watched as someone attempted to pull the woman away when an ambulance and an armed response unit came hurtling towards them.

'Come on, you need to move and let them in,' the bystander said. Leah noticed how their face had drained of colour. Raising a hand to her wounded arm, she winced.

It was nothing compared to what could have happened, she thought.

'My son,' the woman said, taking the person's outstretched hand. 'He's my son.'

The emotion from the woman caught in Leah's throat. She couldn't imagine what it must be like to see your child in that state.

As the woman moved away from the car and the sirens blared, Leah glanced down and saw the side of the boy's face. Most of it was missing, blood spattered all over the inside of the car window, the steering wheel. The front windscreen was shattered, the interior covered in blood.

Leah kept her eyes on what should have been the face of the young lad as the ambulance and armed response unit pulled up. Chaos ensued around her and suddenly, she could hear nothing.

Leah Martin looked down at her hands and realised they were covered in her own blood, the sleeve of her denim jacket soaked, like something from a horror film.

Then she let out her own blood-curdling scream.

–

'It's okay, you're going to be fine. Just take deep breaths,' the paramedic said to Leah as they bandaged up her arm.

Tom stood at the door of the ambulance and looked at Leah with concern. She couldn't remember him arriving. She couldn't remember getting into the back of the ambulance, or what happened to the woman who was screaming for her son.

Looking down at her hands, Leah Martin saw that the blood was gone, had been cleaned away by the paramedic.

'The police will want to speak to you again,' Tom said. Leah's breathing was beginning to slow but the panic still gripped her.

'It's the initial shock, that's all. Just listen to the paramedic, just breathe.'

Leah looked up at her husband. 'Initial shock? I was shot at. Initial shock doesn't come into it.'

Tom's eyes seemed heavy. 'Sorry, wrong choice of words. Are you okay?'

She couldn't get the picture out of her head. She knew that every time she closed her eyes now, that's all that she would see in the weeks and months to come. Whoever that young lad was, he'd pissed someone off. That kind of thing wasn't a tragic misidentification. He'd have owed money. Or drugs. If they'd found Leah first, it would be her lying dead in her car, half her face blown off. That she was sure of.

'Leah?' Tom persisted.

'Yes, I'm fine. Just sore.' The paramedic finished wrapping her arm.

Tom narrowed his eyes; she knew he didn't believe her. Of course he didn't. She'd been avoiding him all day and then this had happened. He turned to the paramedic who'd been treating her and said, 'Is she going to be okay?'

'Well lucky for Leah, the wound is superficial. She's had an anxiety attack too, so her blood pressure is up. It wouldn't harm to see your GP, perhaps get something to calm your nerves.'

'You're going to the doctor when we get home,' Tom said almost as soon as the paramedic stopped speaking.

'Tom, I don't need to see a GP.'

The paramedic smiled and helped Leah to her feet. 'I think it would be best. You've been part of and witness to a traumatic event. It'll take a few days to process what has happened.'

Leah sighed. 'Fine, I'll see a doctor.'

'Okay,' she replied. 'If you want to, we can take you to hospital for a more thorough check or you can go home.'

All Leah wanted to do was go home and hug her son. But then she wouldn't feel safe there either. She'd been shot at after having been sent a named bullet. It wouldn't be long until he showed up at the house.

'No, thank you. Honestly, I'm fine. I'll head home now.'

Stepping out of the ambulance, Leah looked across at the other end of the carpark. A forensics tent had already been erected. She noticed people in white suits, marking parts of the concrete behind a cordon. Her car had been taped off for evidence purposes. She had no idea when she'd get it back. Not that the car was her biggest concern.

'Come on,' Tom said as he puts an arm around her gently. 'The police have requested that all the cars on this level from the halfway mark are to stay as part of their investigation. Mine is parked outside.'

Leah allows her husband to lead her to his car to take her home. 'What happened to the woman?'

'I don't know. I'd assume she's assisting the police.'

Leah nodded, understanding that they would want to question her as quickly as possible seeing that she was a key witness in her son's murder.

'What did the police say to you?' Leah asked Tom.

'They want to speak to you as soon as possible. They've said they'll come out to the house as soon as they can. You're a key witness and a potential target so they want to catch whoever did this quickly.'

The police at the house might deter her ex from making another visit.

The moment she looked down at the boy, half his face blown off and blood everywhere flashes in her mind. The passenger of that car had pointed at her, stared straight into her eyes and then shot at her. Strangely that moment reminded her of what had happened in her life before Samuel came along. What she'd done would never leave her, she knew that. All those things had led her to this very moment. She wasn't a bad person. She'd just made some really stupid decisions.

'Leah, I know what you've been through today is brutal, but we need to talk. I've been messaging you all morning and you've ignoredme.'

'Not now, Tom.'

'Yes now.'

Both fell silent and Leah sighed. 'Just take me home, please. I've got Samuel's party to organise, the house is a mess and if you hadn't noticed, I was shot at today.'

Tom lowered his eyes, as if he was ashamed that he'd started to question her.

'Just let me get all that out the way first, please.'

Tom glared at her and Leah knew she was pushing her luck. But he couldn't force her to say anything. Not after what she'd just been through. And in all honesty, she couldn't face it, admitting to all the secrets she's hidden from him.

Twenty-Eight

Terry Reid sat behind the desk in his office, Richie at the other side and Annie on the sofa. Slamming the phone down, Richie looked at Terry with concern.

'What is it?' Richie asked. 'Neil Collins causing havoc even from the jail?'

'Nah,' Terry exhaled loudly. 'It's the Allison brothers.'

Richie's expression changed, and Annie looked up from the newspaper on her lap.

'Those bastards, they never fucking give up,' Terry's voice was raised. Annie didn't seem to flinch.

'What the hell are they up to now?' Richie asked warily.

'They've crossed the line into our side of the city. There's coke on the streets that isn't our stock, Richie and it's fucking dodgy. Two teenagers died at the weekend, it's all over the fucking news.'

Terry slammed his fist down on the table and the antique record player shook in its place. This wasn't good news for the Reid organisation. If people thought there were dirty drugs on the streets, deals could dry up. He couldn't have that.

'What do you want to do about it?' Annie asked. Terry noticed how Richie frowned at her input.

'No offence Annie, but this really hasn't got anything to do with you.'

Terry eyed his partner, then his missus. As much as it annoyed him how Richie had spoken to Annie, he was right. She couldn't get involved with this side. It would be too risky for her. The Allison brothers were dangerous. They didn't care who they had to hurt to get what they wanted. Terry would have to put Annie on another job to keep her satisfied if she persisted.

'Richie, I don't know how you get around every day carrying that massive chip on your shoulder,' Annie retaliated.

'What the fuck you talking about, Annie?'

'You're jealous because you don't have Terry all to yourself now.'

Richie turned to face Annie and Terry shook his head. 'Oh fuck off, Annie.'

'Ah, come on. You know I'm right. Poor little boy is losing his best friend to a girl,' Annie teased. Terry could almost see the tension in the air between them. He didn't need this kind of aggro in his life right now. Richie and Annie were supposed to be on the same side.

'Right, enough you two. This is fucking serious. I need you two to work together, not against each other. If we let the Allisons off with this they'll run riot Richie. We need to pay them a visit.'

Richie nodded in agreement, backing off from the brewing argument with Annie. Dealing with the Allison brothers could become messy. But Terry knew what they were like, they were hungry for money and power. And they weren't quiet about their business. They just made sure they never got their hands dirty, always had other boys, younger lads on the streets doing their work for them. Animals, some of them. But Terry knew how to fight dirty if he had to.

'I'll get the team together. You're right, we can't let them get away with this. What's the street value on the stuff they've put out there?'

Annie was by Terry now, he could see hunger in her expression. She was keen, he would give her that. But the question he had to ask was why? Kora had never been this interested when it came to the dirty side of the business, always wanting to distance herself from it with no desire to know the details. What was it about Annie that craved the need to get in among this?

'Roughly a hundred grand's worth,' Terry said. 'Which is fucking huge when you think about how much Eddie Allison earned just from sales in the north of the city last year. Thinks he's going places, the fucking prick.'

'How much did he make last year?' Annie asked, eyes darting between Richie and Terry.

'Three hundred by all accounts, that's coke, cannabis and pills. And that was all in the north of the city. Small in comparison to the areas of the city we're supplying,' Richie replied. Terry stared past him and out the window. He needed to breathe through the anger.

The Allison brothers had started out young and initially Terry had been interested in bringing them in on the Reid firm. But they got cocky, too big for their boots and decided they wanted to go it alone. In the beginning, Terry gave them the benefit of the doubt. They'd all been young once, all started from nothing. So he let it slide that they wanted to run the north of the city. In the grand scheme of things, it wasn't a big financial drop for the Reid organisation. However, over the course of the last two years, the Allisons had been building a bit of a reputation for themselves, branching out from simple drug deals on their own patch to other business ventures and

Terry didn't like it one bit. If they crossed the city border with their drugs, they could do the same in other deals.

'They're taking the fucking piss, Richie. I should have reigned them in back in the day. We need to sort this before it gets out of hand.'

This was turning into a turf war and Terry was certain the Reid organisation would come out on top. He hadn't bust his arse for years to lose to some mini wannabe gangsters.

'I'd like to help if I can?' Annie said, taking hold of Terry's hand. He looked up at her, seeing an eagerness in her eyes that he knew couldn't be fed in any other way.

'Well—' Terry started but Richie interrupted.

'No way, Terry. We can't have a woman dealing with this, especially not her.'

Terry frowned, unsure how to react. 'Richie, watch how you speak about Annie.'

'What's the problem with a woman being involved? Oh and by the way, her has a name.' Annie shot Richie a warning glance and Terry sighed loudly.

'I meant that this is no job for a woman. Do you even know what the Allison brothers are capable of, Annie? They'd tear you to shreds if you got involved. Nah, it's not happening,' Richie said.

'Oi,' Terry piped in. 'I get to decide who conducts our business. But I think Richie is right on some level, Annie. It's not safe. Not this job. I can set you up with something else.'

Annie's hand fell from Terry's grip and she rested it on her waist. 'You said you wanted me in. So, I'm in. Let me show you what I'm capable of.'

Terry shook his head along with Richie, who was smiling a little. He was clearly happy that Terry was in agreement. And it was also clear that Richie didn't like Annie, or at least wasn't keen on her presence in the business side of things.

'No,' Terry replied. 'Absolutely not, Annie. Sorry but I'm standing firm on this.'

Twenty-Nine

A few weeks had passed since the discussion about the Allison brothers had taken place. Annie knew that if she persisted enough, Terry would give in and she'd been right. Even Richie had come around to the idea and had spoken up for her, saying that she would be the right person for the job because no one knew her connection to the Reid organisation.

She'd been Terry's girlfriend for a month now, but she felt like she'd been part of his life for a lot longer than that. Annie hadn't said it out loud yet, but she was falling for him. He was charming, handsome and treated her not just as he should treat his woman, but as an equal too. Not only that, but he was taking her mind off her old life. He was keeping her busy, almost enough to drown out the white noise inside her head. And that had been exactly what she'd wanted.

'Do you like it?' the shop assistant asked, bringing Annie from her thoughts and back to the present.

Admiring herself in the mirror, the black dress clinging to the right places and accentuating her curves, she twisted her body and nodded. 'I do. I'll take it.'

'Thank Christ, has to be the hundredth dress you've tried on,' Terry called from the other side of the door.

'Oi,' Annie laughed as the shop assistant stepped out of the cubicle. 'This has to be done right if it's going to work.'

Terry had taken Annie shopping on her request. She had to look the part if she was going to fool the Allison brothers into thinking that she was the real deal.

Stepping out of the dress and placing it back on the hanger, Annie got dressed and joined Terry at the till. She handed the dress across the counter and the woman behind started to wrap it up.

'And you've got accessories, Ms?'

'Yes, I have,' Annie replied as Terry handed over his credit card.

Annie had been in touch with the Allison brothers a week earlier and they'd agreed to meet Annie, and it hadn't taken much persuasion. She'd spoken to them about her proposal of a drug deal and how it could benefit them all. They'd decided to meet her to discuss things and Annie had been excited at the prospect of already fooling them. However, according to Terry and Richie, they would take a little longer to warm to her than she thought because she was a new entity in the business and they'd never heard of her. They *could* have agreed to meet her out of curiosity.

'Annie, you're not known and you don't have a back story. The Allisons might be scum but they're not stupid. They're businessmen just like us. They'll have their guard up with you,' Richie had said.

'Well he didn't sound like he had his guard up when he agreed to meet with me on the phone. So maybe I'm better at this than you think, Richie,' she'd replied.

'Or maybe because you're a woman, Eddie Allison thought there might be more to the bargain than you were letting on.'

That had got Annie's back up but she'd decided to let it slide and instead, prove him wrong.

The woman handed the credit card back to Terry and a bag containing the dress to Annie before they head out of the shop, hand in hand. Terry was quiet and she knew he was thinking about the meet.

The short walk back to the car, Annie thought about their plan and how she would be instrumental in eliminating the problems created by the Allison brothers for the Reid organisation. If this worked, which she was certain it would, then even the north of the city would be Terry's for the taking and it would strengthen her relationship with him, cement her position within the organisation. It might even get Richie onside.

Terry opened the car door for Annie and she climbed into the passenger seat, before Terry threw the bag into the boot and got into the driver side.

'Are you alright? You've been so quiet today,' Annie asked.

'I still don't think this is a good idea. You could end up dead if they work out who you really are.' Terry started the car and fastened on his seatbelt. 'I don't know how you managed to talk me into this.'

'Terry, I'll be absolutely fine. You'll be able to listen to the entire meeting through the earpiece I'll be wearing. You don't have to worry about me.'

'But I do worry,' he said, turning and taking her hand. 'This isn't a game, Annie.'

'I know it's not a game, Terry. If I didn't think I was capable of this, then I wouldn't have put myself forward to do it. I mean let's face it, Richie's not my biggest fan and even he thinks this will work.'

Terry smiled and leaned over to kiss her. 'Just remember your safe word. If you think they're on to you, get the fuck out of there. I mean it.'

'You wanted me to be a part of this, Terry. So watch me.' Annie shook her head. It was slightly annoying that he didn't think the meet would go well. Eddie Allison was an animal, she'd been briefed about the kind of things he was capable of, but he'd be like putty in Annie's hands the second he laid eyes on her wearing that dress. She knew how to work a man. Terry was testament to that.

Running her fingers through Terry's hair and resting them on the back of his neck, she pressed her lips against his. 'I won't have to use the safe word. I promise, I'll get the deal done and out of there quick style.'

As Terry responded to her kiss, Annie's mind wandered and she found herself thinking about how much her life had changed in such a short space of time. She'd been living a conventional life just over a month ago, had experienced some truly awful things. Now she was the girlfriend of a gangster and about to execute a plan that could see her new partner claim more territory in his world. It was now her world too.

Picturing herself dressed up like a moll and meeting two very dangerous men caused a stir of excitement inside she'd never felt before. It was like she was watching someone else's life on screen. It didn't feel real.

But it was real. All of it.

Thirty

Annie sat down on the seat and looked around as a waiter placed a drinks menu in front of her. She smiled and he left the table. The nerves had kicked in now and Annie knew the only way to calm them was to down something strong in one go. She called the waiter back and ordered a double vodka. The last time she drank that in a bar was when she met Terry. It seemed vodka was a lucky charm as well as a relaxant.

As soon as the glass was placed in front of her, she lifted it to her lips and knocked it back in one go. It burned on the way down, snuffing out the jitters almost instantly.

Keeping an eye on the door, she watched as the Allisons enter the bar. First Eddie, then Joe. She got to her feet and stepped out from behind the table. The earpiece and hidden wire were intact and she was confident this was going to work.

They're here. Terry's voice. It was so clear she could be forced to believe he was right next to her. *Can you hear us, Annie?*

'Hmm,' she said quietly.

Eddie Allison approached the table first, his eyes wandered over her and she smiled even though she wanted to kick him where it'd hurt the most. Fucking creep.

'Ms Annie Wicks,' Eddie said. She heard a low rumble at the base of his throat as he raised his hand. She allowed him to take hers. His lips brushed the skin on the back of her hand and he looked her dead in the eye.

'Mr Eddie Allison, it's a pleasure.' She smiled.

The dress is working its magic already, Richie said.

Annie would throw the dress in the bin when she got home later. Shifting her gaze to Joe, who stood just to the left of his brother, she nodded. 'And Mr Joe Allison.'

Joe didn't respond like Eddie, he simply took a seat at the table, not waiting for Annie to sit down first. Eddie shoots him a look as he let go of Annie's hand.

'You'll have to excuse my brother,' Eddie said. 'He's devoid of fucking manners.'

He gestured for Annie to sit down and she did so without breaking eye contact with Joe. He didn't trust her, she knew that immediately. Eddie Allison seemed at ease compared to his brother.

'So, you're new to this game?' Eddie asked.

'I wouldn't say new, I own two clubs in the city and come from a long line of family who've made their money through our kind of trading.' Annie answered with confidence. Joe Allison was flicking through the drinks menu now and ordered two whiskies.

'Funny that, I ain't heard of you before. Have you Joe?' Eddie smiled but it's not genuine.

'Nope, never heard of the Wicks Empire.'

Annie adjusted her position on the seat and kept her expression soft. She cannot show any signs that she is working for the rivals. 'Well, we conduct our business *quietly*.'

Getting the dig in there early was something that could be vital. She saw the exchange between the brothers and knew she had their attention.

'Look, I'm off the radar at the moment and I intend to keep it that way. But I want more for my clubs. You know what it's like, people come in and want the best experience. I think us working together could give them that. And if they get the best, then they'll keep coming back. So if my clubs' takings go up, then that's more money in your pocket.'

Eddie and Joe sat forward. She had their attention.

Terry and Richie were quiet in her ear. She had them hanging on her every word as much as the Allisons.

Slipping her hand into her bag, she gripped the envelope and slid it across the table. Eddie peered inside and showed it to his brother.

'There's ten grand in there. Call it a deposit. And that's just for starters. If you can supply my businesses it means you get to spread yours across the city, and I don't just mean in the north. I'm talking East and West Glasgow here.'

Joe glared at her. 'What about the Reids?'

'Fuck them,' Annie said. She heard laughing in her ear. It was Terry. Of course, he understood it was all for show, but knowing that the Allison brothers thought they were in company with someone else who appeared to give zero fucks about the organisation that ran the city would grate on him. She could just imagine Richie's face. It would annoy him that she'd said that even though it was all an act. 'They're picky about who they do business with and I wasn't going to risk going to them when I know they could refuse my offer. But I know you won't because you're already looking to expand.'

Eddie Allison nodded as a grin spread wide on his face. Joe wasn't smiling but he appeared interested.

'I don't have time to hang about, I want to get moving on this,' Annie said.

Eddie glanced inside the envelope again and showed the contents to Joe. His expression barely changed except for a raised brow. He then slid it back across the table towards Annie. She placed it back inside her bag and got to her feet. The men followed her and now, Joe was admiring her figure too.

'You're playing a risky game, messing with the Reid organisation,' Joe said as his eyes finally moved up from her chest and meet her gaze.

'I could say the same about you two. If the Reids knew this was happening, I'm sure they'd have something to say about it. But they don't have to know. This could be our own little secret, and perhaps in the future, if we expanded enough, we could take Terry Reid and the rest of them out of business. Imagine, us running the city instead of them. Think of the money we could make.' Annie's stomach fluttered with excitement at the danger she was putting herself in.

'Ha, I like you're thinking,' Joe replied.

'Easy does it,' Eddie said. 'We don't want to draw attention to this. Also, we need to know you can deliver on your word, Ms Wicks. And what about the Collins brothers? I assume you know about their business dealings?'

'Yes, of course I do. I'm not going to operate in this city without knowing who my associates are. And before you ask, no I haven't been around each firm asking for a deal before coming to you. I've done my research, I know what you do. And I want to be part of that.' Annie smiled gently and held Eddie's gaze for a moment. She could see the way he was looking at her and she wanted his lurid mind to wander for just a second. 'I'll let you think about it over the next twenty-four hours.'

Eddie Allison held his hand out but this time when Annie offered hers, he didn't kiss it. He shook it.

'We'll be in touch with details, specifics. But I can tell this is going to be a very positive business venture for both of us.'

Annie nodded and pulled her hand from his grip. As she moved away from the table, she could hear Terry in her ear.

You're a fucking genius, Annie. Well done.

Taking a deep breath, Annie approached the door and a waiter opened it for her before she walked through and out to the street.

This life suited her, she was made for it. She had been on fucking fire back there and she wanted to make sure that things only got hotter. Meeting Terry had been the best thing that could have happened to her. He had a numbing effect on her past and that was what she needed. Getting involved in something new and dangerous would help her to forget the pain of what happened before all this had come along.

Thirty-One

Leah Martin sat in silence on the sofa and hoped that Tom would leave her alone to think of something to say. But she knew him better than that; he wouldn't let this go until he knew the truth. She couldn't believe what Charlotte had told him. Of course she meant well, but it really wasn't her place. Leah could handle the past, handle what was lying in front of her.

'Right, what's going on Leah?'

'Nothing's going on,' she lied. 'I'm fine.'

'No, you're not, Leah. Your best friend told me that she's worried about you and that you might be in trouble. Then someone takes a shot at you in a carpark. That's not right, Leah. What is going on?'

She'd never heard Tom using such a firm tone before. He was going to pull the truth from her no matter what. But how could she tell him what she'd done? How could she explain her past without it tearing apart her future? That's if there was a future left. If her messenger meant what he said, then he would be coming after her sooner than later.

'Okay. But you have to let me tell you this from start to finish. No interruptions. I need you to understand everything before you say anything or ask any questions. Okay? And remember, everything I've done in my life was to protect Samuel. You need to understand that.'

Tom nodded, his expression stern. 'Of course I'll understand.'

Taking a steadying breath, Leah got to her feet and left the room before heading out to the hallway where her handbag was sitting next to the front door, containing the picture and the small box with the bullet inside. As much as she knew she was being watched, waiting for the right moment to appear at the door and cause havoc, Leah glanced out of the window, wondering if he was out there right at that moment. The drive and street were empty, but Leah knew that didn't mean he wasn't there. She had to be sensible about this. Keeping her secret hidden was not only important to her, but necessary. However, Tom had a right to know what was going on. She'd involved him simply by falling in love with him, becoming his wife and allowing him to become Samuel's dad.

Pulling the box and the photo out of the bag, Leah felt herself tremble with fear as she stepped through to the lounge. Holding them in her hand by her side, she sat down next to Tom and looked him in the eye.

'Okay, here goes. A few years before I met you, I was with someone else. Something happened and I chose to leave him.'

The sound of footsteps on gravel alerted them both. Tom glanced around and out of the window and Leah's heart banged hard against her chest. It was too late. He was already here before she could explain things.

'The police are here,' Tom said with frustration in his tone. 'Are you feeling okay to speak to them?'

'Yeah,' Leah replied. 'If I can help them in any way then I should. That poor woman, I can't stop thinking about her. How awful to witness your son being shot dead.'

'And what about you, Leah? You were lucky the bullet missed.'

But Leah had already switched off. A wave of relief washed over her; a combination of knowing that she would have to put this conversation on hold and that the police would scare away her ex if he was out there settled her stomach.

Tom got up and answered the door while Leah stuffed the box and picture down the side of the sofa. Stomach churning, she got up and made her way through to the hallway to meet the police.

'Leah Martin?'

Leah smiled politely at the two officers. A male and female. One tall and one short. One blonde and one ginger.

'I'm PC Tennick and this is my colleague, PC Robertson. We'd like to ask you a few questions regarding the shooting this morning,' the female officer said. 'May we come in?'

Tom pulled the door wide, allowing the officers to step inside. They followed Leah through to the lounge and she sat down on the seat where she'd hidden the box and picture.

'How are you after this morning?' Tennick asked, glancing down at Leah's arm. 'You were lucky.'

'Yes, I was. And I'm okay, thanks. Don't think it's hit me yet,' Leah replied as Tom sat down beside her and placed a hand over hers in sign of support. 'The guy had a bad aim,' she laughed harder than she'd meant to. No one smiled and Tennick lowered her eyes. 'Sorry, I've always had bad taste in jokes.'

'It must have been quite traumatic, Mrs Martin. We've a couple of questions to ask you if you don't mind,' Robertson said.

Nodding in response and feeling like an idiot for trying to make light of the situation, Leah was eager for this to be over as quickly as possible.

'Can I get anyone a tea? Coffee?' Tom asked, getting to his feet. Tennick and Robertson shook their heads. Leah asked for coffee and Tom left the room.

'We've gathered some stills from the CCTV footage in the multi-storey carpark where the shooting took place and we were wondering if you would be able to have a look to help us with our enquiries,' Robertson said, pulling some paper from an envelope.

Leaning forward, Leah took the images in her hand and glanced over them. There were three. One of two men getting out of a car and dressed in black. The second contained three men, clear to Leah that they were engaging in conversation. One of the men was the man who was shot dead in his car, she recognised his clothes. The third was a close-up of one of the men who she assumed the police thought was potentially the shooter.

'Do you recognise any of the men as the possible killer from this morning, Leah?' Tennick asked. Her voice was tense, as though pinning everything on what Leah was about to say. Of course, a man had been killed but Leah thought there was something else in the PC's voice.

Glaring down at the images again, Leah stopped herself from gasping out loud. She couldn't show her fear or they would know she was hiding something.

Eyes stared back at her from behind the still image captured by the CCTV and she shuddered.

'Leah, are these the men you recognise from the carpark?' Robertson pressed.

'Yes, possibly. I'm sorry, I don't know for sure...'

Tennick and Robertson looked at one another before nodding. 'The men in the images are under investigation for a series of crimes in the city and we're hoping that this is what we can use to bring them in,' Tennick said.

'I understand. But I'm sorry, today is such a blur.'

'Do you think you'd be able to pick them out if we brought you in to identify them?' Robertson asked.

Leah shifted in her seat. She couldn't do that, it was too risky. Her entire being was about to be blown apart as it was without becoming embroiled in a murder investigation.

'I'm sorry. No, I don't think I'd be able to give a reliable ID.'

Just then, Tom appeared with a mug in his hand and smiled down at Leah. She was thankful for the interruption.

Glancing back down at the image, she knew exactly who she was looking at. The image was grainy but she recognised the man straight away. A face from her past that she didn't want to admit to. Links to a life she was no longer part of.

Thirty-Two

Her heart rate quickened and adrenaline thundered through her body as she watched Eddie and Joe Allison step out of the car and walk towards her. Breathe, she thought to herself. Just breathe.

'Ms Wicks. It's a pleasure to see you again,' Eddie said as he moved closer. She took a step forward and offered a hand.

'Glad to see you both here and that we'll be doing business together,' Annie replied, hoping that she had hidden the tremor in her voice.

Joe hadn't said anything and Annie thought he looked shifty as his eyes darted back and forth. He hadn't met her gaze yet, or acknowledged her presence. Not that she needed his acknowledgement. Upon closer inspection, Annie suspected that Joe was on something. His eyes were wide, his jaw tense and paranoia oozed from him. It set her on edge.

'Joe, open the boot,' Eddie said. 'We want to show Ms Wicks that we're men of our word and can deliver.'

'Hey, I believe you,' Annie said, with a smile.

'Still, come this way.'

Annie didn't falter. She couldn't show weakness or hesitation otherwise she could blow her cover. Stepping towards the car, Joe did as instructed by his brother and when she looked in the boot, she saw exactly what

Terry knew would be there. Thousands and thousands of pounds worth of drugs, all wrapped up in packages of green and brown coloured tape.

'This is the first drop, obviously,' Eddie said as he stared down at the packages. 'Cocaine is our highest earner as you well know. Once this is sold, we'll get more to you. Don't want to hand over all our goods in one go, do we?'

Joe shook his head and lit a cigarette, seeming a little more relaxed.

Annie nodded. 'Excellent, Eddie.' She headed back to the car and lifted the bag out of the foot well and Eddie followed.

She heard Richie's voice in her ear. *Now.*

Eddie and Joe were distracted by the sound of two cars approaching, the headlights casting their shadows onto the ground behind them. Annie's palms were sweating and her chest throbbed. *This is it*, she thought as her hand trailed towards the pocket of her coat and rested there.

'Shit, polis,' Joe said, dropping his cigarette to the ground.

Eddie looked at Annie and then his own car. She could tell he was panicking, he thought they were all fucked. He was right, almost.

The two cars stopped and the doors opened. She watched as the Allison brothers exchanged a glance when they realised who they were looking at and that's when she made her move away from Eddie and towards Terry.

'Ah, Eddie fucking Allison,' Terry said. 'What the hell are you up to?'

Annie stood next to Terry and faced the two men she'd just screwed over. Confusion quickly changed to understanding and Eddie Allison narrowed his eyes. Joe stood by the boot of the car as his eyes darted between his brother and Terry.

'Mr Reid, it's good to see you,' Eddie replied. His acting skills were pretty poor, Annie thought.

'Cut the bull, Eddie. We know you're trying to fuck us over. *She's* with us,' Richie replied. Even now with what was about to go down, Richie still couldn't bring himself to remove the sneer from his tone with regards to Annie. She hated that about him; he still didn't entirely trust her after she'd handed the Allisons over on a plate. Annie knew it was because she was a woman; she wasn't stupid but she wasn't going to let it affect her. And she certainly wasn't going to show any weakness. Annie wanted to prove that she could be just as fierce as Richie and Terry, more so *because* she was a woman.

Eddie Allison locked eyes with Annie and if she didn't know any better, she would go as far as to say she could see a fiery rage burning at the back of his eyes. 'You *fucking* bitch!'

'Now, now,' Annie heard Derek Collins say from behind her. 'That's no way to speak about a lady.'

Thirty-Three

Terry Reid smiled as Eddie attempted to worm his way out of it, but there was nothing he could say that would change Terry's mind. The Allisons had tried to do the dirty on the Reid organisation and it had backfired big time.

'Come on, Terry. This city has enough druggies in it that we can both share the profits,' Eddie said.

'Fuck off, Eddie. You were fucking warned last year, pull a stunt like this again and I'd fucking kill you myself.'

Eddie laughed. 'What? You and your fucking entourage here. Since when were you mates with these tools?'

Derek and Kenny laughed too, but Terry knew it wasn't in humour. Eddie was becoming too big for his boots nowadays; he'd do a deal with anyone if it meant pissing Terry off. It was like a game to him.

'From what I can tell Eddie, you're outnumbered by a long shot here,' Annie said.

'Ah, so you're Terry's latest whore, are you? Got you running around doing his digging for him? Or are you just the rebound after Kora did the disappearing act? Rumour has it old Terry here bumped her off because she was shagging Frankie Conway. Come to think of it Terry, he's not been around for a while either.'

Terry stepped forward and pulled a gun out from his jacket, pointing it at Eddie. Controlling his anger and holding back on putting an end to him at that very moment was the most trying thing Terry had ever done. 'I'm fucking warning you, Ed. Say one more thing to her and I'll put a round of bullets in your fucking skull.'

Annie held her hand up. 'No, it's okay Terry. I can handle this.'

Terry didn't take his eye off Eddie Allison. The Collins brothers stood on either side of their own car and Richie moved closer to Joe.

'Eddie, the only whore around here is you. I mean, you'd only just met me, knew nothing about me and yet here you are. About to do a deal with a woman purely because you couldn't keep your eyes on her face. You made that deal because you thought you'd get some sort of benefit from it, in me. In thinking that you would get to fuck me, you've ended up fucking yourself.'

Annie smiled as Eddie's face contorted. Terry didn't lower his gun.

'So,' Eddie said. 'What now?'

'What do you think, Eddie?' Richie asked. 'You were about to make a deal that stepped into Reid ground. Do you think you're going to get away with that?'

Eddie was silent, eyeing all of his opposition as though weighing up his options. Joe moved from behind the car and stood next to his brother, as if preparing for things to develop. Terry was ready too, he knew this was going to end in a fight. Of course it was. It wasn't just because the Allisons had gone behind his back and tried to deal on his territory, but Eddie had insulted Annie and made reference to Kora and Frankie. A line had been crossed.

'You really think you're the godfather of Glasgow, don't you Terry? You and your little team here, you're nothing. We're coming up in this world and the only reason we're standing here now is because you feel like a failure. You're an old man in a young man's game now. And there's nothing wrong with a bit of healthy competition, Terry. You should appreciate that, given that you've made your way up in the world. I mean, we all know that you're a Mainhill man yourself. You know what it's like to start off with nothing. What was it they called you in the days when you were a boy? Terry the tramp?' Eddie's smile was wide, matching his eyes.

Pulling the trigger, Terry pushed Annie down to the ground as shots began ringing out around them. Eddie Allison was a bastard, he knew which buttons to press in order to get Terry going. This is what he'd have wanted. A shoot out in order to end the Reid organisation and claim the remaining pieces for himself.

'Terry,' Richie's voice called over the commotion. Terry was down on the ground behind one of the concrete pillars next to the car. 'It's Joe. He's after Annie.'

Terry glanced to his right, watching as Derek took Eddie down with one bullet to the knee. To his left, Joe was running, his body low. He was heading around to the back of the car after Annie. Getting to his feet, arm outstretched and ready to kill, Terry heard one final pop followed by Annie's voice. A high-pitched shrill.

She was screaming.

Thirty-Four

Annie was on the move behind the car. Eddie was crying out in pain and Joe was just behind her. She wanted to call out to Terry but her voice felt stuck inside her throat, as though fear had become the blockage, keeping the terror inside.

He was on her now. Joe Allison spun her around and threw her down, his hands gripping her neck to silence her. Her instinct was to grab his hands, try to peel them away but he'd be expecting that. Instead, she raised her left hand and started to claw at his face with her nails, distracting him. It was hard to fight her instincts when she couldn't get air into her lungs. They burned but it would be over soon.

Slipping her right hand into her coat pocket, her fingers wrapped around the gun. Pulling it out, she held it to Joe's side and pulled the trigger. The force of the bullet leaving the gun and lodging itself into the flesh of her attacker forced her arm away and she dropped the gun. The sound was like nothing she'd heard before. A pop, followed by the release of Joe's grip from her throat. He fell down on top of her and rolled onto the ground. Blood. There was so much blood. It was strange that Joe barely made a sound. Then she realised where the bullet must have gone. Straight through and into his lung. She sat up and lifted the gun again but this time she didn't shoot.

Silence ran out around her and the scream finally broke free from her throat as she looked down at the man in front of her, bleeding to death.

'Annie,' Terry called, rushing towards her. 'Are you alright?'

But she couldn't answer and she couldn't stop the noise that escaped her.

The rest was a blur. Terry helped Annie to her feet and bundled her into the back of the car. Before she could realise what was happening, Richie was in the driver seat and Terry was next to her. The gun was in his hand and he was wiping it with the sleeve of his coat.

'Annie, don't worry about this. Derek and Kenny are dealing with this. A team is on their way to dispose of the bodies. You're safe, okay.' Terry's voice was steady, as if this was normal.

What the hell had just happened? How could things have gone from calm to murder in a matter of seconds?

'Annie, where did you get the gun from?' Richie asked as he turned on to a main road from the scene and the car picked up speed.

She looked down at it in Terry's hand, then into his eyes. He knew she'd taken it from his drawer. She'd always wanted to use it; she'd said as much before he'd taken her to the shooting range. But Annie hadn't thought she'd actually need it. She was involved with four of Glagsow's most dangerous men. It had just been an insurance policy for her, a threat to use if necessary. Never in a million years did she think she'd have to shoot someone with it.

'It's mine,' Terry replied, pulling Annie into him.

'What the fuck, Annie?' Richie shouted.

'Oi, if she didn't have it she might be dead now. Shut your mouth and keep driving,' Terry said.

Everyone fell silent then and all Annie could think about was the look on Joe Allison's face as he'd tried to strangle her. It was written all over his face that he wanted her dead.

'I scratched his face, Terry,' Annie said. 'His skin, it'll be under my nails. My DNA will be on him.'

'That doesn't matter, Annie. Our team will sort it. This won't come back to you. I promise you that.'

Annie's arm and shoulder ached from the shot she'd taken. She'd killed someone, taken a man's life, another man's brother. How was she this person now? She'd crossed a line. But at the same time it was kill or be killed. Annie didn't regret pulling the trigger. In fact, it caused a rush of exhilaration she hadn't expected. And if she had to, she would do it again.

Thirty-Five

Terry traced Annie's spine with his finger as she slept. He hadn't meant for things to go the way they did earlier. Eddie Allison had pushed things too far. Saying what he did about Kora and Frankie, about his life growing up in the estate… he'd deserved everything he got. Death was the only option for him. As for Joe attacking Annie, Terry was just glad that Annie had had the brains to take the gun from the desk in his office. It showed him that Annie understood and respected the danger she'd put herself in by becoming part of this world.

Thinking back to when he took Annie to the shooting range, he hadn't realised that her almost perfectly on target shots that day would come in useful. Joe Allison died there on the ground because he'd taken Annie on and underestimated her. They all had. The room lit up as the phone on Terry's bedside cabinet illuminated. Rolling away from Annie, he picked the phone up and stared at the screen.

Derek Collins 03:46: Job done.

Eddie and Joe Allison had been disposed of and Terry took a deep breath. As much as it needed to happen, Terry didn't care much for body count. The less death the

189

better. If people would just do what they were supposed to do, respect the rules and keep to their own territory, then these things wouldn't have to happen. It would make Terry's job a lot easier if he didn't have dead bodies to worry about.

Placing the phone face down on the cabinet, he lay on his back and stared at the ceiling. Now that the Allisons were gone, the north of Glasgow was there for the taking.

With Annie by his side, he really did have it all now.

Thirty-Six

As she lay in the bath and the warm water lapped around her body, Annie closed her eyes and tried to clear her mind. Last night's sleep had been filled with images, all muddled and contorted. Annie knew she was dreaming and had tried to wake herself many times, although she had felt locked in an unconscious state as if it didn't want to let go of her. Images of Jack, Eddie and Joe Allison had swirled around in her head through the night as well as now, as she lay awake in the bath.

Annie slipped under the water, hoping that the images would wash away when she pulled the plug. As much as Annie knew she was safe with Terry around and the Allisons dead, something niggled at the back of her mind. Why didn't she feel more traumatised at what had occurred the night before? And secondly, she was curious about what Eddie had said about Kora and Terry's life as a young lad. As she sat back up and wiped at her eyes, she felt a presence in the bathroom with her.

'Are you okay?' Terry asked.

Looking up at the door, she smiled. 'Fine.'

Silence hung between them for a moment before Terry sat on the edge of the bath. 'You seem distracted. Last night got to you?'

Annie shook her head, attempting to show she didn't care. 'Fine, although that's the first time I've had to shoot someone and hopefully the last. But they both deserved what was coming to them.'

Terry nodded. 'But you don't seem fine, Annie. Some-thing else is bothering you.'

'You seem very sure of yourself,' she replied.

'I'm good at sensing these things. I can tell you're thinking about what happened to Joe and Eddie. I never wanted you to see that side of things.'

Annie didn't react because she didn't want to tell him that his senses were way off. 'Then why involve me, Terry? I'll tell you why,' she didn't stop to let him interject. 'You knew I'd get the deal done and that having a woman like me on your team would be good for bringing people like the Allison brothers down. And if I'm honest, I couldn't give a shit if you'd slit their throats in front of me, Terry. Death is death, isn't it? Doesn't matter what way you go, at the end of the day it's the same outcome. Dark nothingness that lasts for beyond forever. Some people just have it coming to them.'

Eyes wide, Terry broke from her gaze. Regretting her tone and attitude towards him, she sighed. Maybe she'd said too much. 'I just don't want you thinking I can't handle this, that's all.'

Cupping her chin, Terry leaned down and kissed Annie gently on the forehead. 'Okay, fine. I get it, you're a hard lass to crack. If you say you're okay then I believe you.'

'Good.' She smiled, attempting to take the sting out of her words. 'But I did want to ask you something. About Kora?'

Terry's expression was still.

'What Eddie insinuated, about Kora and Frankie and how they'd both disappeared. Was there any truth to that, or was he just winding you up?'

Terry perched himself on the edge of the bath and sighed. 'Annie, Kora was a bitch. She was only ever interested in my money. She got caught cheating with one of the biggest scumbags on the planet and...' He trailed off and Annie wasn't sure she wanted to hear the rest.

'You know what? Whatever happened is in the past. I don't need to know a thing about what happened there. Eddie was trying to get a reaction and I'm giving him what he wanted by questioning you. So don't tell me, I don't want to know.'

Annie had to be honest with herself. There were things she didn't want Terry to know about her and her past. Meeting Terry had come when she was running away from her life before and he respected her desire to keep things from him. He didn't push for her to talk so she was going to do the same. She trusted him, as much as she knew who he was. A gangster. And gangsters have a certain way of doing business. Last night showed her that and now she was one of them.

'Consider me silenced,' Terry smiled and got to his feet. 'Glass of wine?'

She smiled back and Terry walked out of the bathroom. As he closed the door behind him, Annie stared after him, silently willing him to come back. His presence was always a distraction, a blanket that covered the truth which lay inside her. She couldn't tell him what she'd been through, but she wanted him close.

'Red or white?' she heard Terry call from downstairs.

Annie splashed water over her face. 'Red,' she shouted in reply before getting to her feet. She pulled the towel from the rail above her, wrapped it around her body and stepped out of the bath.

Her mobile phone sat on the window ledge and she lifted it, opening the gallery and staring down and into the eyes of her past.

No wonder she couldn't get the past out of her head if all she did was look at pictures of it. A knock on the door jolted Annie and she shut the phone off before opening the door. Terry stood in the hallway, holding two glasses by the stem in one hand and a bottle of red in the other. A wide grin spread across his face and Annie took a deep breath.

'I hope that's steak I can smell downstairs to go with this wine?' Annie said, taking the wine glass from Terry.

'Your senses serve you correctly, madam,' Terry laughed.

Wrapping an arm around Terry and pulling herself close to him, she breathed in his scent. Still new and enticing. 'Terry Reid, you could possibly be the best thing that has ever happened to me.'

'Oi, don't think I'll be cooking you steak and bringing you wine every night. I'm just in a good mood that's all.'

Annie pulled away and looked directly into his eyes. Terry Reid was a gangster, a criminal, a drug dealer and a killer. She knew that. But all she could see in him right now was a good man, who had absolutely no idea what he'd done for her. Provided her with a safe haven, a place to get away from the demons inside her head, even if it were for short bursts at a time.

'That's because I'm here,' Annie replied, raising a brow. 'I'll be down in a minute, I just need to get dressed.'

Terry left Annie at the top of the stairs and headed down to plate up dinner. She moved towards their bedroom and slipped into her pyjamas before catching a glimpse of herself in the mirror. To look at from the outside, Annie appeared perfectly normal. No one would know what had happened to her or to Jack.

Thinking about him now, the emotion that caught in her throat made her feel like she was choking.

Thirty-Seven

Opening the text alert on her phone, Leah took a deep breath.

> **Unknown 08:30:** I'm around. I know where you are. I'm coming for you and my money.

Leah took a breath as she began to type out the reply. He would kill her, had already tried. Who else would have been in that car, pointing a gun at her? If she could just get through today, she'd be able to deal with things tomorrow.

> **Leah 08:31:** It's my son's birthday party today. There are going to be a lot of people around so I doubt you'd want to kill me in front of witnesses. I'll meet you tomorrow. I'll have your money.

Pressing send, Leah waited for a reply. She didn't have to wait long. He stated a time, a place. Leah nodded and replied that she would be there. But she would go alone. She refused to drag anyone else into her mess. Going alone, she was protecting Samuel and Tom.

'Good morning baby,' she said as she stepped into Samuel's bedroom. 'Happy birthday.'

Samuel sat up and rubbed at his eyes. Neither Tom nor Leah had told Samuel what had happened. He didn't need to know. Leah decided she would cover her arm to stop anyone questioning what had happened. 'Happy birthday mate,' Tom said. 'The birthday wizard has been.'

Samuel started to laugh and Leah couldn't help but smile. Things had been strained between her and Tom since the police visit the day before, and Leah had put off telling him about the picture and the jewellery box. She didn't want anything to spoil Samuel's party. He deserved to have the best day and not have adults spoiling it for him.

'Dad, you do know I don't believe in all that anymore. Santa, the tooth fairy or the Easter bunny.'

'Och, don't ruin it wee man,' Tom said, ruffling Samuel's hair.

They all went downstairs and Leah watched as Samuel opened each present. He was not like normal kids; he opened with care and precision. He even refolded the paper at the end. She had no idea where he got that from.

Leah went into the kitchen and made a pot of coffee for her and Tom. It was going to be a long and busy day and they were both going to need it to survive the madness of a football party.

'Hey,' Tom was suddenly by her side. 'How are you this morning? Your arm okay?'

'Yeah it's not even that sore. Kind of dreading the descent of a million ten-year-olds upon our house though. Definitely think I'd rather face another drive by.' Leah poured coffee into a mug and handed it to Tom. 'Sorry. Bad joke. Again. Might need to chuck some gin in these coffees.'

'So, are you going to tell me what Charlotte meant by what she said? *Was* yesterday a coincidence or not?' he pressed.

'I've already told you Tom, not today. Let me get this party out the way and then we'll talk, I promise.'

'Leah, if someone is after you for whatever reason, don't you think I have the right to know. What about Samuel?' Tom shook his head and moved away. He was not just disappointed, he was angry. It was killing her to keep a secret like this, but what else could she do?

They sipped quietly as the sound of Fortnite filtered through from the playroom. 'Really, at this time in the morning?' Leah sighed.

'Oh, come on. It's his birthday.'

Leah nodded but tried to shut out the sound of gunshots. It was too raw, too soon. She could still see half the man's face splattered against the window of his car. Could still hear the woman screaming in grief.

'Tell him to turn it off, Tom. I won't have those sounds in my house.'

Tom gave a long blink. 'Shit, sorry. I didn't think.'

'It's okay. Just tell him to turn it off. I don't want him playing violent games anymore.'

Leah exited the kitchen and headed upstairs to get ready. As she passed the playroom, Samuel called out to her, asked if he could get the paddling pool out for the party once the football coach left. When they'd first moved into the house in Balness, Leah spent a lot of time up in the loft, sorting things into storage boxes and labelling things. It was her way of coping back then with how she was feeling. Being a new mum was a daunting thing, even a few years into it and the loft had been her escape.

'Of course you can, Samuel. But turn that game off. I want you to go and get ready for your party and then you can go out to the garden and help your dad to set up.'

Closing the bathroom door behind her, she slid the lock across and leaned against the sink. Tom hadn't mentioned anything for years about not being Samuel's real dad. She didn't know who Samuel's real dad was herself. That time in her life had been hectic, reckless. Leah didn't need to know the biology; Tom was his dad and nothing would change that. Samuel understood that too and had never questioned his family set up. Leah was thankful for that.

After Leah showered and got ready for the big event, she decided to go up to the loft in the hope that the paddling pool hadn't been shoved to the back. When she got up there, she switched the light on and scanned the space.

Boxes upon boxes lay around the edges of the floored loft, all labelled with keywords such as photographs, baby keepsakes, Christmas decorations etc. The paddling pool sat in its box in the far left corner. Moving across to it, Leah spotted a box next to it which had her name on it. Only her name which she'd written herself. She knew what was in there but hadn't looked at the contents for a long time. Frowning, she knelt down next to it and stared at it for a moment.

Leah peeled back one of the edges and pulled on it, releasing the tape. Lifting one of the flaps, she looked inside. Black tissue paper sat neatly at the top and she lifted it out, revealing a file. It contained important documents for her and Samuel. Documents she'd needed to start her new life, away from her ex and the hectic life she'd lived. Scanning through it, she smiled at how far she'd come, how she'd managed to switch things around. That twenty grand she'd stolen wasn't a cut-throat last minute decision. It had been necessary for Samuel. She knew the risk she'd taken when pocketing the cash. And now that risk had caught up with her. Seeing the man in that picture the police had shown her had brought it all back. It wasn't a coincidence that he was the one who shot that lad in the multi-storey. He was around because her ex was around.

'Leah, did you find the pool?' Tom's voice filtered through the loft hatch and into her space.

'Yeah,' she called back.

Placing the file back in the box, she slid the pool over to the hatch and manoeuvred it down carefully to Tom.

'Cheers. You okay coming down? Some of the boys have started to arrive.' His tone was flat; she knew he was being civil for Samuel's sake. Leah couldn't blame him.

'Yeah. Two minutes,' she replied.

Just as Leah was about to climb down the ladder back into the house, her phone pinged through another text. This time, it was a picture. Leah felt the blood drain from her face as she stared down at the image. Another warning.

> **Unknown 09:15:** I had a little chat with your husband. He's a nice guy. So is your son. A great footballer. I wouldn't want anything to happen to them if I were you. So you'd better keep your promise.

Her stomach dropped then. He was threatening her family, he'd been in their presence. Tapping out her reply, Leah thought about what she'd done. If she could go back and change things, she wouldn't. What she'd done was all to keep Samuel safe. She'd repeat her actions a million times over.

> **Leah 09:15:** I'm fucking warning you, keep away from my son. I told you I'd be there and I will.

Slipping her phone into her pocket, Leah climbed down to the hallway and took a breath. She knew what her ex was capable of. She'd witnessed it first hand herself when she was with him. He wouldn't stop until he had her and his money.

Thirty Eight

Terry Reid hung up the phone and nodded across at Richie. 'That was Derek on the phone. The Allisons have been dealt with and so have their stock.'

Richie nodded. 'We're going to owe them big time for this, Terry. You know that.'

Terry held in the growl inside that was building. He would never owe anyone anything. He owned the city and would not bow down to anyone. Yes, Derek and Kenny Collins played a big part in ridding Glasgow of some of the bottom of the barrel scummy gangsters the city had seen in his lifetime and they would be paid for that in due course. But Terry Reid and the organisation did not owe anything to anyone.

'Nah, Richie boy. We won't. But what we can do is bring them in closer, have them work deeper in the organisation for *us*. They can take hold of the Allison territory, get it back to some sort of normality and calm. From what I've heard, they were running amok there and I don't like what I've been hearing. Threatening businesses, blackmailing them to pay security money, forcing girls into prostitution and addiction. They were nothing but dirty wee bastards, Richie. Dealing dirty drugs, laundering money at a rate no one could afford to pay back just so they could feel powerful. The area is on its arse, worse than Mainhill by all accounts and that's saying something. But I think that Derek and Kenny could turn that around.'

Richie frowned. 'And how do you expect them to do that? Go around and tell the community that they don't have to worry about the Allisons anymore because they're dead?'

Terry got up and moved across the office towards the bottle of whisky. He lifted it in Richie's direction, who nodded in agreement that they should have one.

'No, as much as I think some of them would be glad to hear that. But I do think if Derek and Kenny have another stronghold, and make their presence known along with their own men, then the area will attract less attention. The polis were crawling the streets and the Allisons were putting people like us in the firing line. If the Collinses were to take over under us, then everyone from every town and scheme within Glasgow would be under our organisation. Things would be done our way, which means more revenue for us and no more bodies from the shite they were punting on the street.'

Terry handed a glass to Richie and they drank. The north of the city had become out of control because of the Allisons. Maryhill, Summerston, Lambhill all run by Joe and Eddie's cronies. Having heard about the state of the place, Terry knew that there was only one way to fix things and that was to take over. He had enough men to sort it out. The Allisons' team were young, inexperienced thugs. Terry would see to it that they would no longer be able to inflict their authority.

'How's Annie holding up after the other night?' Richie asked.

'Aye, alright actually. I didn't think she was taking it well at all but then I went up to our bedroom and she was burning her dress in the fireplace. Told me to burn my suit to get rid of evidence.' Terry took another drink and drained his glass.

'Fucking hell.'

'I know. I think she's seen some bad shit in her time to be able to deal with what she did. Either that or she's just a hard nut to crack.'

Richie laughed. 'Bit like you then.'

'Aye, well she's different than Kora, I'll give her that. She's glamorous but she's not after my money like Kora was. She's in it for the thrill, I can see it in the way her eye glints when things kick off. Look what she managed to help us to achieve. Lured two scumbag gangsters to their death and she even pulled the trigger herself.'

'So, she's the one then?' Richie teased.

'Fuck off,' Terry laughed and took a drink.

'Nah, mate I'm serious. You're different with Annie than you were with Kora. I still don't like that she's planted her feet under our table though.'

Terry ignored Richie's last dig and finished his drink. As much as it annoyed Terry at how open and honest Richie was about his slight distrust for Annie being involved in the business, he had to admit to himself that things had moved quickly in that respect, especially after what Kora had done to him. Even Terry was surprised at how quickly he trusted Annie. He thought back to when Kora was first in his life. It hadn't taken him long to let her in either. In fact, Kora divorced her husband quicker than he thought was possible and moved in before it had been finalised. It was what Terry wanted too. In reality, maybe he should have had his guard up with Annie but that wasn't his true feelings for her.

Annie was courageous, ambitious and ballsy. It was as though she was the female version of himself.

Thirty-Nine

It had been two weeks since Lee had paid off Freddie's debt and started working for Terry Reid and the Reid organisation. His official job description, according to Richie, was a senior dispatch and debt recovery agent. In reality, Lee had become a drug dealer, taking on various areas which Terry and Richie had said once belonged to the lad before him. Lee didn't have to ask what had become of that lad; it was obvious by the look on Terry's face. Betrayal of some kind had gone down and Terry didn't have to say out loud what would happen if Lee went down that same path. Lee didn't want to die at the hands of his gangland boss. Not because he was scared of death, but he was scared of what he would be leaving behind. His sister and nephew, alone in the hell of Mainhill and in the hands of Galzo. The very thought was enough to make Lee follow every detail his boss gave him and never would he step out of line.

Lee hadn't had a choice in working for Terry, not really. It was either become an employee, or go back to Mainhill a nobody. He thought back to what Terry and Richie had said, how Lee would be able to look after his sister, get her out of Mainhill and away from the temptation of going back on the junk. Lee knew that the job came with its risks, the main risk of all being that he ended up dead because of his involvement with Terry Reid, but it would be the right thing to do for Maisie and the baby in the long run.

He hadn't spoken to Freddie or his sister about his new position. And he certainly wasn't going to tell Cammy or Rosie. It would mean constant calls and texts about getting their drugs on tick and never having the intention of paying Lee the money back. He wasn't going to get himself into a situation where he found himself bailing his brother out again, certainly not while he was working for Terry and Richie.

In the two weeks that he'd been dealing, around the Mainhill estate but not specifically his street, as well as the outskirts, he'd been flat out busy but found himself to be more well off than he could have imagined in such a short space of time. Terry had paid him nearly a grand for a fortnight's work and there was plenty more where that came from. Lee was doing well, was good at his job. His customers, as Richie referred to them, seemed to understand the consequences of not paying off debt. Terry had taught Lee to be firm, no messing about with the customers. If they knew what would happen, they were likely to pay upfront. Lee had Terry's permission to allow certain customers tick, but once a payment was missed, there would be no going back. So far, Lee hadn't had to get tough with anyone.

A week had passed since Terry Reid had organised a new flat for Lee. The best of the best on the outskirts of the town centre, away from Mainhill estate. 'I don't want you living among your punters, Lee. It's not good for business, they'll not take you seriously if they think you're one of them,' Terry had said once he'd handed him the keys.

As much as Lee hated the fact that this man had held a gun to his skull just two weeks previously, he had to admit that if it weren't for Terry, Lee would still be in the gutter. He respected his new boss. The flat was spacious, modern. It was part of the construction project for afford-able housing in the area and Lee learned that Terry was the main investor. His flat in particular was a two-bedroom with en-suite, with a kitchen diner and balcony. Lee had never imagined living in a place like this. The walls were pristine, white with top of the range fixtures and fittings. The place had been fully furnished too and Terry had informed him that this was part of his salary. Cash flow and a home. Lee really had no reason to complain at all. He hoped that Maisie and the baby would move in with him.

'Ma man,' Freddie called across the street, his arms outstretched as Lee was heading into Maisie's flat. 'No' seen you since you moved out.'

Lee sighed. That had been the whole point. He didn't want Freddie, Cammy or Rosie anywhere near his new place. That would have raised questions. He'd managed to fob them off with a lie about being bumped to the top of the housing association list. However, he wasn't going to allow that to stop him from seeing his sister and nephew. They needed him now more than ever before.

'Mate, what's happening?' Lee said, avoiding Freddie's comment. It was abundantly clear that Freddie had been on one of his benders. Still was by the looks of it.

'Oot ma bin, mate. Been on it for three days,' Freddie replied, confirming what Lee already suspected. 'Need something to help me on the come down. Any blues on you?'

Lee shook his head, mostly in disgust. 'Nah. Why don't you ask your mate, Galzo? Am sure he'll have plenty on him. You might even be able to get some on tick too.'

Freddie clearly didn't hear the sarcasm in Lee's tone and already had his phone out before Lee could finish. A certain amount of sadness washed over Lee as he watched his brother's life spiral in front of him. But Lee knew Freddie was a lost cause. Most of the people Lee and Freddie's age were, with the same family set up as their own. It was why Mainhill was such a shithole. All Lee cared about was getting Maisie and the baby away from the place.

'Galzo,' Freddie practically shouted down the phone in his drunken merriment. 'Aye, I need a favour.'

With Freddie's back turned, Lee headed inside to the flat to see his sister and his new nephew. He couldn't wait to tell her what he had in store for them. A fresh start with money coming in. He couldn't help but smile.

Knocking gently so as not to wake the baby if he was sleeping, he pushed the door open gently and crept into the hall. 'Maisie,' he whispered.

'What?' Her voice came in a slur from the kitchen. Lee turned and saw his sister standing next to the window, a cigarette in one hand and a mug in the other.

'You okay?' Lee asked, peering around the small flat. 'The wee man alright?'

'Aye, why wouldn't he be?' she asked, without making eye contact. 'He's sleeping.'

Lee's eyes narrowed and as he turned to close the front door, he saw a pair of trainers lying on the mat. They were too big to be Maisie's. He raised his eyes as Maisie stepped out of the kitchen and into the hall, lowering her head.

'Lee,' she said. 'There's something I need to tell you.'

'Aye, nae bother Fred. I'll sort ye oot.' Lee looked up at the man emerging from Maisie's bedroom. Galzo.

'What the *fuck* is he doing here?' Lee said, without attempting to keep his voice low. He wanted the bastard to hear him.

'Er, no' that it's any of your concern, mate but am here tae see ma missus and ma boy.'

Galzo stood in the centre of the hall and Maisie's shoulders slumped. Lee couldn't believe that she'd allowed him back into her life again, after what he'd done to her. Eyes darting between the two, Lee fixed his gaze on Galzo and took a step forward.

'I'm fucking warning you Galzo, if you promise her the world and fuck off again, I'll make sure those legs of yours are severed at the fucking knee. Got it? Just remember that she was underage when you got her up the duff, so all it takes is one phone call and you're on the sex offenders register.'

Galzo laughed loudly, with clearly no regard for his sleeping son or Lee's warning. Lee didn't break contact with the lad who had no thought for anyone but himself; he knew that his threat could be carried out if he really wanted it to be. Galzo was dealing on Reid territory and all Lee had to do was pick up the phone to his boss and give a name. But he wasn't going to let his own secret slip so soon.

'Lee, please just leave it,' Maisie said, her words slurring again. Lee turned to look at his sister and right away he could see her eyes rolling. Glazo had done exactly what he'd always done, managed to worm his way back into Maisie's life and ruin her clean streak.

'What are you on, Maisie? Did this bastard give you something?'

'Oi, she's a free woman and can choose to do and take whatever the fuck she wants,' Galzo said, brushing past

Lee and slipping his feet into the trainers. 'I didn't force her into bed, Lee. She went willingly.'

Lee spun and landed a punch right on Galzo's nose, before opening the front door and throwing him out into the communal close. Lifting his hands to his bloodied face, Galzo turned and flew at Lee, who in turn thrust out his arms and shoved him towards the stairs.

'Don't fucking push me on this, Galzo. She's my wee sister and she's only sixteen. You're a fucking grown man of twenty-five and you're giving her drugs when her baby is just two weeks old. Your fucking son. You're bottom of the barrel scum and if I see you anywhere near here again I'll make sure you never walk again. Got it?'

Before Lee got a reply, he closed the door and locked it. Turning, Maisie had already disappeared into the bedroom. Lee went in and saw her standing over the baby's cot, tears brimming in her eyes.

'Why did you have to do that, Lee? I love him,' she sniffled, staring down at her son.

'No you don't, Maisie. He's just made you think you do.'

'He'll never let you away with that, Lee. He'll come back for you, have you done in.'

Lee had to stifle a laugh. 'Nah, that won't happen.'

'How do you know?'

'Just trust me, Maisie.' Lee moved towards his sister and gripped her by the upper arms. 'What have you taken? Are you on the heroin again?'

Shaking her head, Maisie sighed. 'Just a couple of blues, that's all.'

Lee gritted his teeth. That was exactly what Freddie had been on the phone to him for, when he was in this flat. 'What the fuck, Maisie? You've got a baby to look after.'

At that, Lee's nephew started to stir. Poor wee guy hadn't asked to be born into this shitty life but he was stuck with it. Maisie stormed off and back into the kitchen, and Lee bent down to pick him up, following her out.

'Have you registered him yet?'

'Me and Galzo were going to do that today until you stuck your fucking nose in. Now he probably won't come near me ever again and it's your fault,' she sobbed.

'Maisie, if you go to register him today, they'll take one look at you and call social services. At least wait until you're fucking sober. I can come with you to register him.' Lee stopped, took a steadying breath. He didn't want to be hard on Maisie but there was no other way. Lee had to put things straight with her or she wouldn't understand. 'He needs a name, Maisie. You don't want the social work banging on the door. You remember what that was like for us, don't you?'

Maisie fell quiet and Lee rocked his nephew in his arms. 'Have you chosen a name?'

'No, I haven't really thought about it.'

Lee wanted to shake his sister. It was as if she cared about this baby as much as Galzo did. It reminded him of his own mum, Rosie. When Maisie was born, Lee had had to take care of her most of the time and he had just been a kid himself because Rosie was either out trying to buy heroin or injecting it. Freddie was already out causing havoc in the estate, getting into fights, slashing car tyres and smashing windows. All of which their dad, Cammy had found hilarious when he wasn't off his face himself.

'Maisie, if you don't want this baby then you have to be upfront about it. Otherwise you need to get a grip and sort yourself out because this wee guy needs someone to take care of him.'

Maisie stopped sobbing and raised her head, glanced down at her baby and smiled. 'I wanted to name him after his daddy.'

'Galzo? You can't call your baby Galzo, it's no right,' Lee said in horror.

'Not Galzo. Gareth. I want to call him Gareth,' Maisie said.

'And the surname? He's going to be a Whitelaw?'

'Well, I don't know Galzo's last name, so I suppose he'll have to be,' Maisie shrugged.

Oh for Christ's sake, Lee thought but refrained from commenting. As much as he hated the idea of his nephew sharing a name with his waster of a dad, or any of the grandfathers for that matter, he supposed it was better than the child having no name at all.

'Okay, Gareth Whitelaw it is then.'

Maisie's eyes were closing more and more and Lee watched as she moved into the living room and crawled on to the sofa. Lee had to get her out of Mainhill if it killed him.

'Maisie, why don't you and little Gareth come and live with me in my new place? I have plenty of space and you would have your own room. It has to be better than this place, surely?'

Without looking up at Lee, Maisie nodded and said, 'How come you can afford a new flat? Won the lottery or something?'

Lee didn't want to tell Maisie the truth. Not until he got her out of Mainhill and away from Galzo. 'Just say you'll come. It would mean we could spend more time together, especially since the wee man is here now. I

213

want to see you both more often but I don't think it's doing either of us any good to be in Mainhill longer than needed. I can look after you more than Galzo ever could. Little Gareth deserves that at least.'

Maisie had already passed out and Lee was left holding his nephew. This was going to be harder than he thought.

Lee looked down at Gareth and noticed that he'd fallen back asleep in his arms, so walked through to the bedroom and gently placed him back in his crib. How could anyone not want to make a better life for the sake of their child? Lee couldn't allow history to repeat itself, not after what his parents had put them through. He wouldn't.

Pulling his phone out, he called his boss. 'Mr Reid, it's Lee. I have some information on someone who is dealing on your patch.'

As Lee explained the situation to Terry, telling him that Galzo had been dealing in Mainhill and either sourcing his drugs from rival gang leaders or producing his own which was highly unlikely, he knew there would be no going back. Once Terry knew what Galzo had been up to, there would be one and only one outcome. And that would be down to Lee. Maisie might not understand the need for this right now, but in time she would. It was best for little Gareth not to have a waster like that as a dad. In doing this he was protecting his sister and nephew, but also dishing out his own kind of social justice for Galzo taking advantage of his then fifteen-year-old sister, getting her hooked on drugs and getting her pregnant.

'I'll catch up with you later,' Lee said, before hanging up the phone. He sat down on the bed and stared at his sleeping nephew. He couldn't leave now, not with Maisie off her face. What if he woke up and needed milk? She wouldn't be able to feed him. Come to think of it, Lee hadn't fed a baby since Maisie had been one herself. Taking a deep breath, Lee went into the kitchen and pulled out the box of formula milk and read the instructions. He might not know off the top of his head how to feed a baby, but he would know when it was time to do so. All he had to do was listen for the sounds of wailing from the bedroom and that was his signal.

Jesus, Lee thought. Maisie was going to turn out just like Rosie. It seemed history was already repeating itself.

Forty

Placing the phone back in his pocket, Terry Reid looked at Richie with a raised brow. What was it with that *bloody* estate? Why would anyone think it was a good idea to deal on not only someone else's territory, but Terry Reid's? This Galzo fella didn't have a clue what was coming his way.

'What do you want to do about it?' Richie asked.

'I say we let him go on for a bit, let him think he's getting away with it for as long as possible.'

Richie nodded in response. 'Aye. Wee bastards like him need bringing down a peg or two. They always think they're solid until they come up against the big boys. There's always another Angus, eh?'

Terry had to agree with that. Angus had learned his lesson the hard way and ended up face down in the canal with a bullet in the back of his skull. Terry wouldn't hesitate to do the same to this Galzo lad if it meant keeping his reputation at the top of his game. As much as he had others running the drug side of the organisation, Terry needed people to know that he had all ears everywhere. He wasn't just a criminal gangster, he had purchased land just on the outskirts of the city where he planned on building flats. Everyone who was anyone, from the bigwigs in the council to the dealer on the street knew who Terry was and the majority knew not to mess with him. Pissing off a gangster who owned his own construction company could lead to a premature, concrete grave.

'I'll tell young Lee to keep an eye on this lad, report back any activity. We let him think he's going places and then we deal with him,' Terry said.

Richie smiled, rubbing his hands together. 'Wee bastard won't know what's coming to him.'

Forty-One

Sitting at the breakfast table, Annie thought about what she was going to be doing later that day. Having told Terry that she wanted to be more involved with the business side of things, he'd asked her to take over the running of the bar. It wasn't exactly what she'd had in mind and now was the time to speak up if she wanted more than what he was offering. He had to understand that Annie already knew what the organisation stood for and Annie had rid them of one of their rivals just two days ago, so it wasn't as though she wasn't capable.

'Morning,' Annie said sweetly as Terry entered the kitchen.

'You're chirpy this morning,' Terry replied.

Smiling, she got up from the table and kissed him on the cheek. He eyed her suspiciously and Annie stifled a laugh. She loved how Terry looked at her, full of passion and lust. No one had looked at her that way.

'So, I was thinking about the bar.' Annie started as she sat back down. Terry poured a coffee and joined her at the table. 'It's not what I really had in mind.'

'So what *did* you have in mind?'

'Well, when I said I wanted to be more involved, I was thinking more along the lines of the less legal side of things. And I think I've already proven I can handle that sort of thing with the Allisons, don't you think?'

The mug Terry was holding hovered at his lips. His eyes fixed on her and she presented him with her most charming smile. She knew it would be a battle, but it was one she was willing to take on.

In that moment, Annie felt as though she'd split in two. Before meeting Terry, she'd lived in a one-bed flat in Yoker. Her mediocre life had consisted of going to work in the call centre at the Skypark centre in the city of Glasgow, earning just above minimum wage and leaving her with enough to pay her rent and bills. She'd always wanted more from life, but had never found it. Well, she'd almost found her happy ever after, but it had been cruelly stolen away from her in the blink of an eye. They say in the hard times you discover who your true friends are. In Annie's case, it had been no one. They'd all distanced themselves, not sure how to behave around her or what to say. They'd all just disappeared. She had no family to fall back on.

The day she'd met Terry, Annie had felt a spark of excitement, as though she'd found a little of herself again. He'd shown a genuine interest in her, something she hadn't felt in a long time from another person. She was happy to go along with things, push her limits. It wasn't until she'd shot Joe that Annie had realised she'd wanted much more from life, that she wanted to be someone else. She just hadn't thought that person would be a gangster's moll.

'It's too soon, Annie. No offence but we've not been together that long. I've spent years building the business, Richie too. I don't think it would be sensible to let you in on all the ventures right away.'

Annie frowned. 'You don't trust me?'

'I didn't say that. I do trust you but you have to understand that this is business Annie. If you started off as an office junior, you wouldn't be promoted to manager right away, would you?'

Shaking her head, Annie could feel her frustration building inside. How could he not trust her after she'd killed Joe Allison? He had that specific part of her fate in his hands, he was in control of that. She wouldn't exactly do anything to jeopardise that.

'Is this because of what Kora did to you?' she asked, knowing that she was possibly crossing a line.

Annie watched as Terry thought about her question. Eddie had been clear in what he'd said two nights previously down at the warehouse. Kora had slept with some guy called Frankie and then they'd both disappeared. He'd insinuated that Terry had done them both in.

'And what do you think Kora did?'

'Well, Eddie said that she slept with that Frankie guy and they both haven't been seen since.'

Terry had a large intake of breath and Annie's stomach flipped.

'Annie, this has nothing to do with Kora. And that part of my life also has nothing to do with you. I trust you, but not with all the ins and outs of my business. Not yet. Okay?'

Annie ran a hand through her hair. She didn't want Terry to think she thought he was guilty. Even if Eddie Allison was right, it was before her time. Annie knew what she did about Terry and she accepted him for who and what he was.

'Look, I couldn't care less what happened to Kora, whether she left or she's dead. All I care about is showing you that I'm in this because I want to be. I might have started off as a junior, Terry but I moved up to management the second I shot Joe Allison. You have to give me some credit. And if that's not throwing myself in at the deep end then I don't know what is. If that doesn't prove to you that I'm trustworthy with your business and line of work then I don't know what is.'

Terry slid an arm around Annie's waist and looked into her eyes. They were softer now, like she'd made him see sense.

'I'll have to speak to Richie. He is second in charge.'

'That's fine,' Annie replied, kissing him softly on the lips.

'And in the meantime, you'll work at the bar?'

Annie nodded, excited that things could progress for her. Although knowing Richie and how wary he was of her, she knew that if he said no, Terry would respect that.

Terry smiled and instructed Annie to go upstairs and get ready. As much as she wanted a bigger role, starting off at the pub was better than nothing. She needed to look her best if she wanted to prove she could handle more.

Staring at herself in the mirror, she almost forgot about the Annie she was little over a month ago. Things were happening so fast with Terry, not what she'd expected at all. Not that she was complaining now.

'Ready?' Terry called up almost forty-five minutes later.

Annie took one last glance at herself after applying some red lipstick, took a deep breath and stepped out into the hallway, wearing a black trouser suit and killer heels.

'Boss enough for you?' she asked.

Terry nodded and Annie joined him at the bottom of the stairs. They headed out to the car and Gerry drove them to the bar. They were quiet for the short journey as

Annie imagined what life would be like if she was granted more responsibility.

'I've called Richie and told him about what you said. He's meeting us at the pub.'

Gerry pulled up outside the pub. Suddenly, Annie felt herself nervous. She was expecting Richie's immediate response to be no. But perhaps she could talk him round, explain that she was part of their team. The feeling Richie had towards her was mutual but she had to try. As they crossed the threshold, Annie smiled at Hayley who was getting the place ready for opening.

They sat down at the table in the far corner and Hayley offered to bring them a drink. Annie asked for a coffee and she sat back, eyeing the pub.

Terry was quiet as he turned the pages of a newspaper before turning to look at Annie.

'What is it?' Annie asked.

'I know *everything* about you, don't I?'

Frowning, Annie didn't know how to answer. Terry knew she was hiding something and she wasn't ready to tell him. She might never be ready.

'You know enough,' she replied as Hayley places the coffee in front of her. Now Annie wished she'd ordered something stronger.

'Enough that I can trust you? That Richie can trust you.'

'If you didn't trust me Terry, then I wouldn't be sat here with you now. And no offence to Richie but I don't need his trust.'

His eyes narrowed. 'Actually, you do.'

'What? I'm in a relationship with both of you am I?'

'No, but if you want deeper into the business then you need to have the trust of us both. It's as simple as that

Annie. I want you in my life but I won't allow my business to suffer because I go against my partner.'

Now Annie knew exactly where she stood. She had to claw this back before Terry decided against her proposal without Richie's input.

'Look, all you have to know is I am one hundred per cent committed to you, whatever that means.'

'That's good to know. Let's just see what Richie has to say then.'

Richie entered the pub and smiled across at Terry. Ordering a drink from Hayley, he joined Annie and Terry at the table. This was it, the moment Richie would try to tear her apart, make her look and sound as though she wasn't worthy of working with them.

'How's it going?' Richie asked as he drank from his pint glass.

'Let's go out the back,' Terry said, getting to his feet.

The three of them were standing in the back room, part office, part stock room. The lighting was poor and the place smelled like a mixture of old newspapers and stale beer.

'Well, like I said on the phone, Annie wants to work with us. Get deeper into the organisation,' Terry replied.

Richie's eyes darted between them and Annie smiled. 'You want to get your hands dirty, Annie?' His condescending tone annoyed her.

'Yes,' Annie said.

'And you can handle more of what you saw the other night? Killings, debt collection from some seriously fucked up people. People who will cause you aggro and won't necessarily want to pay you right away. I mean no offence Annie, but you're a woman. The folk we supply probably won't take you seriously.'

Annie gritted her teeth, to the point where she thought they would crack and shatter. He was belittling her in front of Terry, perhaps even twisting Terry into his way of thinking.

'Richie, I lured the Allisons into a trap, shot and killed Joe Allison. What the fuck did you do?'

Annie saw Terry's expression flicker.

'Oi, that was a test to see if you could handle shit. You weren't instructed to take a gun from Terry's house and use it.'

'And what does that show? It shows I can use my initiative. I can pre-empt certain situations and in that moment I was right to do what I did. And if I can kill a gangster, I can sure as hell deal with a fucking junkie, Richie.'

Richie nodded slowly but didn't crack a smile. Even if he did agree and think she was capable, he wouldn't say it now. He was quiet for a moment, eyeing Terry. 'I don't like this Terry.'

'Well, we could start her off in debt collecting. Maybe send her round some of the female punters, see how she does?' Terry suggested. 'We won't know until we give it a try, will we?'

Richie shrugged his shoulders, shaking his head. 'It's ultimately your call, mate. Mixing business and pleasure, does that ever work?'

Annie's shoulders tensed. This all felt like she was at a job interview. Why was she putting herself through this? Allowing herself to be degraded by Richie.

'You know what Richie? Fuck you. I've proven myself to be trustworthy, I've killed a man and placed my fate in Terry's hands. If I fucked up, don't you think Terry would have the ability to set up my downfall? He could easily dob me in to the police.'

Terry raised a brow. 'That's not how I work, Annie. If someone betrays me or fucks me over…' He paused for a moment. 'Well, you heard what Eddie said about Frankie and Kora.'

So something sinister *did* happen to Frankie and Kora? Annie's stomach rolled. He didn't have to say anything more. She knew what that meant. It was a warning. Don't fuck him over. Simple.

Forty-Two

Standing in her booth at the shooting range, Annie aimed the gun at the target and hit it dead centre for the first time that week. She'd spent the last three days practising and she felt incredible to finally achieve a hit in the middle. Even though her aim was good, she wanted to perfect it.

Spending time there had been Annie's choice and Terry hadn't had a problem with that. In fact, he'd said it might help her in her new role in debt collection. She might need the skills to show she was in charge when collecting from punters.

Finishing up at the range, she headed out to the car and back to Terry's. Passing through the village she once lived in before meeting Terry, she wondered what life could have been like with Jack. The familiarity of the place sat heavy on Annie's chest as she drove through the heartl of the village. With the window down, she was surprised by how overwhelmed she became by the simple smell of the village bakery. The scent of fresh cakes and bread sat heavy in the air as she passed and Annie was careful not to stare for too long at the place she once called home. Everyone here knew her and knew what happened. She didn't want to face that, it was too horrific. She held down the button and the window eased up, protecting her from the outside. As she exited the village and headed to what was now her new home, Annie breathed a sigh of relief. She turned up the radio and blasted the sounds, drowning out what is going on inside her head.

Pulling into the drive, she saw Richie's car parked in its usual spot. Great, she thought. Another moment for Richie to bash her capabilities. Next time she went to the range, she'd picture Richie's face on the target as she pulled the trigger. She got out and went into the house, happy to be back in the present.

'Terry?' she shouted while removing her shoes.

'Hey,' he said, appearing at the top of the stairs. 'I've got a few things I need you to take care of.'

Annie felt her stomach flip with excitement.

'It's your first debt collection situation.'

Annie climbed the stairs and followed Terry into the office. Richie was sat behind the desk, looking over various papers on the desk. The antique record player was singing softly and Annie felt the tension as she entered the room. It was clear her presence alone annoyed Richie. *Of course it does, he doesn't want to share Terry with anyone, especially not a woman.*

'What's up?' Annie asked, tucking a lock of hair behind her ear and trying not to let Richie bother her.

'We've got a problem with one of our punters. She was notorious for getting her gear on tick off the Allisons and now that we've moved in and taken on their clients, the debt she had with them is now ours,' Richie said. 'She owes us five hundred quid.'

Annie eyed Richie. He hadn't looked up from the desk to acknowledge her and she knew it was a test. Richie wanted to know if she had the balls to go to someone's door and demand they cough up their debt.

'What does she owe five hundred quid for?'

'Heroin,' Terry replied. 'From what Derek has told us.'

Terry stood between them, silent and allowing Richie to take the lead. She could see in Terry's eyes that he too wanted to know if she can do it. Fuck them, if they wanted a show then they'd fucking got one.

'When?' Annie raised a brow.

'Today. Whenever you want.'

Annie approached the table and asked Richie to give her the address. She wasn't going to allow Richie to belittle her. If she could arrange for two of the city's top drug runners to be snuffed out, taking one of them out herself, then she could do this. It's what she'd been asking for all along.

'I'll be back later.'

As she turned to walk out of the office, Terry grabbed her hand and pulled her back. She peered into his eyes but didn't say anything. A reminder of his warning. *Don't fuck up.*

—

Glancing down at her casual outfit of jeans, converse trainers and a leather jacket, Annie was happy with how she looked. She blended in, yet still looked suited enough that when the client answered the door, they'd know not to fuck her about.

Sitting in the car in the estate, she looked up at the flat. It was almost derelict, covered in graffiti. Jagged letters which read, 'Mainhill Fleeto, ya bass' in fluorescent green were spread across the front of the building. Small groups of young teenage boys were dotted between the building she was sat outside and several others. All of them shared two bottles of Buckfast wine between them and as she got out of the car, loud music blasted from one of the windows of the building across from her.

She'd expected to feel something, nerves or fear. But as Annie approached the main entrance, her heart was calm and she felt like this was what she was going to be good at. Finally, she had a purpose.

There was a keypad mounted on the wall to the left but the buttons were charred and the door was already wedged open with a large rock. She moved inside and began climbing the stairs. Flat 1/2 came into her line of sight. She raised a hand and knocked on the door. There was no answer and Annie knew that the girl inside would be expecting debt collection, so would either be out or pretending to be out.

Sounds of a baby crying from behind the door of the flat opposite the one she was standing in front of – Annie turned in response to the noise. The door opened and a girl appeared. She was young, maybe not even twenty yet. She struggled across the threshold with a large pram and the baby inside screamed so loudly the sounds echoed in the communal close.

'Do you need help?' Annie asked.

The girl shook her head as she managed to close the door behind her. 'Need to take him out for a walk to stop him screaming,' the girl said. 'Wee shite hasn't stopped greetin in the last two hours.'

Annie drew her eyes off the delightful girl and turned back to the flat she'd come for. Still no answer. The girl with the baby disappeared out of the building and Annie was thankful that the sounds of the screaming child had gone with her.

Raising her hand to knock again, Annie heard a commotion from behind the door before it was opened. Annie was staring into what could only be described as a hellhole. The small hallway had no carpets, instead cardboard boxes were flattened out on the floor. The wallpaper was hanging off from the top of the walls and the smell inside made Annie gag.

'Can I help you?' the girl slurred as she hung off the door.

'I hear you owe some money to some dangerous people?'

The girl stared at her blankly through intoxicated slits, her eyes barely open. It was likely she'd shot up not long before Annie had arrived.

'I'm here in place of the Allisons. They want paying now.' Annie said, trying to breathe through her mouth as best she could. The girl tried to shut the door and it became obvious to Annie that she hadn't expected a female to come knocking.

Sticking her foot out, Annie jammed the door open and shook her head in warning.

'Look, av no' got any money.'

Confidence boosted inside her and Annie pushed her way into the flat. The girl made no protest and Annie thought she could smell alcohol on her as she passed her, among other things she wished not to know about.

'Then you'll have to find a way of getting it.'

The girl closed the door and let go of the handle, swaying a little as she turned to face Annie. A smirk crossed her lips and she stumbled into the living room. Annie followed her and the décor from the hall flowed in there too.

'What, are ye Joe's bitch or something?' the girl asked.

'Look, I'm not here to fuck about, just get me the cash so I can go,' Annie said. Her patience was wearing thin and the smell of dried urine intensified with every second she spent there.

'I don't shit out money hen, so if ye want it yer gony have to come back later.'

Annie narrowed her eyes and spotted a bag in the corner of the room. It was open and Annie could see notes inside. The girl anticipated Annie's movements and rushed to the bag first, lifting it and throwing it behind her back. Annie gave a menacing smile. 'And if *you* wanted to ram heroin into your veins, you should have saved up your pennies first.'

'Ye cany take it, it's ma rent money,' she sneered, reaching out and attempting to grab the bag from Annie's grasp.

Turning in quick motion, Annie balled her fist and landed it on the girl's jaw, knocking her back. For someone who was pretty off her face, she bounced back quickly and went for the bag again.

Annie didn't want to have to do this, but she had no other choice. Pulling the handgun out from inside her coat, she held it up and raised a brow. The girl stalled, eyeing the gun in Annie's hand and grunting loudly before bringing the bag back into view and pulling out a handful of notes.

'Five hundred,' Annie said as she watched the girl.

'Aye, I know how much I fucking owe,' the girl replied before shoving the notes into a carrier bag and handing it to Annie.

'You'll not mind if I count. I mean, you said you had nothing, then all of a sudden you've got enough to give me plus leftover notes in there.' Annie eyed the bag in the girl's hand before placing the carrier on the table in the corner and counting the cash.

'It's aw there,' the girl said, lighting a cigarette and rubbing at her jaw. 'Ye didny have tae pull a fucking gun on me, I'd have gave it tae ye.'

Annie shook her head. 'Of course you would. Do yourself a favour, don't take drugs if you can't afford them.'

The girl sniggered. 'Aye, a'right maw.'

'I'm serious, if you thought Joe Allison was bad, then you'll be in for a shock the next time you owe this amount out.'

The girl eyed her suspiciously. 'I heard the Allisons done the off and that some other big wig has taken over?'

Annie placed all of the notes back into the carrier and slid the gun back into her coat. Without confirmation of the girl's claims, she left the urine-scented drug den and headed back out to the car. Once inside, she locked the doors and pulled out of the estate.

Her heart hammered in her chest and Annie began to wonder what might have happened if that girl hadn't given in so quickly. She might have had to shoot her. Terry wouldn't have been happy about it. Luckily for Annie, she'd managed to overpower the druggie and things hadn't come to that.

'Fuck,' Annie shouted as she pulled the car onto the main road and headed for the motorway. The feeling of power and courage rushing through her veins frightened her. Perhaps Joe wouldn't be her only victim.

Forty-Three

Cheers from screaming children and party poppers filled Leah's ears and she laughed as Samuel and his friends started tucking into cake like it was going out of fashion. The smile wasn't real though. How could she be happy when she knew that the end of her life was just around the corner?

'Mum, did you see what Rupert got me for a present?' Samuel screeched with excitement as he held up a scooter.

'Brilliant wee man, just brilliant. We'll get out on that tomorrow,' Tom answered before she could. She looked at her husband and offered a smile in thanks.

'Did you say thank you?' Leah asked.

Samuel nodded and turned back to his friends who were tucking into the party food and cake. All of the school mums were in attendance. Debs, Kim, Charlotte and others who weren't part of the Boozed Up Mums WhatsApp group. The place was full and more were due to arrive. As bad as it made her feel, Leah was glad that her house was filled with people. It would mean he would keep his distance, for now at least.

Swallowing hard, Leah made her way across the garden, dodging kids kicking footballs around and popping balloons. She stood in front of her friends who knew nothing of what had happened the previous day at the carpark.

'So, how you finding this? A living hell?' Kim laughed, holding out a glass of fizz.

'It's not that bad. The kids kind of entertain themselves,' Leah replied, taking a large gulp from the glass. Eyeing Charlotte, she could tell her friend felt the tension. 'Can I talk to you for a minute?'

Charlotte nodded and followed Leah as she headed to the edge of the garden. Stopping and turning to meet her friend's eye, Leah sighed before taking another drink.

'Okay, I'm just going to say this. What the actual fuck do you think you're playing at? Telling Tom that you think I'm in some sort of trouble? Are you completely devoid of knowing how to keep things to yourself? You're supposed to be my friend, Charlotte.' The words hissed through her teeth and Charlotte winced.

'I'd say I'm sorry Leah, but I'm not. You told me something really fucked up and I don't think you should be going through that by yourself.'

Leah noted the other girls watching from the corner of their eyes. They knew something was up.

'Just remind me never to confide in you again, Charlotte,' Leah spat. As she went to move away, Charlotte reached out and grabbed her arm and Leah cried out from the pain.

'Oh my god, what's wrong?'

Leah moved a hand instinctively to her bandage, breathing through the pain. 'I cut myself, that okay with you?'

'Leah, if you want to treat me like this because you're scared then that's fine. But I'm not going to apologise for looking out for you. You're my best friend. You'd do the same for me.'

Deep down, Leah understood why Charlotte spoke up but that didn't make it easier to smile and nod along. Instead, she went inside the house and headed straight for the kitchen. Charlotte didn't follow. Leah was alone, standing by the kitchen window watching her son's birthday party in full swing. Her friends, school mums and dads, neighbours all laughing and chatting in her garden. She couldn't be out there, pretending everything was perfect when in fact, she'd been shot at by a disgruntled ex the previous day and he would be waiting to meet her tomorrow, ready to kill her regardless if she gave him his money back or not.

Reaching for the drinks cabinet, Leah eyed the bottle of tequila which stared back at her. She hadn't named their WhatsApp group Boozed Up Mums for nothing. Knocking back a shot, Leah winced as the liquid burned the back of her throat and made her gag instantly. It wasn't quite the same without a few gins in her system first.

'You make a habit of doing shots at a kid's birthday party, do you?'

The voice startled her. Leah spun around and her heart almost leapt out of her chest. Mouth drying up in an instant, Leah parted her lips to speak but words failed her.

'I hear you were involved in a near miss yesterday?' he said, raising a brow as he leaned against the door frame.

'How did you get in here?' Leah's voice rasped. 'Get out or I'll phone the police.'

He stepped forward, close enough that she could smell his breath. 'No you won't. You don't have the balls. Contacting the police is like signing your own prison sentence, *Leah*.'

Trembling, Leah glanced out of the window in the hope that someone would see that she was in trouble. No one was looking in her direction.

'Are you here to finish me off since your brother didn't do a very good job yesterday?' Leah spat. 'I mean, Derek has a pretty crap aim, bullet was nowhere near me.'

Kenny Collins grabbed her arm and dug his fingers into her bandage. 'Don't get fucking smart. He was never going to kill you, not until you pay back what you owe. You've upset too many of us. You know how this works, there's no such thing as an easy out.'

Grabbing Leah's face, Kenny dug his nails into her cheeks and drew her face close to his. 'Remember, tomorrow. If you even think about not showing, your lovely little family out there won't make it to the end of the day. I've got a bullet with each of their names too. Got it?'

Letting go, Kenny disappeared out of the kitchen and she heard him close the front door. Waves of fear washed over her as she began to suck in air in deep gasps. Grabbing for the tequila, she drank straight from the bottle.

Party poppers in their tens began to sound from the garden, along with children stomping on balloons and screaming in unison as Samuel's friends began playing a game. Leah rushed up to the bathroom and the tequila left her body as she retched.

She was going to die tomorrow. There was no getting away from it. She couldn't tell Tom about this, he'd make her go to the police and by then, they'd all be dead.

When Leah became a mother to Samuel, she'd vowed to protect him from anything. If that protection came in the form of death, then she would do it.

Forty-Four

'Five hundred quid,' Annie said as she threw the bag onto the desk. Terry looked up at her and closed the window on his computer screen. She hadn't been away for too long at all. Punters in debt usually came up with every excuse in the book as to why they needed an extension.

'She just gave it to you?' he asked, pulling the bag open and peering inside. Annie was right, five hundred quid was staring back at him.

'No,' Annie replied. 'She tried to tell me she didn't have the money she owed. In fact, she let me in. Don't think she realised who I was or why I'd turned up at her door. In a way it was a good thing, meant she let me in, or at least I didn't give her much of a choice. Told me she didn't have any cash and then I found that.'

Terry glanced back down at the money and wondered what exactly Annie did to retrieve it. He'd heard of this girl, always in debt to the Allisons, who'd allowed her debt to them to rack up. Word had it that she paid back her debt in other ways. Selling herself on the streets was one of them. But apparently the most common was to pay for her drugs by having sex with the Allison brothers themselves. And if they didn't want her, they pimped her out to others in order to clear her debt. That was most certainly not how Terry and the organisation conducted their business. He was many things, but he was absolutely not a sex trafficker.

'So you just took the money?' Terry pressed, sliding the bag into the desk drawer.

'Well,' Annie smiled, taking the gun out from the inside of her coat and placing it on the table. 'I was persuasive.'

Laughing, Terry sat back on his chair. 'I assume you didn't have to use it?'

'Well, I didn't shoot her if that's what you're asking.' Annie sat down opposite Terry. 'Although, I was disappointed at how easy it was to make her give it up once I showed her I wasn't messing about.'

Annie had surprised Terry. She'd adapted to his way of life so quickly, it was like she'd been born to do this. She would be an asset to the organisation. She already was.

Terry had a few more collections lined up for her, most of them similar to the one she'd done. If Annie had a particular way of doing things to get the job done, then he was happy to let her proceed. He'd decided already that he wasn't going to put her up against any male clients. Annie could handle herself, that he was clear on. He only had to think of Joe Allison to be reminded. However he would make sure she handled only the female clients from now on. He handed her a list of the jobs that needed doing, and Annie smiled down at them, reached over to kiss him and said, 'I'm going for a shower if you fancy joining me?'

Winking, she left the room and Terry watched her go. Adrenaline seemed to be the thing she sought out the most and she was always looking for it. He still wanted to know what her drive was from the point of when they met until now. Something was pushing her to keep going and even though she'd assured him things from her past weren't going to get in the way, Terry wasn't convinced.

Annie reminded him a lot of himself, private and driven. It was how he'd managed to earn his money. Never mix business with pleasure, that had always been his motto. But now he was deeply involved with Annie whom he'd brought into his organisation and yet he still didn't truly know a lot about her. He did know that he trusted her enough to bring her in and he didn't want anything to come between them. Terry hadn't felt like this about anyone before. Danger and lust combined with a soft affection for Annie meant that he had to be careful not to push her on what she didn't want to tell him.

He entered the bathroom and opened the shower door. Annie stood there, naked and covered in bubbles. Her soft pale skin and fiery red hair drew him in.

'Ah, couldn't resist me, eh?' Annie said, pulling Terry into the shower. He was fully clothed but he didn't care.

'Annie?' he said, taking hold of her upper arms and staring into her eyes. 'If there is anything you want to tell me, ever, then you know I will be here for you if you need me.'

He saw a flicker in her stare, like he'd touched a nerve. There was something she was holding back, but unless she was ready to reveal that herself, she wouldn't tell him.

'Terry,' Annie replied. 'Is there something *you* want to tell me?'

'No,' he replied. 'Just that I'm here for you.'

At that, he kissed her on the forehead despite the bubbles and allowed himself to fall under her spell again. What had she done to him? He was a gangster. A hardened gangster. And she'd softened him. No woman had had this kind of effect on him.

Forty-Five

Opening the bathroom door after having cleaned herself up, Leah took a deep breath and returned downstairs. Kenny was gone and he wouldn't be back. He'd done his job for the day in warning her about turning up for her meeting. She knew better than to fuck with him, or any of the others for that matter.

'Hey,' Charlotte met her at the bottom of the stairs. 'Look, I don't want to fight with you. So I've come to apologise. I should have kept my nose out of your business.'

'No,' Leah sighed. 'I'm the one who needs to say sorry to you. I spoke to you about my problems for a reason. I needed to get things off my chest. But you're right, I am in trouble. But I can't tell anyone what kind of trouble. I need to deal with this on my own, Charlotte. And don't bother trying to talk me out of it.'

Charlotte's eyes softened and it caused the lump in Leah's throat to swell and tears threatened.

'I'm not going to do anything to make your situation worse. Just remember that I will help you if I can. All you have to do is ask, you know I'll drop whatever I'm doing to be there for you. And for Samuel and Tom if necessary.'

Leah grabbed hold of Charlotte and hugged her tight. She was the first one to chat to Leah on Samuel's first day at nursery. He had screamed the place down as she had walked out the door, holding back tears. Charlotte's daughter had started on the same morning and they had gone to the local coffee shop together and had laughed at how they were always complaining of their kids never giving them a moment's peace yet the second they were free they were aching to have them back in their arms. They'd been best friends ever since. The other girls, Kim and Debs, they were lovely too but Charlotte was that one girl she could always count on. Leah supposed that was why she got so annoyed at her for telling Tom about being worried about her. Leah knew Charlotte meant well. She always meant well, yet Leah could never reveal her secret. No one would understand.

'Thank you Charlotte. But I have to take care of things by myself. I promise, I'll be fine.'

Leah spent the rest of the afternoon in the garden, chatting with the girls, drinking an appropriate amount of gin for a kid's party and trying to forget that this was the last day she would be alive.

Forty-Six

Annie had been excited to plan her romantic meal for two. She was going to cook for Terry, lay the table and make sure that his phone was switched off. He'd been working so much lately that she wanted to take his mind off everything, allow him some time to relax with her. It was also a bit of a celebration too, now that she was working with Terry within the organisation.

Stepping out of the supermarket that morning, Annie made her way across the carpark and opened the boot of her car. Piling the bags of food and wine inside, she closed the boot and moved around to the driver door. Just as she was about to open it, she heard a commotion. A car door slamming, a woman shouting. Across the opposite end of the carpark, Annie saw Richie, standing by a car she didn't recognise. It wasn't his Range, the one similar to Terry's. It was a small car, blue. Possibly an older Nissan Micra. A woman stood at the driver door, holding it open. She was waving her arms around, as if she was frustrated, although Annie couldn't be sure because she couldn't hear what the woman was saying. Not clearly anyway. All she heard was *I'm sick of this* and *Why can't we just go somewhere?*

Watching closely, Annie could see that Richie was beginning to move away from the woman and as she turned, Annie saw it was the woman from the photo in Terry's drawer. It was Kora, Terry's ex. It was definitely her, there was no doubt. She had the same long brunette hair which curled at the ends. The same as in the photo. Annie remembered thinking the girl was pretty.

She was becoming more and more irate with Richie and Annie wondered if she should go over and say something, but before she could decide, something happened that stopped her in her tracks. Richie had pulled Kora in close to him, was hugging her tight to his body. Kora had wrapped her arms around Richie and then leaned up to kiss him. Not just on the cheek like a friend. She'd been screaming at him one minute and the next, they were all over each other in public.

'What the hell?' Annie whispered. The rumour was that Kora was dead; it had been insinuated that Terry had done her in when Terry found out she'd had an affair with Frankie Conway. The Allisons had said as much the night they'd died. Terry had even insinuated to Annie that the rumours were true, but Annie had chosen to ignore them. Now she was looking right at Kora, alive and well.

Pulling out her phone, Annie quickly took a few pictures. She wasn't sure what she would do with them, but having them was better than not. What the *hell* was Richie doing with Terry's ex? They were supposed to be best friends, business partners? How long had this been going on for?

Annie watched as Kora got back into the blue Nissan Micra and drove out of the space, while Richie walked along the path towards the entrance of the supermarket. He hadn't seen Annie. Should she tell him what she'd seen? Should she tell Terry? Knowing what he might do to him after Kora had cheated on him, she thought better of it. There was a possibility that the person Kora had cheated on Terry with was Richie. Right under his nose.

That was a stupid and highly dangerous thing to do when engaged to a gangster.

Climbing into the car, Annie stared down at the images on her phone before pulling out of the parking space. What the hell was Richie thinking, getting involved with his best friend's ex? He was putting so many business deals at risk, not to mention his friendship.

Annie remembered the first time she'd met Richie. All over the young barmaid at the pub he was. It seemed Richie didn't give a shit about the people around him. All he cared about was getting it whenever he wanted, no matter who got hurt. The ironic thing about this was, Richie had always been open about how he wasn't sure he could trust Annie. A quote popped into her mind then: 'he who cannot trust others, cannot be trusted *by* others.' That seemed to fit this situation well.

Annie would keep a closer eye on Richie now. She wasn't going to let him make a fool out of Terry. But she could also use this to her advantage. Perhaps if she were to show these images to him, he would back off.

Whatever was going on, Terry was in the dark about it.

Forty-Seven

The last stack of cash had been counted and Annie placed it into the sack at the side of the desk before getting to her feet and punching in the code to the safe that Terry had left for her. Opening the door, Annie placed the sack inside and locked the safe again. She'd counted almost five grand and that had only been collections she'd made from a fraction of the small female-run businesses in the city. Terry had said that Annie would get a better response from them than he would and he'd been right. Since taking them on, payments had come without question or complaint. The bigger firm's takings were still to come but Terry and Richie would deal with those.

Annie had never seen that amount of cash before let alone been the one collecting it. Having retrieved payments from just a few establishments, Terry had been impressed with Annie's ability to get things done. She didn't ask questions as to why people were so forthcoming about their payments. It didn't take a genius to work out why they hadn't made a fuss. Annie was hardened to most things if she didn't think about the ins and outs.

'Do you fancy a drive later?' Terry asked as he opened the safe on the back wall of the office.

'Where to?' Annie replied, watching as he typed in the code.

'How about down Loch Lomond way? We could get Gerry to drive us, take a bottle of champagne and some food?'

Annie's brow furrowed; Terry wasn't normally the romantic type but she would go with it. The corner of her mouth lifted into a smile and Terry nodded.

'Ah, we're like one mind,' Annie replied. 'I was at the supermarket early this morning, picking up some stuff to make us a romantic dinner to celebrate us working together now.' She smiled and he leaned over for a kiss.

'Awe, you're a gem Annie. Okay, excellent. The weather will be glorious down there.'

'I've never been,' Annie replied.

'You've *never* been down to Loch Lomond?' Terry cocked his head to the side.

Annie shook her head. 'Never really thought about it. No reason to go.'

'No reason to go?' Terry repeated, obviously dumbfounded by Annie's words. 'Annie, it's the most peaceful place I can think of. If this job has taught me anything, it's when the opportunity arises to spend some time in a peaceful environment, take it.'

Annie couldn't remember what peace felt like. Had she ever experienced it? Possibly before Jack. After Jack, definitely not. Her heart swelled with a sadness she'd thought was beginning to disappear. Clearly it was still there, heavy on her chest.

'Okay, you twisted my arm,' Annie said and she saw a smile creep onto Terry's face. It felt good that she made him smile like that, that he wanted to do things for her that would make her happy. Peace and happiness it seemed were a long way away but Annie would settle for what she had right now, because she knew in time with Terry, things would get better. She just had to hope that he wouldn't press her on her past.

Annie finished up at the desk and went into the bedroom. Sitting down on the edge of the bed, she resisted the urge to look at her phone. She would have to delete the images from her past sooner or later. But right now she just couldn't bring herself to do it. Deleting them meant that part of her life was gone forever, even though it was her fault things had gone so wrong in the first place.

Her fingers tingled as she placed them on her pocket where the phone was hidden. She took a deep breath and told herself no. That was then. This was now. She couldn't look at his face. Whether it made her smile or made her cry, Annie knew that looking back at that time in her life would hold her there. The whole reason for being with Terry, working for him and sharing a life with him was to forget what happened. But the urge got the better of her and she took out the phone and glanced down and into the face of Jack. Tears swelled and a sob almost escaped. Guilt, fear, love and loss formed a ball of despair inside her chest and Annie clamped a hand over her mouth to keep from crying out.

–

Terry pulled the car into a parking space outside a grand building in Loch Lomond, stepped out and opened the boot. Annie followed him and offered to carry one of the bags. She took a peek inside and noticed he'd packed food. Nice, she thought.

They walked out of the small carpark and along the edge of the building, overlooking the loch. She noted the name on the sign; Loch Lomond Lodge at the Cameron.

It was like something she'd never seen before. The architecture was stunning, but it wasn't long before she realised that this wasn't the place Terry was taking her. As they headed away from the lodge, they took a small pathway and headed down towards the water. The sun was still high, the temperature comfortable.

'Where are you taking me?' Annie asked.

'It's a surprise,' Terry replied. Annie accepted this; she'd find out soon enough.

After around a five-minute walk, the trees which towered over the path finally cleared, revealing a deep blue sky above. Annie immediately saw the small island which was situated just north west of where they were standing. A wooden jetty extended in front of them and Terry kept walking and that's when Annie noticed the boat at the end of it.

'No, seriously Terry. Where are you taking me?'

'Over there,' he replied when they reached the boat. 'Incharden, one of my favourite places in the world.'

Annie regarded the boat and then looked back across to the island. Fear crept into her belly. She hadn't been close to open water like this since Jack had died. The guilt of not being able to stop it from happening had become too much and she'd attempted to take her own life, slipping under the surface as she lay in the bath one night after cutting herself. 'Don't worry, we'll have lifejackets and Innes here does this trip at least eight times a day,' Terry said, as if reading her fear. Of course, he'd read her wrong but she was glad of the distraction.

Annie glanced at the man in the boat and smiled weakly and he returned the gesture. Innes seemed older, around his sixties perhaps and looked like a typical Scottish fisherman in his green waist high waterproofs and a skipcap. Terry held out his hand and she grabbed it a little too tightly as he helped her to step into the boat.

'These are for you,' Innes said, handing over two lifejackets to Annie and Terry. As much as they were supposed to assure her the trip across the loch would be safe, it made her more nervous. 'Welcome back Mr Reid.'

'It's a pleasure to return, Innes. How's the missus?'

'Och she's fine. Busy getting the place ready for the next flock of tourists, ye know how it is.'

Annie glanced at Innes and then Terry. Of course he knew Innes, Terry appeared to know everyone.

They sat down and the boat wobbled and bobbed in the water. With one hand squeezing Terry's tighter than normal and the other gripped on the side of the boat, Annie felt her stomach flip as the boat began its journey across to the island.

'You okay over there?' Terry asked over the sound of the engine. Innes was in front of them, staring out at the water and appeared incredibly calm.

'I'll be fine once we get off,' Annie replied, hoping that sea sickness wasn't something she suffered from on top of the anxiety she was feeling. She didn't know, having never been on a boat before.

The journey took fifteen minutes, but to Annie it felt like an hour. The boat docked at the jetty and as soon as they stepped onto land, all the fear and anxiety left her as she looked back across the water to the mainland.

'Wow,' she said under her breath, feeling her fear slowly dissipate.

'Told you it would be glorious.'

She turned back to Terry and noticed that Innes had already made his way along the jetty towards the large Incharden Hotel. Terry told her that Innes and his wife

Audrey owned the island and everything on it and were friends of Terry's family. Annie didn't question it.

'So we're going into the hotel then?' Annie asked.

'No, we're heading around to the other side of the island. It's only a mile and a half walk but it's so secluded and you get some cracking views.'

'Terry, are we camping?'

Terry laughed. 'No, just picnicking.'

They walked together to the other end of the island and when they arrived, Annie was blown away by the beauty of the place. A small white sand beach welcomed them, with water so blue she could have mistaken them to be on a private Caribbean holiday resort; with the sun shining down on them and the silent surroundings it was better than perfect. The terror of the boat ride was wiped from Annie's memory.

A large fleecy blanket had been laid on the sand prior to their arrival, with an ice bucket to the side containing a bottle of champagne. Annie gave a sideways glance at Terry who was smiling widely. Placing the bags down on the blanket, Annie walked towards the water and removed her shoes. The cold Scottish water on her skin felt refreshing, like it was washing away all the terrible things that had happened before meeting Terry.

Staring out at the loch at the smaller island to the east and the rest of the view ahead, Annie realised she could stay here forever. It was like the fresh air and the surrounding water made everything go away, so long as she didn't have to be in the water she would get through the hard times.

Taking a deep breath, Annie turned back to the picnic spot Terry had organised prior to arrival and stopped when she realised what she was looking at.

'What are you doing?' she asked, stunned and now beginning to shake. 'Why are you down there?'

Terry didn't reply, instead he reached into his shirt pocket and pulled out a ring. Annie's eyes widened at the sight of how beautiful it was, how the stunning surroundings matched the moment and how much her life was changing by the day.

'Annie Wicks, I have never been more stunned or overwhelmed by a woman in my life and by the way you have made me feel,' Terry said as Annie began walking towards him.

Stopping in front of Terry, who hadn't moved, Annie stood above him and smiled widely as he asked her to marry him. A smile could mask a thousand dark thoughts and memories and up until now, Annie had been able to hold herself together.

Tears spilled over and her heart and stomach ached with guilt and happiness all at once. But she couldn't get the word out. Instead, she nodded and Terry placed the ring on her finger.

Marrying Terry would be a life changing thing for Annie and exactly the thing she'd needed. He'd come along at the right time, helped her to move on with her life. She loved that he was able to give her what she needed and in time she was sure her feelings for him would grow. But Jack would never leave her alone. He would always be there in the back of her mind because if it wasn't for her, he would still be alive.

Forty-Eight

Lee Whitelaw stood at the bottom of Maisie's flat, smoking a cigarette as he waited for his sister. She'd agreed to move in with him for a few weeks. Admitting that she needed help with the baby had been a turning point. Galzo hadn't been back to see Maisie or the baby since Lee had punched him in the face, which had been three days ago. Maisie had come to her senses, realising that Galzo only saw her for one thing, an earner. Selling her drugs had been easy up until this point, but Lee wasn't going to allow that to happen, not now that there was a child to think about.

As much as Galzo hadn't been anywhere near Maisie, he was certainly still present in Mainhill itself. Dealing on Reid territory was the single most stupid thing Lee thought anyone could do, but excitement stirred inside Lee as he watched Galzo walking around the estate, bold and cocky, selling weed and coke to the teenagers hanging around in groups.

Lee took out his iPhone and filmed Galzo moving around the estate, taking Reid money and thinking he owned the place. Of course he'd already told Terry and Richie about what Galzo had been up to. This video evidence was purely so Galzo couldn't talk his way out of it. Everyone would benefit from Galzo being dealt with, including Terry and Richie. Galzo was making them out to be idiots the longer he got away with dealing in Mainhill and Maisie was suffering purely from his presence. Lee knew this was the only way to get rid of Galzo so Maisie had a decent shot at getting sober and becoming the mum that little baby deserved.

Sliding his phone back into his pocket, Lee leaned against the wall and finished his cigarette. Galzo glanced over, a filthy expression crossing his face. As much as the lad probably wanted to knock Lee out, Lee knew he wouldn't do it. Lee was from Mainhill, grew up there. Galzo was from the outskirts originally, came from a village that was nothing like the hell of Mainhill, but had always wanted to be part of the estate since he was a school kid. He wouldn't stand a chance if he started, there would be too many hoping to get in the thick of it and lend a hand to Lee. Not that Lee needed anyone to help knock the shit out of Galzo. He could do that with both eyes shut. Galzo was all bark when it came to facing men. Women were his target.

'Ready,' Maisie said, pulling Lee's attention back. 'Let's go.'

'Brilliant,' Lee said, leading his little sister towards the taxi waiting at the side of the road. He opened the door, the luggage already inside, and took the pram from Maisie, allowing her to climb into the taxi. The driver got out and helped Lee lift the pram inside and just before he climbed in himself, he turned to see if Galzo had caught a glimpse of what was going on.

He'd moved onto the next group of teens but had stopped, his full attention on Lee who gave him a sly smile before climbing in the taxi.

'Did he look over?' Maisie asked.

'Naw,' Lee lied because he knew Maisie was hoping Galzo would suddenly become a stand-up dad and boyfriend. Lee knew that was never going to happen.

–

Lee opened the front door of his new flat, courtesy of his new boss and Maisie's eyes looked like they were going to pop out of her head.

'Oh my god, Lee. How the fuck can you afford this place?'

Inside, Lee closed the door and turned back to his sister. 'I've got a new job.'

'It must pay well,' she said, taking her shoes off and going off to do her nosey.

Lee glanced down at little Gareth who was beginning to stir and lifted him out. 'A'right wee man. This is your new home, much better than that shithole we've just come from. You're going to love this place.'

'Lee,' Maisie said, immerging from the large kitchen diner. 'Thanks bro.'

'Anything to get you back on your feet, Maze.'

Forty-Nine

As he slid the ring onto Annie's finger, a memory flashed into his mind of when he'd brought Kora here not so long ago. She'd said yes. They'd both been happy. Then Frankie Conway had come along and…

Terry pushed the thought of his ex out of his head. Now was not the time to be thinking about her. Or Frankie bloody Conway. Pulling Annie in and hugging her tight, he felt close to tears himself but he managed to keep them hidden. He knew this would have been the perfect place to propose to Annie and he couldn't have asked for a better outcome. She'd said yes to becoming his wife. He was going to have Annie by his side for the rest of his life and yet he still didn't know a lot about her, only what she'd shown him. Did he truly know who Annie Wicks was? Where had she come from? Did she have family? The biggest thing he had to ask was, what was she running from? He wasn't stupid. Although knowing very little, he knew she had secrets that she was keeping from him. Yes he was keeping things from her, like what happened with Kora, so he couldn't exactly ask for information without volunteering his own. On the other hand, Terry was turned on by the fact that Annie was mysterious. Something about the blank space she possessed sat well with him and he couldn't explain that.

He felt her body jerk against his and pulled away to see her face. She wasn't just crying with happy emotion, she was sobbing. Not the reaction he had hoped for even though she'd said yes.

'Are you alright?' Terry asked.

'Yes,' she managed to choke out. 'I've just… No one has ever done anything like this for me before and I'm overwhelmed, that's all.' Annie smiled and suddenly her eyes light up and the tears stop.

A wave of panic set in then and Terry wondered if Annie had just said yes because she didn't have the heart to say no. He hoped that wasn't the case. He had loved Kora, of course he had but he'd never felt like this about anyone in his life. Annie was like the part of his life that had been missing. But he had to know for sure that she was marrying him for the right reasons.

'Are you *sure* this is what you want, Annie? I won't be offended if you were to tell me it was too soon. I know we've only been together a short time and our relationship has been intense, not like a normal relationship. But I can't see my future without you. I can't and that's why I asked you to marry me. It doesn't have to be an instant thing, we can have a long engagement if that's what you want.'

Annie started to laugh and Terry realised he was babbling.

'Shut up, Terry. If I didn't want to be with you or see myself with you long term then I wouldn't be here at all.' She wiped the remnants of tears away from her cheeks and looked down at the engagement ring that Terry had slid onto her finger. He could see she loved it.

If someone had told Terry just a few months ago that he would have met someone like Annie, who he would integrate into his business and ask to marry him, he would have told them to fuck off. Terry wasn't a soppy man, he was a gangster, a man who was in charge of the city's drug and security trade. However, he knew that when he fell, he fell hard. Now he had created a scene you'd find in a romance film and he knew that Richie would have something sarcastic to say about it. Of course he would; Richie wasn't the type to stick to one woman. He also wasn't keen on Annie at all. From the moment he'd met her, Richie was open in his inability to trust her. Terry hadn't let that stop him from developing things with Annie.

They sat down on the blanket and Terry popped open the champagne from the ice bucket, thankful that he'd met Annie. She would make an honest man of him in some respects. His idea to propose had been on a whim, but it had felt like the right thing to do. Seeing the power Annie had possessed after her first debt collection job had been the thing that helped Terry to see that life without her would be less interesting, less exciting.

Terry poured champagne into two plastic flutes and handed one to his new fiancée. Special didn't cover it. Annie ticked all of the boxes: exciting, adventurous, fearless. How could he not want to marry her?

'So, the wedding,' Terry started but Annie held her hand up.

'Let's just hold off on that right now,' she sipped the champagne. 'There's plenty of time.'

She leaned over and kissed Terry so passionately, she knocked him over and spilled champagne all over him. They had sex right there on the small, white sand beach under the Scottish sun.

Later, as they headed back to the main jetty on the island, Annie asked about the rest of the surrounding islands. Terry took great pleasure in educating his future wife on the small islands surrounded by the Loch. All of them were owned by Innes and his wife Audrey. Innes inherited them from a bloodline that went back further than he'd been able to find out.

'That one over there,' Terry pointed to the island to the north west of where they were standing on the path, 'is Inchcarrach. It's the second biggest island of the group. There is a hotel on one side and two or three cottages on the other.'

'That's it?' Annie asked. 'How do they sustain it?'

'Millionaires hire it out for weeks at a time, throw big parties, weddings, that kind of thing. There are others, most uninhabitable due to their size but the rest are all run by Innes and Audrey's sons and their wives.'

'So there's Incharden, Inchcarrach and…?' Annie pressed.

'To be honest, I can't remember the names of the others. But they're all Inch something,' Terry said as they reached the main jetty. As much as he wanted to keep her here overnight to celebrate their engagement properly, there was work to be done back in Glasgow. Innes was waiting for them. The sun was going down and there was a chill in the summer night air.

'We'll come back here, Annie. I'll take you a tour around all the islands,' Terry said as he helped Annie into the boat.

'Congratulations you two,' Innes said.

As they began their journey back to the mainland, Annie seemed much more comfortable than she did on their way out. Leaning in to him, she let Terry wrap his arms around her, shielding her from the Loch breeze.

'Maybe we could get married on one of these islands?' Annie said.

Terry nodded. 'Whatever you want, Annie.'

And he meant it. Terry would do *anything* for Annie. No matter what that meant and no matter whether he came to know about her past. If this was how he felt about her now, nothing could change that.

As they enjoyed the short journey across the Loch back to the mainland, Terry's phone buzzed in his pocket. Pulling it out, he opened the message sent from Lee. It had been forwarded to him and to Richie. He watched footage of a younger lad dealing drugs in Mainhill.

> Galzo dealing on Reid territory. It's time to sort this little prick out.

Lee had informed him just days ago about Galzo and Terry had chosen to let him go on, dig a deeper grave for himself. Now that he had physical evidence, Terry would use it to rid him of this problem.

–

'What's that?' Annie asked, looking up at the phone in Terry's hand.

'Just some business to attend to when we get back,' Terry said through gritted teeth.

'That doesn't sound good,' Annie replied, seeing the look on her fiancé's face.

'Nah, it's not good. Not good at all.'

Annie chose not to press further. Whatever was going on, he would deal with things himself and if he needed her input, he would ask for it.

As the boat made its way across the water back to the mainland, Annie felt a lot calmer being on the water. There was no point in allowing the panic to consume her because she was still alive. A neighbour had found her that day and called an ambulance, thankfully. At the time, Annie had wanted to die but having survived, she knew that death wasn't necessary. Jack had already died, there was no need for another death. She felt guilty for thinking that way but she had to be fair on herself. She'd come through a lot in the last few months, came out feeling stronger than she believed possible and now, she'd found Terry and things were getting better.

Glancing down at the rock on her finger, she smiled. Being engaged to someone she wasn't in love with wasn't a bad thing because she believed in time her feelings for him would grow. As much as Terry ran businesses that meant people often met a violent end, he never showed that side when he was with her. And he was successful and wealthy because of his work and she would reap the benefits of that working with him too.

Richie was another story. Having seen him with Kora and knowing that he wasn't to be trusted meant that one day, Annie knew, Richie would be out and Terry would only share his future success with her.

Walking into the pub that day had been the single best thing that had happened to her. Of course, Jack was the exception. Always would be. What happened to Jack was her fault yes, but that didn't mean she could never be happy again, did it?

Fifty

Pulling up outside the luxury apartment complex, Annie smiled. 'And you own all of these?'

'I'm not just drugs and guns you know,' he winked at her as he stepped out of the car. 'I do have other skills.'

Looking up at the place, she felt a sense of pride come over her. She was going to be married to a man who made all of this happen. It felt good.

They reached Lee's door; he was already standing there awaiting their arrival after he'd buzzed them into the building. He was young and handsome with muscular arms and bright blue eyes. Annie almost blushed at how she saw him.

'Boss,' Lee said. Terry held a hand out and they shook. 'Richie not here today?'

'Nah, he's keeping a close eye on you know who.'

Lee nodded and stood aside to let them in. 'This is my fiancée, Annie.'

'Nice to meet you Annie.'

Annie gave him a smile as he led them through to the lounge.

'Annie, Terry, this is my sister Maisie and my nephew, Gareth.'

Annie glanced down at the girl sitting on the sofa and immediately recognised her. The girl from the building where Annie was doing her debt collection. Maisie was the girl coming out of the opposite flat with her baby in the pram.

'Oh, hi,' Maisie said. 'I think we've met?'

'Yeah,' Annie replied. 'Back in Mainhill. I was…' She hesitated, unsure how to explain what she'd been doing that day in the estate. 'Visiting someone.'

'Maisie and wee Gareth here are staying with me until my sister can get back on her feet. That a'right boss?' Lee asked Terry. Annie noted the look of apprehension on Lee's face.

'Why wouldn't it be?' she asked, deciding to step in. Terry caught her eye before smiling down at Lee and Maisie.

'Aye, no problem.'

They sat down on the sofa and Maisie told Lee that she was going for a shower and asked him to watch the baby, but before he could respond, the girl had already left the room and the sound of the bathroom door being locked echoed down the hall.

'She's struggling a bit being a new mum,' Lee said. 'She's only sixteen. The guy who got her pregnant is a waster. In fact it's the same guy who's dealing in the estate.'

Annie noted Terry's change of expression. 'Lee, can I have a word?'

Terry and Lee got to their feet and Lee glanced down at the baby in the crib next to the sofa. 'Erm…'

'I'll keep an eye on him,' Annie said, giving a tight-lipped smile. She wasn't here to be a babysitter but she couldn't say no, and she hadn't been asked to be part of the conversation between Lee and Terry.

'Cheers.' Lee stepped out of the room and Terry followed, but not before he turned to face Annie with a smile on his face and said, 'Get some practice in, eh?'

He closed the door behind him and Annie felt her stomach drop. 'I don't think so,' she whispered, sitting back on the sofa and hoping the baby didn't wake up.

The flat was silent; she couldn't hear the water running from the shower. She couldn't hear Terry or Lee's voices. All she could hear were the short intakes of breath from the tiny human she shared the room with.

Getting to her feet, Annie peered into the crib and watched the baby sleep. She barely blinked as she took in the sight. Tiny fingers. Tiny fingernails. He was incredibly small, perfect. How could a girl at sixteen, who, by the sound of it had issues with staying sober, produce such perfection?

The baby began to stir and soon he was wailing, his tiny lungs sucking in as much air as they could so he could let out a cry louder than the last. Annie panicked when she realised no one else was around to pick him up and soothe him.

'Shit,' she whispered. Reaching down, she scooped him up in her hands and stared down at him. 'Little guy, I don't really know what to do with you here.'

As she began rocking him and his little voice whimpered, she saw the baby look at her and a feeling of dread crept over her. She froze for a moment, guilt, fear and heartbreak consuming her. She quickly laid him back in his crib and opened the lounge room door. 'Lee, Maisie, the baby's crying.'

Lee emerged from the kitchen and passed by Annie. She watched him pick the baby up and begin to soothe him. It seemed to Annie that Lee found it easy to soothe the baby, as if he was his own.

'Not quite the maternal type then?' Terry asked, laughing a little as he stood by her side.

'Yeah about that,' she laughed gently, 'just so we're clear, no kids. I don't do vomiting and shitty nappies.'

'Really?' He looked almost disappointed and didn't return her attempt at humour.

'Really,' Annie replied. 'I like the freedom. Having that kind of responsibility just causes heartache and stress. I like wine, nice food and being able to enjoy a hangover without having to—'

'Aye, okay I get it Annie. No kids.'

Shocked by the sudden expression change, Annie noted how disappointment faded and was replaced by irritation.

'You *want* kids?'

'No, it was just banter, Annie. No need to get so serious.'

Terry moved back into the lounge and left her standing in the hallway as Maisie emerged from the bathroom, a towel wrapped around her tiny frame and wet hair dripping over her shoulders. The baby was still crying, but screaming less.

'Think he's hungry,' Annie said, attempting a smile and feeling as though she owed Maisie an explanation.

'Aye, wee shite's always hungry. Lee will do it,' Maisie replied, going into one of the bedrooms and closing the door.

Nice, Annie thought. *She's not winning the mother of the year award then. Not that she's old enough to be one.*

Taking a deep breath to ease the constriction in her chest, Annie thought about what Terry said about her not being the maternal type and his attitude when she'd said no kids. Why had Terry behaved like that? They'd only just got engaged, barely been together long enough for that. Now he was talking about children. Annie felt freaked out. Almost trapped. Things were great with Terry, but she couldn't possibly be expected to want to bring a child into the relationship. A gangster and his missus didn't exactly spell out perfect parenthood, and it wasn't as though she'd had a glowing reputation as being a mother the first time round.

And how could Annie put herself through that again? How could she ever allow herself to want another child after what she'd done? Or to word it better, what she'd failed to do. Her beautiful baby boy. Dead because of her. She couldn't keep him alive. The most basic thing a mother should be able to do and she couldn't fulfil it.

Listening to the baby in the lounge as young Lee tried to soothe him while his useless mother shut herself in her bedroom, her chest ached. Holding him and feeling warmth from the little one's skin… Annie didn't know how she was still standing.

Eyeing the door of the flat, Annie headed straight for it and before she knew it, she was standing at the back of the building, sucking in great lungfuls of air and wishing it had been her who had died instead of her baby. Being around Terry had made her forget her past life. She hadn't expected to be faced with a new life when walking into the apartment.

Staring out at the carpark, Annie decided to steady herself. She couldn't let this affect her anymore, she had to be strong for herself. But she mustn't ever tell Terry about what happened before she met him. She couldn't. He wouldn't be able to look at her in the same way. She couldn't even look at herself in the mirror without hate coursing through her veins.

Turning, straightening her back and fixing down her jacket, Annie strode back into the apartment building and back up to Lee's flat and pretended everything was completely normal.

But there was nothing normal about Annie, or her life. Nothing normal at all.

Fifty-One

Hearing the door closing, Terry knew Annie had left. He wasn't sure what had just happened, but he knew that whatever it was, something was bothering Annie and he wanted to know what. If he was going to marry this woman, then he needed to know everything, not just what his background check had thrown up, which was practically nothing.

'Boss, what are you going to do about Galzo?' Lee said quietly as he placed the baby back into the crib at the side of the sofa. 'Bearing in mind he's not only dealing on *your* turf, but he's also fucking my sister about and trying to get her back into drugs.'

Terry looked up at Lee and saw nothing but anguish on his face. He could see that Lee really cared for Maisie and that was the way it should be. But he couldn't allow Lee's emotions to get in the way of business. And Terry couldn't let this little shit get away with taking the piss for much longer.

Terry nodded, got to his feet. 'Right, Lee. Let's get one thing straight. I'm not a problem fixer, I'm a businessman. I am not going to sort this guy out for you on a personal level. He's fucking with *me* and that's the only reason. I want you to arrange to meet this guy, tell him you're looking for some gear. I want to know the time and place of this meeting. You tell him fuck all, I don't want him suspicious that you're working for the Reid organisation.'

Lee pursed his lips. 'Okay, what happens when you get there?'

'You fuck off and get on with your job. Got it?'

'Aye boss, got it.'

The front door opened and Terry heard the sound of Annie's heels in the hallway but she didn't appear in the lounge. Instead, she hung around in the hall, waiting for Terry to finish his business with Lee.

Good, Terry thought. He wasn't sure what to say to her after her strange reaction to his suggestion of her not being the maternal type. What was that all about? She's a woman, most women wanted kids, don't they? Terry definitely did, but the way she shot the idea down had hit him somewhere inside him he hadn't known existed.

Fifty-Two

Just as Annie was about to face Terry after what had happened, Maisie Whitelaw stepped out of the bedroom and into the hallway. Annie looked her up and down, noticing just how young and small she was. To look at her, you'd never have known she'd just had a baby.

'Oh, I thought I'd heard you two leave?' she said to Annie, not stopping as she passed her in the hall and went into the kitchen. Annie stood by the kitchen door.

'No, I went out for some fresh air.'

'Right,' Maisie said. 'Has the wee shite stopped screaming yet?' She laughed, but Annie didn't return a smile. Not even a raised corner of the mouth.

'Sounds like it,' Annie replied. As she stood there, regarding Maisie, Annie wondered what kind of life the girl had led to get to a point of having a baby at sixteen. She didn't look well either.

'Good. I cannae listen to him screaming all day again. Goes right through me, ye know?'

Annie smiled. 'Fancy a cuppa?'

Maisie nodded and they went into the kitchen together. Annie closed the door as Maisie busied herself getting mugs and teabags from the cupboard.

'So your brother is helping you out with the baby then?' Annie queried.

'Aye. Fuck knows what kinda state I'd be in without him.'

'And the dad? He's not around?'

Maisie stopped what she was doing, turned her face to the ceiling as if trying to stop tears from coming. 'Naw.'

'Shame,' Annie replied.

'Not really. He's an arsehole. Fancies himself as a bit of a gangster. I loved him and all that but he was dangerous for me, you know what I mean? I was kind of addicted to him. Still am I suppose.'

Annie nodded, understanding a little of how that felt. 'Not having them around is a bit like withdrawal, eh?'

'Aye, something like that,' Maisie said as she filled the kettle.

Sounds of baby Gareth crying filtered through from the lounge and into the kitchen, even with the door closed. Sighing loudly, Maisie went through and reappeared with the baby in her arms.

Annie watched as she attempted to make tea with one hand while cradling him in the other. Stepping in, Annie took over. 'Here, I can make the tea.'

'Actually, could you just take him?' Maisie said, holding him out to her.

Annie awkwardly held the child while Maisie turned her back on him. 'I love my son, I do. But sometimes I wish I'd not been so fucking stupid to get pregnant in the first place.'

Annie heard a crack in Maisie's voice. Poor girl. Poor child, Annie thought as she looked down at him. He'd stopped crying now as she gently rocked him back and forward.

'He likes you,' Maisie said, plastering on a fake smile. 'I know who to go to for a babysitter then.'

Annie laughed, but knew that the answer she would always give was no. She couldn't be around babies or children.

'What about other family, or friends? Surely there are more people who could help out other than Lee. The organisation has a lot of things coming up, and Lee might become busy with Terry in the weeks and months to come,' Annie said.

'No way. My parents are druggies and I wouldn't leave a dog in Freddie's care. He's my other brother. I love him but he's a bit of an idiot, not far off becoming a full-blown junkie himself. That's how Lee started working for Terry in the first place. He paid off Freddie's debt after Freddie was late in paying. For Lee it was either work for Terry or be killed by him. I know what option I'd have gone for. I'm young and have made some shitty decisions but it doesn't take a genius to work out that was his only option…'

Annie felt her eyes widen at the sheer honesty coming from Maisie's mouth.

'Oh shit, sorry. I shouldn't be saying things like that to you. You're kinda like the gangster's moll, aren't you?' Maisie said, her face scarlet with embarrassment.

'Ha,' Annie failed to suppress her laughter. Maisie reminded her a little of herself with how open and brutally honest she could sometimes be. 'I suppose I am. Although I think moll makes me sound a lot older than I am, so maybe just missus is fine.'

Maisie smiled and looked down at the baby who was now asleep in Annie's arms. 'Right, that's it.'

'What?' Annie asked.

'You're never leaving again. How did you manage to get him to fall asleep?'

Annie glanced down at Gareth. 'Maybe all this gangster chat was just too boring for him.'

Fifty-Three

Standing in the estate and looking up at his parents' council house, Lee hadn't realised until now that he had escaped hell on earth. The flat Terry had provided had opened his eyes to the disaster Mainhill really was, with young kids on the street causing mayhem, discarded needles on the ground, broken glass all over the park and boarded up windows not only on the flats but the council houses too. The only houses that looked remotely decent were the bought properties, and those were owned by people who moved in when Mainhill first went up in the early Seventies. The only reason those people stuck around was because they were tied into owning their properties, but it didn't matter what they did to make them look nice, they were in the middle of one of the worst estates in Glasgow. Lee almost felt sorry for those people, even the ones who he'd stolen the wheels from. But he had to look after number one. That's what everyone in life did, wasn't it?

'Oi, Whitelaw!' Lee turned in the direction of the voice and saw Galzo headed straight for him, a glint in his eye and a balled up fist. But Lee knew it wouldn't go any further. He didn't have the balls to stand up to Lee, not really.

'Who the fuck d'ya think you are? Think you're a hard man do you, throwing punches playing the doting big brother?' Galzo said, stopping in front of Lee.

'Fuck off Galzo. You're nothing but a wannabe gangster. Do you even know the kinda shit you're bringing to your own doorstep, dealing on Reid territory?' Lee said, stepping in towards his enemy, shoulders pushed back and showing no fear.

To Lee's surprise, Galzo took a swing, but Lee anticipated it and caught his fist in his hand, twisted his wrist and punched him in the jaw with the other. It was quite pathetic how Galzo went down so quickly. He was the one acting the hard man but couldn't deliver on his word.

Glaring up at Lee, Glazo got to his feet. People on the estate were beginning to stop and take notice of what was unfolding.

'Don't bother trying to get up and fight, Galzo. You and I both know you won't win.'

Galzo's shoulders slumped slightly and his stance became less forced. 'What the fuck is it to you that I'm on Reid grounds? It's no' as if you've got anything to do with them, is it?' He spat.

'Naw, I don't,' Lee lied.

It was easy to do, considering that Lee wasn't dealing on the estate. Terry and Richie had said they didn't want Lee doing that. They'd seen it before, a lad dealing on his own doorstep. It never ended well, people taking the piss with payments because they thought they were mates. He'd been put on the Blackhill run, a few miles away. No one knew him there and that was fine by Lee. It also meant that Galzo really was in the dark about Lee's involvement with the Reids.

'But if you've got an interest in my sister and want to have any kind of relationship with your son, then I don't think it's the best idea to go getting into something with the Reids you won't be able to get yourself out of. And I don't want my sister caught up in a turf war. It's bad enough she got herself involved with you in the fucking first place.'

Galzo gave Lee a death stare but Lee knew there was no threat. Not yet anyway. Galzo was nothing on his own. But he knew some dodgies and it was risky for Lee to challenge him at all. But when it came to Maisie and Gareth, he would do anything he thought necessary to protect them.

'You know what?' Galzo sniggered. 'I don't think you really understand the danger you've put yourself in acting the hard man with me. Aye, you might have a good right hook, but would you be able to stand up to me if I pulled a blade on ya?'

Lee rolled his eyes and forced a laugh. 'A blade? Really? That's the only way you'd get the better of me, ain't it?'

'Well, if you were bleeding out on the fucking street, and your sis was up in that flat smashed out her wee face, then I'd be free to take that wee lad a' mine and fuck off, wouldn't I?'

A rage began burning in Lee's chest, but he had to stay calm. Don't rise to it, he thought. Terry and Richie would be here soon enough to deal with him. A couple more days and things would be finished with the prick. 'Aye, so you would Galzo.'

Galzo raised a brow at the same time that the corner of his mouth lifted into a sneer. 'Fucking watch me, Lee. Thing is, you don't know whether I'm at it or not. So you wouldn't see it coming. And I know you, you won't tell

Maisie about this because your such a doting big fucking brother that you won't want to worry or upset her. And on top of that, she wouldn't believe that I would do something to her anyway. And maybe I wouldn't. You'll never know.'

'Galzo, for a guy who's taken a few bangs in the mouth from me, you seem to be awfully sure of yourself. Do yourself a favour and fuck off or the only person getting knifed around here'll be you, a'right?'

Galzo sniggered. Started laughing. But he didn't move closer to Lee. There was a look on Galzo's face that told Lee he didn't want to risk it. That was good, that meant that he was wary. If he *was* more wary of Lee, then he wouldn't see the Reid's coming.

But the words that stuck in Lee's mind were what Galzo said about taking Gareth. Lee couldn't allow that to happen. Wouldn't allow it. However, Lee knew that Terry was going to take care of Galzo, he just hoped it would be sooner rather than later, for Maisie and little Gareth's sake.

Fifty-Four

Getting out of the car and watching them through the window of the restaurant, Annie Wicks felt sick at the sight of Richie Jackson and what he was doing. It was bad enough that she'd seen him in the carpark with Kora, Terry's ex. But to see that it definitely wasn't a one-off and that Richie was betraying Terry made her angry for her fiancé. Especially with all the digs Annie had been getting about Richie not being able to trust her and how she shouldn't be let in on company policies and plans.

Glancing down at her phone, at the image she'd first taken of them together in the supermarket carpark, she grinned. What kind of a gangster conducted his business in public? Richie was supremely idiotic in Annie's eyes. If he had half a brain in his head, he'd at least see Kora behind closed doors if he wasn't going to end it with her.

Lifting the camera, she zoomed in on the couple sitting together at a table near the corner of the window. Smiling and laughing together. Annie snapped a few more pictures before sending them to her own email address. She had to have a backup plan in case Richie were to destroy the phone. Because she was going to tell him, confront him about his affair. How could she look Terry in the eye herself if she was keeping a secret like that from him? She was supposed to be marrying him. But it wasn't just about that. It wasn't as though she was a stranger to keeping secrets. In having this information, in confronting Richie it would mean he'd have a choice to make. Lay off Annie and keep his affair secret, or get his legs broken. Simple.

Taking a steadying breath, Annie crossed the road, the heels of her shoes clicking on the concrete with every stride. Pulling on the heavy glass door, a waiter smiled at her, asked if she wanted a table. Shaking her head, she nodded in the direction of Richie, indicating to him that she knew where she was going.

Her heart pounded in her chest as she moved closer to the table, a mixture of excitement and disgust coursing through her as she pulled out the chair opposite the couple and sat down.

'Er, who the hell is this?' Kora said, turning her attention to Annie.

Annie studied the woman's face. Long brown hair, curled at the ends. Dark eyes. The eyes of a liar. Annie was glad Kora had treated Terry so badly. If she hadn't Annie wouldn't be sitting here now. Engaged and ready to move on with her life.

'Annie, what the *fuck* are you doing here?' Richie Jackson hissed. He was rattled and so he should be.

'I could ask you the same question, Richie. But then I already know the answer to that, don't I? You've not exactly conducted your business on the quiet, have you?'

Richie's eyes bored into Annie as she sat back in the seat. A waiter approached and asked Annie if she wanted a drink.

'Oh yes, a vodka. No ice. Make it a double please.'

As the waiter left, Annie turned to see Kora try to get to her feet. Richie pulled her down by the wrist and shook his head.

'Excuse me, I don't know who you think you are hen, but you'd better take yourself back to where you just came from,' Kora said, aggression in her tone. Raising a brow at her, Annie laughed gently.

'So you've not told her then?' Annie asked Richie.

'Annie, don't do this.' Richie said. 'Not here.'

Kora's eyes darted between Richie and Annie and her eyes widened. 'Oh my god. Is she your wife or something?'

Annie laughed loudly as the waiter returned with a double vodka. She thanked him and sipped at it as she watched Richie squirm.

'No, she's not my wife. Nothing like that,' Richie said and lifted his pint glass. 'Jesus Annie, what the fuck are you doing?'

Ignoring Richie, Annie turned to Kora. 'Kora, I'm Terry's fiancée.'

Blood drained from Kora's face then and her eyes darted around the room as if looking for the nearest exit. 'Is he here?'

'No, do you think Richie would still be in one piece if he was?' Annie said, sipping again at her drink. 'I know all about you, Kora. About what you did with Frankie, but do tell me, were you cheating on Terry with Richie too?'

Kora shook her head but her eyes told a different story.

'Oh my god,' Annie glared at Richie before resting her eyes on the woman Terry had almost married. 'So even though she was shagging some other guy, one of your rivals, you had an affair with her anyway? Bloody hell Kora. You know how to work your magic on the gangsters of the city, I'll give you that.'

'Annie, it wasn't like that and you have no idea what you're getting yourself into here,' Richie sneered, leaning across the table at her.

'Do *you*? You know who Terry is, don't you? Because it doesn't seem like you do.'

They fell silent at the table and Annie got to her feet. 'Look, Richie. If I've managed to find out about this, what makes you think Terry won't?'

'Do you know what Terry did to me?' Kora spat. 'If it wasn't for Richie, I'd be dead right now.'

'I don't care, Kora and to be honest what I'm about to say really has nothing to do with you.' Annie eyed the man who claimed Terry should have kept her out of the business. 'This is about me and Richie. You've had a problem with me since the day I met Terry, or at least since the day I said I wanted in. You've given me a hard time. You've said I'm not worthy of working within the confines of the criminal underworld. But I've proven myself time and time again so here's my proposal. Keep your mouth shut about me, start showing me a bit of respect and I won't tell your 'so called best friend' that you've been sleeping with the woman he was engaged to. And just so you know, I have evidence of your affair, tucked away somewhere safe. So it won't just be my word. It will be concrete proof. Hope I'm clear on that.'

Kora and Richie fell silent and it felt as if everyone in the restaurant was watching them.

Lifting the glass, Annie drained the vodka and turned her back on the couple. As she walked out of the restaurant, she glanced at the waiter who served her as she passed him at the bar. 'He'll pay.'

As Annie got back into the car, she locked the door and popped a mint into her mouth before heading home to Terry.

Fifty-Five

Maisie Whitelaw sat with her mobile phone in her lap. Her foot tapped nervously on the floor as she bit at the edges of her thumb nail. With Lee out and Galzo on his way, she was both excited and scared. What if Lee came back and caught Galzo in his flat? What if she wasn't strong enough to tell him to leave her and Gareth alone? She still loved him so much but she knew he wasn't good for her. He did something to her she couldn't control and no matter how he behaved or what he said, she just couldn't keep away from him. Telling Galzo where Lee lived probably wasn't her best move but she had to see him if there was any hope of their relationship getting back on track. Was it ever on track? When Maisie thought about it, they'd never been official. It was always just casual sex between them. But it had been going on since she was fifteen. That was why Lee had been so annoyed when he found out. Yes, Maisie knew it was wrong because by law she'd been underage, but she knew what love was. The age difference didn't matter to her. Or to Galzo.

Glancing down at little Gareth asleep after his last feed, Maisie smiled. No matter what happened between her and Galzo now, she would always have a connection with him.

She thought about what she'd said to Annie, about being addicted to Galzo and how she knew he wasn't good for her. Being madly in love and addicted to someone was the same thing, wasn't it? When you had the prospect of being with that person, it was almost impossible to resist.

Hearing a car pull up outside, Maisie got to her feet and saw the love of her life step out and on to the street. Her heart picked up speed when she saw him and she couldn't help but smile. The idea of being in the same room as him was overwhelmingly exciting.

She met him at the front door and when he stepped inside Lee's flat, he glanced around the hallway. 'How the fuck did your brother afford this beast?' he asked.

That was the one thing she wouldn't let slip to Galzo. It was important to Lee that his work with the Reid's remained a secret. It was bad enough she'd allowed her heart to rule her head and told him where to find her.

'His new job pays well,' she replied.

'Fuck me, Maze, it doesn't half.'

Moving away from her, Galzo walked through to the lounge and she followed him. He'd barely looked at her since arriving and suddenly a pang of sadness washed over her.

'Ah, ma wee man,' his voice boomed.

'Ssh!' Maisie hissed. 'If you wake him it'll take me ages to settle him again.'

Galzo turned and scooped Maisie into his arms, kissed her hard. She almost melted at his touch. 'So, I've had a wee thought. Hear me out.'

'What is it?' Maisie looked at him expectantly. He put her down and sat her on the sofa before he began pacing the floor. 'I think you and the wee man should come and live with me. I can take care of you both. You wouldn't need to work. I could give you both money. I mean, a man should be with his missus and son, right?'

Maisie felt her heart begin to swell. Was he serious? He really wanted her?

'Galzo, I mean yeah. Of course I'd want to live with you. I love you, you know that.'

Galzo smiled widely and sat down next to her, gripped her hand and squeezed it. 'I mean, yeah. I love you too.'

Maisie knew Galzo didn't mean it. But he could learn to love her, couldn't he? Surely he still fancied her, otherwise he wouldn't be here, making the effort. Maisie wasn't stupid though. She knew he'd been with other women his own age. He was nine years older than her and she'd heard the rumours. He was often nicknamed 'shagger' for his reputation. It killed her that he'd been intimate with others, but none of those had had his baby. She could use that as an advantage.

'I want us to get married,' she blurted out.

Galzo's smile faded then, and his grip loosened. 'We don't need to get married, Maze. I'm here, aren't I?'

'I know, Galzo. But it would show me how much you want to be with us if we got married. I wouldn't have to worry about you being away from me because we'd have that connection.'

Galzo stood up and started to laugh. 'Maze, you've got to relax. If we were married, I wouldn't be chained to you. I'd still be able to go out and do what I want. And getting married is expensive, you know?'

The excitement Maisie had felt when Galzo first arrived slowly dispersed. She knew it was a long shot and his answer had told her everything she needed to know. Fighting back tears as she glanced down at her baby boy, Maisie got to her feet and led Galzo out to the hallway. He pulled back, spun her around and kissed her hard. The way he used to at the beginning of their relationship.

'What room first, eh?' he said, tugging at her shirt. Maisie pushed him away towards the front door.

'No, Galzo. If you don't want to commit to me and your son, then I don't want you around.'

A frown spread across his face as Maisie lifted her hand to open the door.

'You're a fucking cock tease, you know that, Maze?'

'And you're a let-down. I knew you weren't capable of anything more. Lee was right about you.'

'Don't bring your fucking brother into this. He's an arsehole. And I'll tell you something, there isn't anything that is going to stop me seeing my boy in there. Do you get that?'

Without responding, Maisie pulled open the door and waited for Galzo to leave. She wasn't scared of him. Heart-broken, disappointed yes. But not scared. 'If you were any decent guy, you'd have stuck around from day one and you didn't. You fucked me over so many times, left me hanging. Made me think there could be more between us. But you just had to go out and sleep with so many others while I was carrying your baby. Just fuck off Galzo. I should never have asked you here.'

Eyes wide, Galzo grabbed Maisie by the face and squeezed so hard she let out a cry. 'You're nothing without me, ya wee bitch. A stupid wee druggie, aren't you? I mean let's face it, it wasn't hard to get you into bed. All I had to do was dangle a bag of powder in front of you and you came running like a dog sniffing out a fucking treat. I'll make sure my boy knows who I am. If you even think about trying to poison him against me I'll fucking have you.'

Maisie's jaw almost hit her collar bone in shock at the venomous words trailing from Galzo's lips. How could he say such things to her when she was the mother of his child?

Letting go, Galzo pushed Maisie out of the way and left the flat, slamming the door behind him. Maisie slid down against the door and began to cry.

As much as she hated him, she'd also never loved anyone more. How was that possible?

Getting to her feet, Maisie made her way towards the bathroom. *I must look a state*, she thought to herself. Opening the door, she was distracted by a gentle knock on the front door. So gentle she barely heard it. Wiping away the tears on her face, she reached for the door handle, but as she pulled it open, a force from the other side knocked her to the floor.

Looking up, she saw Galzo towering above her. Rage burned in his eyes and his hands were balled into fists. 'Jesus, Galzo. What the fuck are you doing?'

But he didn't answer, instead blows rained down on her, knocking the wind from her lungs. All Maisie could do was pull her tiny frame into a ball and hope that her ordeal would be over soon.

Fifty-Six

The atmosphere at the dinner table was stale that evening, and Terry Reid didn't know how to start off the conversation with his new fiancée, but he knew the best thing would be to start as if things were fine.

Taking a drink from the wine glass, he looked over at Annie and smiled. 'I still can't believe you said yes.'

Her stony expression faded into a smile and she too lifted her glass. Taking a sip and setting it back down, she laughed. 'I still can't believe you put me on a bloody boat.'

'How was I to know you were scared of open water?'

'It was beautiful though,' she sighed. 'Look, I'm sorry about earlier at Lee's flat.'

Terry nodded, skewered half a meatball onto his fork and smiled again. 'Can I ask what that was all about?'

Annie exhaled loudly, as if contemplating telling him something important. She fell silent again and Terry knew not to push her. There was clearly something wrong and he didn't want to upset her.

'Kenny Collins called earlier,' Terry said, changing the subject. 'Neil's been released this morning.'

'Oh? What does that mean for the deal with Derek and Kenny then?' Annie asked, seemingly happy with the subject change.

'Well I don't know yet. But Richie seems to think he's a liability and if I'm honest I kind of agree with him.

He can't hold that temper of his and when someone or something gets in his way, that's when things kick off.'

'And that's bad for business. Especially at the clubs.'

'Exactly,' Terry replied, placing the fork in his mouth. 'When the police turn up because a fight has broken out at one of their clubs, and Neil loses the plot it only puts our stock and our money at risk. If any of our dealers are caught in the crossfire, which has been known, it's a loss for the organisation and money out our pockets.'

Annie smiled across at Terry and got to her feet, moving across to the counter and pulling another bottle of red from the rack. It felt good to talk to Annie about business. She seemed to understand the ins and outs for someone not long on the scene. And Terry trusted her more than he trusted anyone else. That was why he wanted things to be smooth between them.

'Annie, about what happened back at Lee's place. I don't want you thinking I was trying to put pressure on you to have a baby. I mean, I'm not a hundred per cent sure I want to but it's one of those things society makes you think you should consider. Isn't it?'

Annie sat back down at the table and poured more wine into their glasses, having finished the last bottle. But she didn't say anything in response and that worried Terry. He trusted Annie, of course he did. But with everything that happened with Kora, he didn't want anything to happen that would ruin what he had with Annie.

'Yeah, I suppose it is. I do want to marry you and to continue to work alongside you and to grow the business. Perhaps even have a little branch of my own. But just so we're clear Terry, I can't be a mum. It's not something I'd be good at and I don't want to try.'

She finished pouring the wine almost as soon she finished speaking. Terry had known Annie was a strong person from the moment he met her and that was what he loved about her. Fine, she didn't want kids, he could live with that. What he couldn't live without was her. He'd already been through it with Kora and that had almost ended him.

'Okay,' he replied. 'That's fine. So long as I get to marry you, then I don't care what we do.'

Annie placed the wine bottle on the wooden table and ran her foot up the inside of Terry's leg, with a sly grin creeping across her face at the same time.

'And what you said there, about having a little branch of your own to busy yourself with? How about a club? Or a clothes shop?' Terry asked.

'No offence Terry, but I don't want you to *give* me a business. I want to plan it myself, build it up on my own.'

Terry smiled. He was hoping that she would say that. It would give him one less thing to worry about. 'Good girl,' he said. 'I love an independent woman.' He winked and took a sip of wine from his glass.

'I've got something on later tonight, so I'll be out for a few hours after dinner. I'd take you but it's a situation I don't want you part of. Might get a bit… well, you know what I mean.'

'The less I know the better,' Annie replied. 'I don't need to know. I'll be here, soaking in a bath with the rest of this bottle.'

Terry nodded. Annie was right to not want to be involved. As much as he trusted her, he didn't want to expose her to more murder and bloodshed. That side of things should be for Terry and Richie to deal with.

This Galzo lad couldn't possibly want to live a long life if he was selling his shitty drugs at a cheaper rate to Terry's regulars, on Reid territory.

Fifty-Seven

Maisie Whitelaw pulled herself up and onto the sofa. Every limb in her body ached, every muscle burned from the beating she'd taken. Galzo sat on the floor, his head in his hands as he sobbed.

'I'm so sorry, Maisie. I don't know what came over me. You just push my buttons, you know.'

Emotion took over as she watched him, sobbing and apologising. She felt sorry for him. Of course she did. She loved him. Was in love with him. How could she just sit there and plead hatred when really, she felt the exact opposite, even though she was sure he'd cracked a rib.

'It's okay. I'm fine.' She winced as red-hot pain sliced through her.

Galzo seemed to notice and he got to his feet and went to her. As much as Maisie loved him, she now feared him too. 'What can I do?' he asked, gripping her hand and running his fingers over her bruised face.

'Get me something for the pain,' she whispered. Her voice cracked and she began to cry.

'Here,' Galzo said, handing her a small tin. She knew what was inside. Knew what it would mean. But at this moment in time, all she cared about was going to a place where she would forget everything that had happened.

She took the tin from him and they smiled at one another. 'I'll make things right Maze. I swear I will. I promise, I'll never lay a hand on you again. I want to be a dad to that wee boy. I promise.'

She closed her eyes as he kissed her head, wishing that he had been a better man from the start. Wishing that she had been enough for him in the beginning. Then maybe she wouldn't be in this mess. But then maybe he did love her, so strongly that it scared him to the point where he lashed out?

Galzo got up and she heard him go into the bedroom where little Gareth was asleep. Lee would kill him when he found out. And he would be so angry at her for inviting Galzo to see her, for giving him the new address. What had been the point of moving out of Mainhill if she was going to allow Galzo to find her?

Maisie went into the bedroom to check on little Gareth, who had slept through the whole thing. Thankfully. The little lad didn't need to hear all that. How could she be a mother to him? How could she raise him when she herself had been dragged up by Rosie and Cammy? Watched Rosie allow Cammy to get so high he didn't know his arse from his elbow and knock her about during a bad trip. In fact, Lee had been the one who'd looked after her when she was young. All she could remember was doing anything she could for Rosie's attention, only to be cast aside for Rosie's need to consume drugs and booze.

She kissed Gareth on the head, gentle not to wake him. Galzo stood over their son, beaming down at him. Pain shot through her ribs once more and she had to stop herself from crying out.

Maisie turned and went back into the lounge, leaving Galzo with the baby and returning to the place where the tin was waiting for her. Funny how one needle and a little brown powder would erase the pain of what Galzo had put her through. Love, hate and fear had become one emotion, one feeling. Did he love her? Did he even fancy her?

Maybe if she took enough heroin, she would never have to wake up to find out.

Sitting down on the sofa, Maisie prepared her hit. She hadn't done this in so long. Since before she became pregnant. But she hadn't forgotten what it felt like. Of course, she knew that she was chasing that first hit. No one ever had the same hit as the first time they'd taken the drug. But that didn't stop them looking for it.

Now, all Maisie wanted was to forget. And that was what heroin would do for her. If it killed her, Maisie knew that Lee would look after Gareth, because he'd taken care of her when Rosie couldn't.

Wrapping the belt from her jeans around her upper arm, Maisie pulled on it as tight as she could and found the vein, before injecting the needle.

Once finished, she sat back and waited for the rush to hit her. It wouldn't take long. It never did.

'Better?' Galzo asked, appearing in the lounge. Maisie nodded slowly as the pain in her ribs subsided.

She opened her mouth and Galzo slid a cigarette between her lips, lit it and placed the lighter back in his pocket. Then, he placed an ashtray next to her before Maisie's eyes closed completely, and an intense feeling of pleasurable calm warmed her.

'That's it,' Galzo's voice came from afar. 'The pain will be gone soon.'

Fifty-Eight

Lee Whitelaw sat on the wall at the bottom of the stairs that lead up to his parents' council house. A cigarette between his fingers and his phone in his pocket, he thought about the possible outcome of Terry and Galzo's meet. Lee knew Terry well enough now as his boss to know that he took no shit from anyone. Lee had also been on the wrong side of Terry before; it was just lucky for Lee that Terry had seen potential in him. Maybe that could have been Galzo too, if he'd gone about things the right way. Not that Lee would want to work with him. It was bad enough Galzo had managed to get his sister to fall under his spell and that she'd had a baby to him by the age of sixteen, but working with him? Thankfully, that wasn't the reason Terry would be conversing with the prick this evening.

Glancing over at the gathering of a few teenagers on the grass at the front of the flats, Lee couldn't help but laugh as both young lads and girls drank from bottles of Buckfast wine and cider, while dancing to some hard-core and house music. That used to be him and Freddie back in the day. The only difference between them now was Freddie would still go out and behave that way, join the teenagers and get smashed in the street. Lee was beginning to build a career now working for the Reids and he liked where things were going. It had only been weeks, and he already had his own flat as part of his wage.

'What you doing sitting here?'

Lee turned to see his brother perched on the wall beside him, as if Freddie had heard Lee's thoughts. Lee hadn't spoken to his brother in a few days. He couldn't bring himself to even look at him, knowing that Freddie was mates with Galzo. Maybe it was time to tell Freddie the truth about his pal.

'Waiting for someone,' Lee said, taking a long draw on the cigarette. 'What you been up to?'

'Nothing. There's fuck all to do around here, is there? How come I've not seen your new place yet?' Freddie asked, his words a little slurred.

'What you on, Fred?'

'Just had a few bevies,' he replied. Lee offered him a cigarette and lit it for him. 'So, I hear Maisie and the wee man are living with you? Maw's raging.'

'What's she raging about? She didn't give a fuck about Maisie when she was a baby, so why would she be bothered by her grandson?' Lee spat.

'A'right mate, calm down,' Freddie said, pulling on the cigarette. Taking a half bottle from his pocket, he took a large mouthful.

Lee glared at Freddie and shook his head. 'Don't fucking tell me to calm down, Fred. You've not got a fucking clue about what's going on, do you? You're just as bad as Rosie. And Cammy for that matter. Not one of you have bothered to see how Maisie's doing, not one of you could give a shit for that wean. Especially you.'

Freddie turned, his brows raised in shock. 'What the fuck do you mean by that? She's my fucking sister. Of course I care.'

'Really? Then why is it you have never asked her who the dad is? And if you had half a brain in that skull of yours…' Lee jabbed a finger into the side of Freddie's head. 'Then you would know who got her pregnant.'

Freddie pushed Lee's hand away and got to his feet in defence. 'What are you on about, Lee?'

'Your mate, Galzo. Ask him about Maisie.'

Freddie fell quiet, his eyes drifting along the estate. Lee followed his gaze and saw the man himself walking towards them.

'Go on. Ask him who the dad is.' Lee said the words loud enough for Galzo to hear, fully expecting him to launch into an argument. But he didn't.

'Oi,' Freddie shouted, moving towards Galzo. Lee remained perched on the wall, waiting for the boss to turn up and deal with the situation. It was an added bonus that Freddie was now angry with his mate. It was about time. 'Have you been shagging my sister?'

Galzo opened his mouth to speak, but before he could say anything to Freddie, they all turned in response to the sound of a car speeding into the estate. Terry Reid pulled up beside Lee in the estate before stepping onto the road, followed by Richie.

'A'right boss,' Lee said, giving a nod. Terry greeted him silently. Both Freddie and Galzo turned to Lee with a look of bewilderment.

'*Boss?*' Freddie asked.

Lee ignored his brother but kept his eyes on Galzo. It was clear to see that he was slowly piecing together what was about to happen and Lee felt a stir of excitement in his stomach. Seeing the realization on Galzo's face that Lee was in fact working for Terry and had set the whole thing up was like waking up on Christmas morning as a kid with everything on his list.

'This him?' Richie said, gesturing towards Galzo. Lee nodded in confirmation and Richie approached Galzo, calm and confident. 'In the car, mate.'

'Eh?' Galzo asked.

'You heard him,' Terry intervened. 'He said *get* in the car. We've got something we want to discuss with you.'

Lee smiled as Galzo turned to him. 'Awe, I get it now. You're a grass. That's it. Fred, your brother here's a grass.'

Lee hadn't expected it, but Freddie swung a fist at Galzo and caught him on the side of the face. Galzo fell against the side of the Range and Richie gripped him under the arm and forced him inside then climbed in beside him.

'Lee,' Terry raised a brow.

Lee understood that his boss was telling him to get in the car too. He was part of this but not in the same way as Galzo. Without hesitation, Lee got up from where he'd been sitting on the wall and walked towards the car. The music still blasted from across the street and it appeared that no one had witnessed what had happened.

'Lee, where are you going?' Freddie asked.

'I'm going to work, Fred.'

'You *work* for Terry Reid?' Freddie's eyes were wide, but his fist was still clenched from when he punched Galzo.

'Look,' Lee said, pulling the keys for his flat from his pocket and holding them out to Freddie. 'I'll text you my address. I'll meet you there in a couple hours. But *don't* tell Cammy and Rosie where I live. I don't want nothing to do with them. Got it?'

Freddie took the keys in his hand and nodded.

'Right, I'll see you later. Oh and good left hook, Fred.'

Closing the passenger door, Lee heard the locks activate. Turning towards the back, Richie held a gun to Galzo's head. 'Keep still, keep your mouth shut and you'll get a chance to explain yourself. A'right?'

Galzo did what he was told and Lee faced out to the road. Terry was quiet. That was never a good sign. Lee knew he was at his most dangerous and angriest when he was quiet.

Driving out of Mainhill estate and towards the town centre, Lee knew exactly where Terry was taking them. The same place he'd taken Lee when Freddie owed the Reids money. As much as Lee knew that he was safe, and on the right side of Terry, he couldn't help but feel a little sick at the thought of what he was going to become witness to. Pulling out his phone, Lee sent Freddie a text of his new address and reiterated for him to go there and wait for him. He wanted to be okay with his brother. It was important for Maisie to have them both support her, even though Fred would need help with his addictions too. Sliding the phone back into his pocket, he settled back into the passenger seat.

'Galzo, isn't it?' Terry said, his eyes glancing up at the rear-view mirror. 'You've got some explaining to do, lad. I hear you've been fucking Lee's wee sister about on top of dealing drugs in the estate. Did you know I own Mainhill?'

Lee didn't turn to see Galzo's reaction. He wasn't sure he *wanted* to see the look on his face.

'Terry, I think this little prick's been taking the piss out of us. What do you think?' Richie said. A painful grunt came from Galzo's side of the car.

'Aye, I think so too, Richie. Taking the piss out of Lee here, too.'

The rest of the journey, they were silent. When they reached the substation on the outskirts, Lee's legs felt like they'd turned to jelly. As Terry got out of the car, Lee followed and soon, they were all standing in the middle of the deserted carpark, with Richie pointing the gun at Galzo's skull.

'Right,' Terry said, beginning to pace. 'Why don't you start off with how much money you've made off taking the piss out of me?'

Lee glared at the lad who had fucked up his sister's life and could feel the corners of his mouth lift into a smile. This was the best outcome for Maisie. If Lee hadn't been working for Terry, then he wouldn't have cared less that Galzo was dealing in the estate. What he did care about was his sister and his nephew, and working for Terry definitely had its advantages.

'I don't know what you're on about,' Galzo hissed.

'I don't think it's a good idea to lie here, Galzo. Especially when you've got a gun pressed into your nut,' Lee said.

'This is you, isn't it? I mean, you hate the fact that me and your sister had a good thing going so you decided to wreck it. How do you think she'd feel if she knew you were doing this to me?'

Lee took a deep and steadying breath. 'Naw, Galzo. You've been taking advantage of Maisie since she was fifteen. She was young and impressionable and you asserted power over her. She thinks she loved you but really you've wormed your way into her head and now she's had your kid. It's fucking sick.'

Richie glared at Terry and then Lee. 'You're telling me I'm holding a gun to a paedo's head and I've not pulled the fucking trigger yet?'

299

Terry held his hand up and gestured for Richie to stay calm. 'So, you're a pervert as well as a piss taker then?'

'Look, Terry, I've no' been dealing drugs on your patch mate. I widnae dae that, I swear.'

Lee could tell that Galzo was beginning to sound desperate, but there was no turning point. The only way out of this for Galzo was death.

'That's not you then?' Terry held his phone up to Galzo face, showed him footage that Lee had sent of him dealing on the estate. 'I think that's most definitely you, sunshine. You've got a thing about kids, don't you? Selling them drugs and trying to get them into bed?'

'Yer a fucking pervert. Simple as.' Richie butted the gun off the side of Galzo's head and he let out a groan.

Lee's phone buzzed in his pocket and he took it out, stared down at the screen. Freddie was calling him. Ignoring it, he ended the call but almost immediately, it began ringing again. Lifting the phone to his ear, he could barely make out what Freddie was trying to say.

'Lee, now's not the time to be taking personal calls,' Terry said. But Lee didn't process it, too busy trying to calm Freddie down.

'Freddie, what is going on?' Lee said. Glancing up at Galzo whose eyes were on him, both men understood what was about to happen.

'*Lee man, she's in a bad way. All sorts of fucked up. Blood everywhere. The wean man, the wean's gone! The wee man's no' here. What the fuck, Lee, what the fuck do I do?*'

Dropping the phone to his side, Lee rushed towards Galzo, grabbing the gun from Richie's grasp before Richie had time to react. He knocked Galzo to the ground and started laying into him with his feet, kicking into his chest and stomach.

'It was you, wasn't it? She's lying up there almost fucking dead because of you, isn't she? You piece of fucking shit! Where's the wean? Eh? What have you done with him?'

Galzo was shouting at Lee to get off, that he didn't have a clue what he was on about. Lee didn't believe a word of it, it only fired him up more.

Lee felt Terry attempt to pull him off; however Lee's newfound strength was fuelled by rage. Richie stood by with his arms folded across his chest and watched as everything unfolded.

A red mist descended on Lee, and before he could control himself, his finger was over the trigger, pulling on it without hesitation.

Everything was still. Staring down at Galzo, Lee's finger still hovered over the trigger. He took in the scene, a bloodied mess where Galzo's face used to be. He was dead.

Fifty-Nine

Richie Jackson unlocked the door of the flat and pushed it open. It had been a long day and an even longer night. But it was worth it to snuff out the life of a street player who thought they would get away with screwing over the organisation. He'd been surprised that Lee was the one to kill off Galzo, but it showed Richie and Terry what he was capable of. He was the sort of man they needed on board.

Stepping inside, he noticed how tidy and fresh smelling the place seemed. Unlike the rest of the flats inside the building. Although the tenant of this particular flat wasn't the same as the rest of his tenants who were mostly prostitutes, working the streets of Barrhouse. Richie had seen an opportunity. Not only was he their boss, but their landlord too. It meant two incomes from each girl and that was enough to put a smile on his face. This was a side business Richie had on the go. Something that he kept from Terry, an income only he received. It wasn't as though Terry would want in on it but he would voice his opinion on the situation, that he didn't like it. Richie didn't care, it was a good way to earn and if the girls were in need of cash, then he was happy to provide them with a client if it meant he got a good cut.

Tonight, Richie moved through the one-bedroom flat and as he pushed the kitchen door open, he watched as the girl he was renting to danced around in her bare feet to the radio as she cooked an omelette.

'Oh, Jesus. You scared the bloody shit out of me,' she said, startled by Richie's presence.

'Sorry. How are you?' he said, placing the keys into his pocket. Looking her up and down, tonight was the first time in a long time he'd seen her smile. 'In a good mood I see?'

Smiling, she placed the spatula in her hand on the counter and approached him. As she slid her arms around his waist and pulled him in, Richie had to fight every urge to lift her up and carry her through to the bedroom.

'Why wouldn't I be?' she asked, her lips so close to his he could almost taste her. 'If it wasn't for you, I don't know where I'd be. That's why we can't let that bitch ruin us, Richie. We love each other and that means more than anything. Doesn't it?'

Richie ran his fingers through her hair and stared into her eyes. 'We shouldn't have crossed that line, you know. As much as you two aren't together anymore, it shouldn't have happened. And as much as I don't like the woman, Annie was right.'

Richie thought about Annie's proposal, how she'd backed him into a corner. No, he didn't trust Annie, he didn't think that it was a good idea to have her in the business but who was he to make that judgement. He was sleeping with the woman who used to be engaged to his best friend and business partner. The woman who was supposed to be dead. The woman who Terry thought he'd killed.

'But it did happen, Richie. And I couldn't be happier about that. Terry was a stop gap, even if I had to almost die to realise that. You're the real deal and I want you more

303

than I've wanted anyone in my life. And what about what he did to me when he found out about Frankie? He could have killed me, Richie. I was almost dead and you saved me. If Terry hadn't left you to dispose of me, I'd have died on that kitchen floor. I was so lucky he didn't check and finish me off.'

Richie thought back to that night when he'd agreed to get rid of Kora's body. It had felt like a punishment seeing her like that. Having slept with her a few weeks prior to that evening, even before she'd had a thing with Frankie Conway, Richie had started to develop a thing for Kora and seeing that she was almost dead had startled him. Thank god Terry had left as quickly as he had and Richie was there to see that she was actually still breathing.

Shaking his head, Richie felt like the worst person in the world, stuck in the most difficult position. A position he'd put himself in, no less, but it didn't make it easier. He'd taken her back to his, let her stay for a few days before allowing her to settle and stay hidden in the rented flats until she got on her feet and could get away. But as the weeks had gone on, Richie found himself becoming more and more attracted to Kora. Just weeks later, they'd ended up having sex in the hallway of the flat when he'd gone to check on her. They'd been together ever since. It had been so easy to lie to Terry since he thought he'd killed Kora. And it wasn't like he'd planned to fall in love with Kora. It just happened the more he spent time with her.

Richie smiled at how open she was being. 'Kora, what *have* you done to me?'

Laughing, Kora allowed Richie to lift her up and sit her on the kitchen counter. Parting her legs, he leaned in as close as he could and kissed her hard.

Richie knew he had crossed a line – worried that if Terry found out, he'd take revenge on them both. It wouldn't matter that they'd been best friends since they'd been kids, or that they were in business together. Terry didn't allow lines to be crossed when it came to loyalty. Richie had fucked up big time and he wouldn't be able to change it now.

To add to his worry, Annie knew what was going on. He got that she felt a loyalty to Terry even if the blackmail was for her own gain. If he was honest with himself, he used to share that loyalty. He still did to a certain degree, but he had crossed that line and he knew that there was no coming back from that.

–

Lying in bed with Kora resting her head against his chest, Richie thought about what it would do to Terry if he found out not only that Kora was still alive, but that Richie had moved her in and was having an affair with her – and about what it would do to the organisation. Because if this all came out, one of them would end up dead. Eventually, regardless of Annie's blackmail, Richie knew that he would have to end things with Kora and tell her to leave the flat. He didn't want to end things between but he had no choice. Terry would find out eventually and then they'd both be dead.

Sixty

Pulling into the drive, all Terry could think about was having a couple of whiskys while Annie massaged his shoulders in the bath. What a fucking night. He hadn't expected all of what had unfolded to happen. All he'd wanted was to snuff out the little prick who was screwing him over, who'd turned out to be a pervert too. Instead, he had become involved in a family feud. But then again nothing about that damned estate surprised him. In fact, it seemed worse now than it had when he had lived and worked there as a kid. Or maybe now that he was an adult and seeing it from an older perspective he just thought it was worse. Either way, Mainhill was a means to an end and there was no way he was going to allow some wee bastard to fuck that up for him. He'd had it all thought out in his head how he'd kill Galzo, but then Lee suddenly exploded into a rage and murdered the lad right in front of them.

Terry had been surprised that Lee had been capable but it had also shown him the potential that lay ahead of Lee. Galzo was dead in seconds and Lee had acted as though he'd just killed a spider. Unfazed and calm.

Annie's car was in the driveway and he sighed with relief when he saw it as he opened the front door. Calling out to her as he kicked off his shoes, Terry headed straight for the drinks cabinet and pulled out his favourite bottle.

'Annie?' he called again. 'You in?'

Placing the bottle down on the counter, Terry climbed the stairs towards their bedroom, expecting to find her in the shower or the bath waiting for him. Entering the bedroom, he noticed how Annie's side of the built in wardrobes were lying open. Some of her clothes were gone. And her shoes. On closer inspection, the suitcase that had been sitting on the top shelf of the wardrobe was also gone.

'Awe, you fucking haven't,' Terry said to the empty bedroom. Making his way through to the office space, where he'd first taken Annie after meeting her in one of his pubs, he glanced at the wall where his safe was located. 'Annie, please tell me you fucking haven't.'

Terry roared in anger and pulling back the frame which covered the safe, he punched in the code and opened the heavy-set door. It took Terry a few seconds to process what stared back at him. Nothing but an empty space. There had been ten grand in sacks sitting inside that safe earlier that morning – money that Annie had put in there herself, along with cash collections Terry and Richie had made themselves. All of it equating to twenty grand.

'Annie! What the fuck have you done?'

Rage building in the pit of his stomach and rising quickly to his chest, Terry slammed the safe door shut so hard the whole room shuddered.

Pulling out his phone, he tried calling Annie. As it began to ring, a vibration came from the other side of the room. Glancing over at the sofa in the far corner, he saw it. Annie's phone was perched on the arm, glowing out at him as his name came up on the screen. Throwing it across the room, Terry ended the call and dialled Richie. After four or five rings, he picked up.

'What's up mate?'

'Is Annie at yours?' Terry asked, the anger making him breathless.

'No, why *would* she be?'

'Fuck!' he screamed, dropping his hand to the side of his body before using the other to open and then slam the safe door shut again. He wanted to pull the thing from the wall cavity and chuck it through the window. Placing the phone at his ear once more, he could hear Richie asking what was wrong.

'It's Annie. She's *fucked* me over.'

'What do you mean?' Richie asked, suspicion in his tone.

'She's gone, Richie. Taken twenty grand of my *fucking* money with her.'

'Couldn't she have just gone to deposit the cash?' Richie suggested.

'Naw, mate she's packed her stuff. I've tried phoning her but she's left her phone here. She's done a *fucking* bunk. I can't believe this.'

Spinning around to face the window, Terry launched his phone against the table and the screen smashed, tiny pieces of glass splintering off and landing on the thick carpet.

How could she do this? *Why* would she do this?

Moving along the hall and back towards the bedroom, Terry stood in the middle of the floor at a loss as to what to do. She'd left him, stolen his money. But hadn't taken the car. It was obvious why. She'd have known he'd be able to track the location of the car, so she'd left it behind for anonymity.

Glancing down at Annie's bedside table, staring back at him, was absolute confirmation that Annie had well and truly screwed him over. She'd taken off the engagement ring and left it behind. All twenty grand's worth of diamonds stared up at him, with a handwritten note next to it.

> *I'm sorry to do this to you Terry. It's nothing to*
> *do with us. I just have to go. A x*

Scrunching up the note and throwing it down next to the ring, Terry went downstairs and lifted the bottle of whisky he'd taken out. Opening it, he took a large gulp straight from the bottle. Then another. And another.

Why had she decided to go now? They'd only just discussed their future, how she wanted to branch off with her own business within the organisation. They'd just got engaged and discussed getting married.

Maybe Terry's luck with women had run out? Maybe they were all just like Kora. Unreliable, untrustworthy bitches.

Shaking his head, Terry felt the unrelenting shame creep over him that he could have been so stupid to make the same mistake twice. The twenty grand Annie had stolen may as well have had Frankie Conway's face on each note. Giving Annie the safe combination was the single most stupid thing he'd done.

Sixty-One

Leah and Tom waved off the last of the party guests. It had been a long day. Samuel could barely stand from all the football, games and presents. He was exhausted and Leah's heart swelled for him but at the same time she'd had the same smile plastered across her face while pretending that everything was normal when in actual fact a psycho from her past had broken into her house during the party to remind her of her debt.

'So you enjoyed your party?' Tom asked as he closed the front door.

'Best day ever,' Samuel replied with a yawn. It was half past eight in the evening, way past the time Leah had planned for everyone to stay but she'd seen her son having such a good time that she herself didn't want the day to end.

Once Samuel was in bed, Leah sat on the sofa with a gin and waited for Tom to ask her again what was going on. But he didn't. He simply kissed her on the cheek and went to bed without saying a word. In a way, she was glad she didn't have to discuss things with him. But she was terrified that their last interaction would be on bad terms.

The WhatsApp group was going constantly, the girls chatting about the next tequila night and suggesting that Leah set up a jewellery stall at the next school fair. Leah barely processed any of the messages. Instead she got up and went to the hallway. At the top of the stairs, she quietly pulled down the loft hatch and climbed into the loft.

Sitting down in front of the box where she'd been looking at the file earlier that day, she pulled the file out and opened it. Had it really been ten years since she'd become a mum? That time had gone by in a flash and so much had happened. The best thing being that she'd met Tom, who'd quickly taken on Samuel as his own. They'd never discussed the option of Tom adopting Samuel, it didn't seem necessary. Sam viewed Tom as his dad from the second they'd started spending time together and Leah couldn't have asked for a better find.

Taking a sip from her glass, Leah's eyes filled with tears. She'd made it as far as ten years without her past catching up with her. Ten years. Tomorrow, all her hard work was very likely to come to an end. She knew her ex wasn't going to let her live. Of course he wasn't. She had stolen twenty grand of his money and disappeared.

She read the page in front of her.

Hereby Declare as Follows

I absolutely and entirely renounce, relinquish and abandon the use of my former name, **Annie Wicks**, and assume, adopt and determine to take and use from the date 1st December 2010 hereof the name of **Leah Smith** in substitution for my former name of **Annie Wicks**.

No one had called her Annie in ten years. No one in her life right now knew her as Annie and never had done. Not Tom and certainly not Samuel.

Leah knocked back the last of her gin. Tomorrow she was going to come face to face with her past. Terry Reid would get his money and his revenge. But Leah still held a card close to her chest that, if she played just at the right time, could save her life.

Sixty-Two

Ten years earlier

The shrill ring of the phone made Annie jump. Closing the dishwasher, she made her way through to the hall and picked up the receiver.

'Annie, it's Derek. I need to speak to Terry. It's an emergency.'

Annie frowned. 'He's not here. Can't you get him on his mobile?'

'Don't you think I've tried that? Fuck!'

'What the hell is the problem?' Annie felt her stomach lurch. Derek was normally the calm one out of the Collinses.

'It's Neil. He's back in the jail. The stupid bastard has killed a fucking polis in one of Terry's pubs. The place is crawling with pigs. They've found counterfeit cash in the tills and dodgy booze in the stock room. You need to find him now.'

Annie felt sick. How stupid did Neil Collins have to be to do something like this? When Terry got a hold of him, the police would be the last thing Neil would have to worry about. Hanging up on Derek, Annie pulled her mobile phone out of her pocket and tried Terry but it went straight to voicemail. She tried Richie and even Lee Whitelaw because she knew that's who he was with. All phones went straight to voicemail. Of course they did. No way to trace them when a murder was being committed. She wasn't stupid. Annie didn't bother leaving a message, she didn't want to leave evidence of Terry's knowledge of the counterfeit money or booze. The police could use what she said in those messages in court if things ever came to that. She really had become a gangsters moll, hadn't she?

Annie paced the hall, back and forth. What the fuck was she supposed to do? She had no idea where Terry was or how long he was going to be. If the police had evidence of counterfeit money and booze on one of Terry's premises, they would come looking for him. In the grander scheme of things, it was a miniscule problem but one they couldn't afford to have. She would have to go out looking for him.

Grabbing the car keys for her Porsche, Annie left the house quickly and drove to the only place she thought she might find Terry. Lee Whitelaw's flat.

Pulling up outside the luxury apartments, Annie got out of the car and took a deep breath. She wasn't looking forward to telling him about Neil Collins. She knew how he would react and it was lucky for Neil that he was currently behind bars.

As Annie approached the main entrance, someone was on their way out and held the door open for her. Once in the lift, she tried to consider what to do if Terry wasn't there. She would have to wait, and if Terry was away for hours, it might give her more time to work out how to explain things to him without him flying off the handle.

Stepping out of the lift, Annie made her way along the hall towards Lee's apartment. Knocking on the door, she waited for an answer. When no one came, Annie tried the handle. The door opened and, stepping inside, she noticed a distinct metallic smell in the air. She recognised it right away. The night she killed Joe the same scent lingered in the air, on her clothes.

'Lee? Terry are you here?' Annie called gently. The smell of blood grew stronger as she moved through the flat. And for her to be able to smell it, there must be a lot. 'Lee? Terry?'

Annie peered into the kitchen but there was nobody in there. Stopping, she stared at the lounge door. It was closed. Without hesitation, she pushed the door open and the smell was like walking into a brick wall. It hit her head on and she had to resist the urge to gag.

Standing by the lounge door, Annie took in the scene in front of her. Maisie was laid slumped on the sofa and looked badly beaten. But not just that. A needle lay next to her on the sofa, foil and a spoon on the floor. Annie could barely look at it. Barely look at her.

'Oh *shit*! Maisie?' she called, taking a step forward. There was no response. 'Maisie, are you okay?'

Watching her chest with an intense gaze, Annie hoped she would see signs of life but it was hard to tell because she herself was shaking so much.

'Fuck,' Annie said as she reached into her pocket with trembling fingers to retrieve her phone. Finger hovering over the 9, Annie thought about what she would say to the police when a sound from the bedroom distracted her.

The baby. He was crying.

'Shit,' Annie said, shoving the phone back in her pocket. Following the sound, Annie pushed her way into the bedroom and glanced down at the baby in the crib. He was wide awake, eyes peering up at her. Just like Jack had not long before he died. Sudden infant death syndrome they'd called it. Not that the title made it easier. If anything it had made her feel worse. She couldn't stop her baby boy from slipping away at just a few weeks old. He'd been healthy, her pregnancy normal. So why did he have to go? Staring down at Gareth now, her heart ached the same way it did that morning she lost Jack. Almost six months without him. In some ways it felt like a lifetime ago. She'd forgotten how he smelled, how soft his skin was and the little blonde hairs on his head, so fluffy and small.

Scooping him up into her arms, Annie couldn't stop herself. Pulling him close, she inhaled his scent. He smelled exactly the same as her own baby boy. A sob began to build inside her then and all the emotion and pain from that morning came flooding back. But then baby Gareth stopped crying and closed his eyes, seeming to settle in her arms. This baby needed someone to care for him. Not just now, but for the rest of his life. Annie could give him that. That maternal instinct hadn't just go away after Jack died. It lingered, as strong as the day she found out she was going to have him. But she'd suppressed it, pushed it down deep into the pit of her stomach, even told Terry that she didn't want children because she couldn't face or admit the grief of losing a child.

Pulling herself together, Annie glanced around the room as she looked for a blanket. Finding one, she wrapped him up carefully and placed him back in the crib, before moving out of the bedroom and into the kitchen. Bottles. She needed bottles and formula milk for him. Gathering up as much as she could after going through the kitchen cupboards, she shoved everything into a plastic bag, along with nappies and a pack of wipes.

Peering into the lounge, she saw that Maisie remained in the same position as she had been when Annie found her. Annie didn't feel guilty. This was the right thing to do. That little boy deserved a mother who appreciated how lucky she was to have him, not some junkie teenager who would get off her face at any opportunity. If Annie left him there, and Maisie survived what had happened to her, then Gareth would only become like his family, like the kids on that bloody estate. If she left him here, and Maisie died, he'd grow up without a mother and still become a statistic. Annie could give him so much more than anyone else. He deserved a good mother and Annie had another chance of becoming what she'd always wanted to be.

Moving into the bedroom, she scooped Gareth into her arms and took a deep breath. This was it. If she did this, there was no going back. She couldn't change her mind halfway through. There were too many adults in this little baby's life who would let him down. She refused to be one of them.

Creeping out of the flat and into the communal hallway, Annie closed the door as quietly as possible, wiping the sleeve of her jacket across the handle.

'Okay baby boy, it's time to get you away from here,' she whispered.

Exiting the building, Annie rushed across to the car and opened the boot, removed a series of blankets and packed the passenger foot well before placing baby Gareth on them. Then, she climbed in and drove back to Terry's in the hope that neither the police nor Terry would be there. She needed clothes and money if she was going to make this work. All of those things were at Terry's house.

The journey back was slower than normal, as Annie was driving much more carefully than she would normally. What if she was pulled over for a routine police check? Annie's heart pumped in her chest. She couldn't think like that right now. She had to focus on her plan, which was barely a plan at all.

Even though Annie had moved in with Terry just a little over two months earlier, she'd decided to keep the flat that she'd lived in when pregnant with Jack. She couldn't face giving up the home she'd lived in with her baby boy, even if he'd only been with her for a few weeks. The encounter with the biological dad had been a one-night thing after a night out. She could barely remember what he'd looked like and she didn't have a contact number for him, so he knew nothing of what happened. She'd been single throughout the pregnancy and managed to gather everything she'd needed for the baby arriving. So she still had baby clothes, nappies and an environment fit for a baby. She hadn't been back at the flat since moving in with Terry and he knew nothing about it, nor Jack for that matter.

She felt guilty at the thought of leaving Terry without an explanation. But he was an adult and he didn't have to rely on anyone to get him through each day. This baby did.

Terry would hate her for this, possibly even want to kill her like he thought he did with Kora. The thing was, Annie was smarter than Kora, understood Terry a lot more than she ever had. Annie knew the risks involved in what she was about to do. This wasn't a selfish choice. It was entirely selfless. She was doing this for Gareth. She couldn't help her own son, but she wasn't going to fail a second time.

Pulling up outside Terry's house, she was glad to see the place in darkness. Leaning down and kissing Gareth on the head as he lay contented by the low thrum of the engine, she said, 'I'll be back in a minute, baby boy. I *promise*.'

Annie rushed into the house and ran up the stairs, two at a time without bothering to turn any of the lights on. Pulling open the wardrobe doors, she dragged the suitcase out from inside and started chucking in as many clothes and shoes as would would fit. Zipping the case closed, she stopped for a moment and took a breath as she stared down at the diamond on her finger. Pulling it off, she laid it on the bedside table and pulled the case along to Terry's office.

That was when the guilt became unbearable but she couldn't let it get in the way of what she needed to do. Annie pulled the frame away from the wall and typed the code into the safe. Sighing loudly in relief, she took the bags of cash out of the safe and closed it again. There was twenty grand inside the bags in total. That would be enough to get her started. Babies grew fast.

Pulling out her phone, Annie called a taxi to come for her at the house. She couldn't take the car, if she did Terry would find her quickly. If she had any chance of being a mum then she had to leave it, she had to leave everything behind. One day she would pay Terry back, if she could. She didn't *want* to steal from him. He'd been so good to her.

Annie deleted the call to the taxi company and left the phone on the arm of the couch in Terry's office before going outside and taking Gareth out of the car. As she clutched him to her chest, she hoped that Terry wouldn't show up before the taxi did. How would she explain having Gareth in her arms and twenty grand of Terry's cash at her feet.

Thankfully the taxi pulled up outside the house and Annie climbed in, with the help of the driver, before telling him the address of her old flat.

Smiling down at Gareth, she kissed his head. Finally, she had her baby. She had her son.

Sixty-Three

Present Day

It was early, too early for anyone else in the house to be awake on a Sunday, especially after the tenth birthday party of the year. Leah had got up and cleaned up the house quietly. She'd wanted to leave the place tidy before going to meet Terry.

Leah was dressed and ready to leave the house. Standing by the front door, she took a last look around and held in her tears. She'd given Samuel a life he'd never have had if she'd stayed with Terry. Samuel would have grown up with Maisie and Lee, surrounded by gangsters and drug deals among other things. Who knew what he'd have ended up like? Leah didn't regret what she'd done. Not one bit. She would sacrifice herself if it meant keeping her son safe, with Tom as his dad.

Leah left the house quietly and headed along the street towards the meeting point to which she'd been ordered to go. Terry had been clever, he'd made sure he was never seen up until this point. Now that she thought about it, the man in the pub that night had been Lee Whitelaw. His eyes were what made her remember. The guy in the car at the multi-storey shooting had been Derek and then Kenny had turned up at the house. Terry had sent all his men to do his dirty work for him. Somehow they'd managed to track her down and now she was in this situation, walking towards her own death.

Crossing the road, Leah headed down the country road towards the Farm Estate. No one would be around at that time in the morning, not even dog walkers. Terry had clearly sought the place out, made sure he was in a position that no one would be able to see what they were doing. That didn't surprise her. Even though the village was seventy miles from where Terry lived, it wasn't a shock that he'd found her. He'd know everything about Balness and Leah's life. The school Samuel went to, the jewellery business, the pub. Everything. He'd have had his men investigate it all.

As she headed down the road to Farm Estate, Leah could see Terry sitting on the bench in the distance, waiting for her. Turning his head, he looked straight at her and Leah's stomach flipped.

Finally reaching the bench and legs like jelly, Leah stood in front of Terry Reid and took a breath. It didn't shock her that he was on his own. He was very sure of himself. She knew he'd think being there on his own would scare her more.

He'd aged, a lot. Greying temples and a few lines at the edge of his eyes. He was still as handsome as he was back then. Her feelings about him had changed, but he was still as attractive now as he had been. That was the charm he possessed and how she'd fallen for him in the first place. She felt a stir inside her belly, the same she had the first night she'd spent with him. It was unexpected.

'Long time no see, Annie,' he said. 'I have to admit, age agrees with you. You look… well.'

Leah felt herself begin to blush. This wasn't what she'd expected at all. She'd expected violence, being thrown into the back of a car or van and driven to a deserted place to be killed.

'I don't know what to say,' was all Leah could manage. No one had called her Annie in ten years. It sounded odd now.

'Well, I've had ten years to think of what I would say to you if I ever came across you again.' He seemed calm, and Leah knew that wasn't a good thing. 'Sit down, Annie.'

Doing as she was told, Leah sat at the opposite end of the bench and remained silent. Whatever he wanted to say, she would let him. If he asked her about her disappearing act all those years ago, she would lie through her teeth to make sure he never made the connection between that and Gareth going missing. She would die to protect her son.

Sixty-Four

Terry Reid stared at his ex-fiancée, taking in everything about her. She looked exactly the same as the last time he had seen her, except for a few lines at the sides of her eyes and slightly shorter hair. He couldn't quite believe he was looking at the same woman he'd asked to marry him ten years ago. As much as he was confident that he would finally catch up with her, he was still surprised that the day had finally come.

She couldn't meet his eye, looking at everything except him. Terry thought back to when they first met in his pub in the east end of Glasgow. Fiery red hair, although toned down more than the last time he'd seen her. Blue eyes. Her personality matched her looks. Yet now, she seemed different. A shell of who she used to be.

'So, Annie, I'll get right to it,' Terry said. 'Where's my money?'

Annie stared back at him, her expression neutral. 'Before we start, my name *isn't* Annie. Not anymore. But you already know that, don't you?'

Terry's eyes narrowed as he looked on at the woman he once wanted to marry. He hadn't expected to feel so calm when he saw her. 'Yeah, I heard. Leah? Doesn't really suit you, does it? But then, neither does being a mum. You said you didn't want kids.'

She drew her eyes away from him. 'It just happened. It wasn't planned.'

'And my twenty K, was that planned?'

Annie didn't reply, instead she hugged herself harder. 'How did you find me?' she asked.

'Lee Whitelaw saw you in the city. Followed you a few times to make sure it was really you. Funny thing is, I told him it wouldn't be you, that you'd have been an idiot to have stayed in Scotland after what you did. But I was wrong. Then he said you tried to confront him one night in your local but you were hammered so he left. Then of course there was the hit at the multi-storey. That was Derek. You saw him. Police came asking questions, didn't they? I watched all that unfold myself. You did well not to grass him in. But then you didn't do that for him, did you? That was to make sure we didn't blow your cover on the Joe Allison killing. Then of course Kenny met your man, Tom, is it? Aye, stood chatting to him for a bit while watching your boy play football.'

Annie's eyes darted in his direction. Yes, now he had her right where he wanted her. She would have to do anything he said because he could tell that all she cared about was keeping her family out of this.

'Seems as though my money got you everything you wanted in life, Annie. Now it's time to give it back.'

Sixty-Five

'I have your money, Terry,' Leah said, her voice trembling a little.

Terry glared at her. He didn't believe her. Not at all. Not that she blamed him. But he didn't question or interrogate her. Instead he asked an odd question.

'You remember Lee Whitelaw, don't you?'

Her stomach dropped again and she felt her defence mode kick in.

'Yeah, I remember Lee. Nice lad,' was all she could manage. 'How is he?'

'Fucked up. His nephew went missing the night you left. They think the wee lad's dad took him.'

'What do you mean, took him?'

'Stole him. The same way you stole from me. You understand the concept, Annie,' he spat. 'Anyway, that night was hell. Turns out the dad was killed that night, and Lee thinks the baby was taken somewhere before the dad died. They never found him. I know people think I'm a hard man and for the most part I am, but seeing that family in that state, not knowing where that baby went was fucking harrowing.'

Leah breathed steadily, in through her nose and out through her mouth. Hearing that made her shiver.

'How's the girl doing? What's her name again?'

'Maisie,' Terry replied. 'And I don't know how she's doing. No one does. Lee and his brother Freddie found her that night, all sorts of fucked up. They didn't think she was going to make it through the night. Then she disappeared too. Just upped and left. Lee thinks she went looking for the wean. But no one really knows.'

Breathe, Leah told herself. Just breathe. She expelled air slow and steady. She knew Terry, knew what he was when she was with him all those years ago as Annie.

If someone crossed him, they always ended up dead. All except Kora.

Annie would never have let that happen to herself. Leah would have to resort back to her old ways if she was going to survive this.

'You sent me a bullet with my name on it.'

'Yes, I did. It was a warning.'

'I got that.'

Terry turned, took Leah's hand in his and she froze in fear. 'How did we get to this, Annie?'

Leah shook her head. In all honesty, she didn't know herself.

Sixty-Six

Terry Reid was a dangerous man, someone she wished she'd never become involved with. At the time, all she'd been looking for was a distraction after losing Jack and Terry had certainly been a distraction. She'd quickly become embroiled in business she'd known nothing about. Drugs, guns, murder. At the time, she'd soon almost forgotten about her old life as plain old Annie Wicks and had become the gangster's fiancée. If it hadn't been for Maisie, there was every chance that Leah would still be living as Annie Wicks, possibly married to Terry. Now though, she feared him.

'Tell me what happened back then?' Terry asked.

'You know what happened,' Leah replied.

'No. All I know is that one minute, we were talking marriage and business and the next I come back to find you gone and twenty grand missing from my safe. A little note saying that you had to go. Why?'

Leah sighed. How was she going to go about this? She couldn't tell him the truth about the baby.

'I don't know. I just had this moment where I thought about what I was getting myself into and I freaked out.'

Her iPhone dug into her thigh as she readjusted herself on the wooden surface and remembered that she had something that could distract Terry.

'I don't buy it, Annie. You were fine, we'd *just* got engaged. You owe me a proper explanation.' Leah shivered upon hearing her old name as it snaked from Terry's tongue.

'I think we both know I owe you a lot more than just the truth, Terry. But you're right. I didn't just freak out. I just, I don't know…' Leah hesitated. 'Got caught up in the moment. I thought my lust and passion for what we had would turn into something more. But it didn't. I got swept away with the idea of love, but in reality it never came. I'm sorry if that hurts you, I am. I didn't mean to hurt you I really didn't.'

'Okay,' Terry shifted on the bench. 'If you didn't want to hurt me, then why not just tell me to my face?'

Leah shook her head. He was too close to the truth, too close to realising that she wasn't being fully honest with him. 'I was a coward. I didn't want to see the look on your face when I told you. We'd moved so fast, Terry. You've got to admit that yourself, surely? I mean, how long had it been since Kora left before I moved in?'

Terry turned sharply, giving her a look that almost pierced through her. 'What the fuck has Kora Anderson got to do with this?'

'Nothing,' Leah replied. Would now be the time to tell him about Richie and Kora? It might help deflect the situation away from her for a bit while she figured out how to get out of this. But then, maybe he already knew. It had been ten years since she'd left, ten years since she'd confronted Richie. And when she thought about it, Richie hadn't been one of the men keeping an eye on her. She hadn't come across him and Terry hadn't mentioned him. Perhaps he and Kora had done the off so they could be together in peace?

'I was just saying that we did move so quickly. I mean, you still had a picture of Kora in your house, didn't you? That day I found the gun?'

Terry sniggered. 'Aye, that's right, the day you went snooping through my desk the morning after I'd met you.'

Hearing a click, Leah turned to see that he was pointing a gun at her. Raising her head, she met his gaze and knew that she had to do something to stop him from killing her, because he would. She had no doubt about that.

'Terry, I know you're angry with me and you've every right to be. But I have something for you that I hope can somehow make up for what I've put you through,' Leah said, reaching into her handbag.

'You'd better not pull any stunts or I swear Annie, I'll fucking shoot you right here right now.'

She took the envelope out of her bag and handed it to Terry, all the time keeping her eye on the gun. While holding the gun in his right hand, he took hold of the envelope in his left and glared at it.

'It's twenty grand in cash. Count it if you need to, I wouldn't blame you if you didn't believe me.'

Opening the envelope, Terry glanced inside and then lowered his gun. He fell silent and Leah didn't know how safe it would be to get up and leave him. It wouldn't be the end of it, surely. He wouldn't just let her walk away. Not now that he'd found her.

Glancing down the country road, Leah saw Charlotte heading towards them on her morning jog. 'Oh, hi Leah.' Charlotte approached, sounding out of breath. Terry glared at Leah before getting up from the bench and moving away from her.

'Hi Charlotte,' Leah said, keeping her voice steady.

'Are you okay?' she mouthed.

Leah nodded. Charlotte hesitated before she smiled and said, 'Can't stop love, on my way to earning my twenty-five-mile medal for this month.'

Relief took over then as Leah watched Charlotte carry on with her run and move around the corner. It was good that her friend was moving away, she didn't want her anywhere near Terry.

Terry resumed his position next to Leah, gun pointed towards her. 'You're coming with me.'

'No Terry, I'm not. You've *got* your money, I've said all I can say. Just leave me now, please.'

He released the safety catch and Leah heard it click. She remembered what it felt like to hold a gun to someone. She remembered what it felt like to kill. All those feeling would be coursing through Terry right now, adrenaline taking over.

'I wasn't asking, Annie. Now get up and walk with me. I'm not going to hurt you if you just do what I say.'

Don't panic, she thought to herself. *Just do what he said and when you get back to the main part of the village, you can call someone to help you.*

She started to walk with him, the gun pressed into her back as he walked just a footstep behind. Leah thought about the time they'd gone together to the shooting range. Even though it was ten years ago, Leah could remember everything there was to know about how to shoot a gun. She'd practised enough times. Thing was, the only gun near to her right now was the one that Terry had pressed against her back, so shooting him wasn't an option.

As they emerged from the country road and into the village of Balness, Leah looked along the road towards the house. Terry's car was parked not far from her drive. It

331

seemed her house was still asleep. Charlotte was nowhere to be seen and the street was empty. No one around to help her.

'Where are you taking me, Terry?'

'You'll see.'

They reached Terry's car and he opened the door, instructing her to climb in. She did as she was told and hoped that Samuel wasn't at his bedroom window, watching his mother being held hostage. She thought about running, but held no doubt that Terry would shoot her in the street and drive off. Terry had never been convicted for murder and she knew he'd killed many a gangland rival. Why would her death be any different?

As Terry climbed into the driver seat, he kept his eyes in front of him as he started the car. Driving through Balness, Leah glanced at her house and silently said goodbye to her family. Leah thought of the podcast she often listened to, the one about people who go missing and there is no trace of them ever again. The family never find out what happened to them. That was going to be her.

'Buckle up, Annie. We're going for a long drive,' Terry said.

Sixty-Seven

The car pulled into the car parking space and suddenly Leah felt like it had only been weeks since she'd last been here. The day that Terry had brought her here and put her on that boat was a day that she'd always remembered as a lucky escape. A life with Terry wouldn't have been exciting forever. It would have turned dangerous for her eventually. He was a gangster after all.

'Let's go,' Terry said, appearing at the passenger door and holding it open. 'We're taking a little trip down memory lane.'

Her phone in her pocket was her only lifeline and she was glad she'd put it to silent earlier. He hadn't mentioned anything about her having a phone and she hoped it would stay that way. But Leah knew that going out to Incharden would play havoc with the mobile phone signal and that even if she was able to call for help, she might not get through to anyone.

Stepping out of the car, Terry held the gun to her back again as he guided her down to the jetty. The same place they'd got on the boat the first time he'd brought her here.

'You remember this place?' he asked, his tone calm and sending an icy finger trailing down her spine.

'Of course I remember it, Terry. Ten years isn't a long time,' Leah replied.

'It is for me.'

They reached the jetty and a boat with an engine attached to the back bobbed up and down in the water. Leah regarded her situation. She was pretty much screwed. There was no one around and with a gun to her back, she had no choice but to do what she was told.

'Climb in, Annie.'

'Terry, I've told you my name is Leah now,' she said as she carefully stepped into the boat.

'Shut up and just do what I say, will you. I'm sick of people forgetting who they're fucking dealing with.'

Frowning, Leah watched as Terry climbed in after her and started the engine. She pulled the life jacket which was sitting on the floor over her head and looked out at the water. It was calm, almost like before the storm. It filled her with dread.

The boat eased away from the jetty and Terry steered it in the direction Leah had suspected. They were going out to Incharden. But why? Why would he be taking her there?

The same familiar nausea crept in that she'd experienced the first time around, only this time Terry wasn't comforting her like he had when they came out here ten years previously. Now he was the threat.

The short journey across the water felt like a lifetime but as the boat pulled into the jetty, Leah's heart sunk when she saw the small hotel and the difference in it from when she last saw it. Her memories of this island had projected beautiful images into her mind whenever she had thought of it. But now, staring up at Incharden Hotel, it looked more like something out of a horror movie.

'What happened to this place?' Leah asked, almost forgetting the circumstances as to why she was here.

'Innes and his wife died not long after you left me, Annie. He left this place to me in his will. His sons packed up and left for Australia. They still own the other islands but they're completely deserted. No one comes here anymore,' Terry said as Leah climbed out of the boat.

Stepping onto the jetty, she was careful of her footing as the wooden platform bobbed on the surface of the water. Making her way across it and onto the sand, Leah stared up at the hotel and a little part of her died inside. It was just her and Terry here. No one else. They were miles from the mainland and Leah knew that Terry had brought her here to kill her.

'I want to show you something,' Terry said. As Leah turned around to look at him, she wasn't surprised but terrified to see that the gun in his possession was still pointed at her.

'What is it?' Leah asked, trying to remain as calm as she could.

'You'll see. Come on.'

Terry took hold of Leah's wrist and walked her around the edge of the hotel building. The place still smelled the same as it did before, although now there was a black cloud hanging over what she'd once deemed one of the most beautiful places in the world she'd ever visited. If hell was an island, she thought.

Things had changed a little the further in they moved. The woodland around them was overgrown; moss surrounded the tree trunks and everything was green and full. If Leah didn't know any better she would have said she was trekking through the rain forest. Terry pulled at her wrist, silently insisting that she keep up with him. She stumbled a little, almost losing her footing. Moving her hand down to her pocket, Leah felt her mobile in there, covered by the long jumper she was wearing.

Please god let there be enough battery left.

They'd been walking for around ten minutes when Terry told her to stop. She did as he said and a sudden wave of panic took over. 'What are we doing here, Terry?'

'You see this island? I've always loved it, always wanted to be here when I was back in Glasgow,' he said, tucking the gun away inside his coat. Leah realised she still had her lifejacket on.

'This place was like my safe haven when the pressure of the organisation became too much. As much as I may look like I'm holding my shit together, Annie, I'm still just a guy trying to keep my head above water, you know what I mean?'

Leah nodded but tried to concentrate on her breathing technique. In for three, hold, out for three. Not that it helped. She still felt helpless.

'Ten years ago, I had it all, Annie. I had you, a thriving organisation, a best friend. I had my future in the palm of my fucking hands and then,' Terry stopped and snapped his fingers. 'It all went to shit, fell apart when you left.'

Terry stepped to the side and started moving his foot back and forth across the ground before stamping on it. Leah glared down at the soil, noticing the mound under Terry's feet.

'Terry, I'm sorry. I am. If I could go back and change it so you wouldn't get hurt then I would.' Leah heard the desperation in her voice.

Terry pulled his lips into a thin line, his eyes wide. 'I'm not hurt, Annie. I'm angry, *really* fucking angry. And you know what I do when I'm angry, don't you?'

Her knees were weakening with every second she stood in front of him, staring down at the mound beneath him. Her eyes traced the ground, to the left and to the right. Before she could comprehend what she was seeing, what she herself was standing on, large mounds began popping up all around her.

'Jesus, Terry is this what I think it is?' she whispered, hoping against all hope that she was wrong. This wasn't the man she'd met a decade ago. Back then, she was the broken one. But now, as she looked down, she knew that whatever had happened since she'd been gone, Terry Reid was so broken he'd lost his mind. Gone insane.

'These are graves?' she said, fear scratching at her throat. She found it hard to breathe.

'Normally I have someone on my side, there was always one. You or Richie. But you both fucked me over, Annie. And I never let anyone walk all over me, or take advantage.'

So he *had* found out about Richie? Or had he done something else to betray Terry?

Her heart crashed against the wall of her chest. Leah looked up at a gap in the trees to see a patch of blue sky peeking through the greenery. She knew what he was saying.

'They're all in here, waiting for you Annie. All the traitors, all the people who fucked me over or tried to. Your spot has been here all this time.'

Leah followed Terry's gaze and when she did, there was one mound just to the right of the others. But beside it was a plank of wood, laid flat on the ground. Her own grave.

Sixty-Eight

He watched as Annie clasped her hand over her mouth in shock. Of course she was shocked. It wasn't every day that you got to see your own grave. But that day had come for Annie Wicks. She well and truly deserved this, like the rest of them.

'Get in,' Terry said, lifting the wooden plank he'd placed over the hole.

'Terry, don't do this,' Annie replied. 'I gave you your money back, I've apologised. Can't we just leave it at that?'

Terry laughed loudly. Was she serious? How could she possibly think that she would get to walk away? 'Annie, you know who I am. You were engaged to be my wife. You knew what I did to people who crossed me and you turned a blind eye to it. Just like Kora did. Oh but now that it's you in the firing line all of a sudden you think I'm going to go all soft on you?'

'Terry, please?'

He couldn't stop himself, he was upon her, hands around her neck. Squeezing. Gripping. As he looked into her eyes, he saw Kora Anderson staring back at him. He should have killed her when he had the chance the first time around, made sure she was really dead, before she went ahead and tore his friendship with Richie apart. Bitch.

Annie dug her nails into Terry's hands as she tried to claw her way free. He closed his eyes, loosened his grip. Allowed Annie to fall to the ground. Staring down at his ex-fiancée, he too fell to his knees next to her as she hunched over, sucking and gulping in as much air as she could.

The day he'd found out about Richie and Kora's affair was a day he'd never forget. It hadn't been long after Annie had left. Maybe two, three weeks? He'd been sat in his office, listening to some Beethoven, trying to stay calm. He'd been angry with the world after Annie had left him. No explanation, no warning signs. Nothing. Just gone. Vanished from his life.

Richie had come into the office, face white as a sheet and eyes red around the rims. Terry had known something was terribly wrong, but he would never in a million years have imagined what was about to come out of Richie's mouth.

'I've got something I need to tell you, Terry. And you're not going to like it, but I have to be honest with you.'

Terry had sat forward on his seat, the music playing softly around them. 'Jesus, Richie. What's wrong? Are you ill or something?'

Richie had been quiet for a moment before he had raised his eyes to meet Terry's. 'I've been having an affair with someone. Someone you know. Someone you were close to once.'

Terry had frowned, leaned back in his seat. 'What are you talking about?'

'I didn't mean for it to happen the way it did. It was just sex, in the beginning. But I ended up falling for her, Terry. Big time.'

Jesus fucking Christ. Annie, Terry had thought. 'Annie? That's why she left?'

'No,' Richie had said, holding up his hands. 'Not Annie.'

'Then who Richie? For fuck's sake just spit it out.'

Richie had taken a deep breath, clearly nervous. Terry already knew their friendship was dispersing with every word that came out of Richie's mouth.

'Kora. I've been seeing Kora.'

Terry had hesitated, wondering if this was some kind of sick joke and Richie was just taking the piss. Having one of his comical moments. Not that it was funny. But Terry couldn't help but snigger. 'You've been shagging a dead woman? I tell you something Richie, your patter's getting worse.'

'It's true, Terry. That night I walked in and you asked me to take care of the body, well when you left I realised she wasn't dead. But in all honesty, I'd been seeing her before that. I'm not proud of it but you had to hear this from me. I was going to end it with her.'

Terry had got up from his chair then. 'Tell me you're kidding Richie.'

'Deadly serious. I'm sorry Terry. Annie knew but I had to tell you first.'

Terry had moved to the window, stared out at the grounds of his house. Breathing through the rage building in his chest.

'You mean before she did?'

'No. I feel like shit for what's happened,' Richie said.

'Let me get this right. You said you'd been seeing Kora *before* I asked you to dispose of the body? Then when you saw she was still breathing you helped her?'

Richie had nodded.

'Then you proceeded to carry on with your affair, even after the Frankie Conway situation. You saw what that did to me and you carried on anyway?'

'Aye,' Richie had replied quietly.

Terry had flown across the room then, throwing punches. Richie fought back, but Terry was too big and overpowering. It hadn't lasted long. Blood pooled beneath Richie's head. Terry had gone into a black hole and when he came out of it, his best friend, Richie Jackson was dead.

–

Annie sat up now, clutching her throat. Silence hung over them, aside from the birds singing above them in the trees. Terry stared at Richie's resting place on the island, just a few feet away from where he and Annie were sitting now.

'I was going to tell you, Terry. I was. I'm surprised he told you at all. He must have been worried that I would get to you first and...' Annie stopped speaking. 'I should have told you straight away. I'm sorry.'

'You're all liars, Annie. All in it for yourselves. You, Kora, Richie. The one person out of all of this who hasn't tried to fuck me over is Lee Whitelaw. And you know why? Because he knows the meaning of the word loyal. Our lives imploded at the same time, Annie. His nephew went missing the same time you left. We helped each other out, you know.'

Annie sat forward, wiped the tears from her cheeks and cleared her throat. 'What happened to Kora?'

Terry smirked, pointed to one of the graves. 'She's in there. I took care of her almost as soon as Richie. Buried them together.'

He saw the look of distress on Annie's face and moved towards her, shuffling along the ground to be next to her.

Gripping her face and pinning her against the tree, he pressed his nose against hers. 'They're all in there, Annie. Every single one of them. Even your kill is in there, Annie. Joe Allison, his brother. All of them.'

Turning her head, forcing her to look down at the graves of Joe and Eddie Allison, he heard her gag. It filled him with euphoria, all this power.

Annie struggled under his grip. 'Get off me, Terry.'

'Or what? You'll scream? Who's going to hear you all the way out here, Annie? It's just us.'

Getting to his feet, he pulled Annie up with him and pushed her towards the hole in the ground he'd dug for her.

'If you've got any peace to make with the world, now's the time to do it Annie.'

Sixty-Nine

Leah tried to keep her balance as Terry threw her towards the hole but she lost her footing, stumbled towards it and almost fell in. Landing just a foot or so away from her own grave, Leah spun her body around and saw Terry towering over her.

Scrambling along the ground, Leah pushed herself up and ran towards the edge of the island, zigzagging through the trees and the bushes that surrounded her. He had the gun, she knew that. And at any moment she expected a bullet in her back. But she couldn't give up. She had Samuel to think about.

She heard Terry calling after her but she kept moving as fast as she could. He was upon her, felt his fingers grasping at her hair and she was pulled back, landing flat on the ground. Terry climbed on top of her, pinning her to the ground so that she had no choice but to stare up at him.

He pressed the gun to her skull and Leah closed her eyes. This was it, the moment her life would end.

Click. Click. Click.

'Fuck!' Terry screamed, loosening his weight on her.

She opened her eyes and saw that he was fiddling with the gun. It had jammed. Terry got to his feet and as he attempted to pull her up, she aimed her balled fist right for his crotch, using an upright motion and connecting as hard as she could and gripping with her fingers. Inflict as much pain as possible and get as far away as possible.

Crying out, Terry fell to his knees and dropped the gun. Leah lifted it and threw it as far into the trees as she could and ran towards the jetty. As she ran, she struggled to get her phone out of her pocket. Running, keeping an eye on her footing and checking to see if Terry was behind her, Leah dialled.

'Please, help me. I'm on Incharden Island. He's trying to kill me and—' Leah felt the phone being pulled from her hand. A hard blow to the head sent her flying forward. White noise filled the inside of her head as white-hot pain coursed through her.

Her sight was blurry but she could see the sky peering through the tops of the trees as she was pulled by the feet back towards the burial site Terry had used the island for.

She was falling now, into a black hole. Soil and thick clumps of dirt were beginning to pile on top of her. Blinking away tears and dirt that scratched her eyes, Leah tried to open her mouth to speak, to plead with Terry not to do this. She was being buried alive – how could this be the way her life ended?

As the dirt piled on heavy, weighing her down, the darkness began to creep in.

Leah felt herself slipping away, easing her way out of life and into death.

Faces flashed into her mind. Samuel and Tom. As much as she loved them, she couldn't help but feel content at the idea that maybe she might soon be with Jack. Her beautiful baby boy Jack.

Heavier now, she felt her body begin to sink and pin to the soil beneath her as she fell unconscious. Jack was the last little face she saw.

Seventy

Opening her eyes, Leah tried to sit up, gulping and gasping for air. She felt a hand on her shoulder, a gentle squeeze. Panic rose up and out of her throat as she tried to scramble to safety – when she turned to see Tom sitting beside her.

'It's okay. You're safe. I'm here,' he said, pressing his face close to hers. She could see him clearly now, his eyes red and brimming with tears.

'Tom?'

'Yes, you're safe.'

Glancing around the room, Leah looked from left to right. Terry was nowhere around and she was alive. She began to sob as Tom pulled her close, tucking her into his chest with his arm. She was alive. But how? She recalled what happened on Incharden. Terry had thrown her into that hole after he'd smashed her over the head. He'd piled the dirt on top of her, hoping to bury her alive.

'How am I here, Tom? How did I get out of there?'

'You called for help? Remember? They were barely able to make you out but the police were able to track the location of your phone and they found you. That bastard...' Tom breathed. 'He was filling that hole up when the police got there.'

Leah let out a sob.

'They arrested him, managed to get you out and onto the boat where an ambulance was waiting.'

345

They arrested him, Leah thought. 'Oh god. The others. Tom, there were more graves. He told me.'

'I know, the police found them. The whole island is a crime scene. It's all over the news. There's a police officer stationed outside the door right now. Jesus Christ Leah, what were you thinking going off with him like that?'

Leah rested her head back on the pillow and raised a hand to her husband's cheek. She spotted dirt beneath her fingernails, remembers trying to claw her way out of the grave.

'I didn't want him anywhere near you or Samuel. It was bad enough he had found me.'

'You're going to have to tell me what happened between you both back then, Leah. I want to know why he wanted to kill you.'

Leah closed her eyes, saw the look on Terry's face as he pinned her to the ground, ready to shoot.

'Okay,' she said.

And she told him everything. No detail untouched. Leah laid herself bare and for the first time in just over ten years, she told Tom about Jack, how she met Terry and the money. About how she took Samuel from the Whitelaws.

Seventy-One

The trial of Terry 'The Bossman' Reid came to an end today at the High Court in Glasgow. Terry Reid, 46, stood accused of the murders of various criminal gangsters and associates which had gone unsolved for just over a decade.

The missing person's cases of drug runner Angus McDonald, drug runner and stolen goods pedlar Gareth 'Galzo' Pickering, and criminal brothers Joe and Eddie Allison had gone unsolved, until their remains were recovered on the island of Incharden, which was owned by Reid. Their bodies were recovered after a distress call went out to emergency services by a woman who cannot be named for legal reasons. When police arrived at the scene, they were astounded to find that Terry Reid was in the process of burying a woman, who was a key witness for the case. Fortunately, the woman was saved and the case was able to go to trial.

Forensic officers found a total of six graves on the island, four of which belonged to the above named. One other belonged to that of none other than Richie Jackson, Terry Reid's right-hand man and business associate.

The crime community as well as police were shocked to find Jackson's body on the island and had no explanation for it. Terry Reid to this day has made no comment on Jackson's death.

The last grave contained the remains of Kora Anderson, one-time lover and fiancée of Terry Reid. She'd gone into hiding after it was reported that their love affair ended on bad terms and her family reported her missing in 2011.

Post-mortems concluded various reports on how each of the victims died, but they all echoed the same name. Terry Reid.

The 'Bossman' also stands trial for various drugs and gun trafficking charges and as this report goes to print, various apartment complexes around the country which were contracted to Reid Constructions have had the tenants removed and the apartments are being excavated, as authorities are led to believe that there could be a higher body count, with the possibility of victims having been hidden in the foundations of the buildings.

Lee Whitelaw, a known associate of Reid's has also been sentenced to a minimum of twenty-five years as an accomplice in the deaths of Gareth 'Galzo' Pickering, Richie Jackson and Kora Anderson.

Members of the victims' families are said to have breathed a sigh of relief and cheered when the sentences were read out in court today. Reid showed no emotion as he was led away from the dock, whereas Mr Whitelaw hung his head and sobbed.

As this report goes to press, it is understood that the notorious Collins brothers have been arrested in connection with the murder which took place in the

St Enoch Centre car park. They're also wanted in connection with the deaths of other gangland criminals in the city. If convicted, they could face many years behind bars.

Seventy-Two

'Jesus, Maisie are you okay?' Annie called, shaking Maisie by the shoulders. She opened her eyes slowly and peered up at Annie through bloodshot slits.

'What the hell happened?' Annie cried, checking Maisie over. 'Who did this to you?'

'Galzo,' Maisie croaked. 'Bastard started laying into me before he left.'

Both women turned their attention to the door as the sound of baby Gareth crying alerted them.

'Annie, I can't get up.'

'It's okay, I'm on it,' Annie said, leaving the room quickly to tend to the baby. Maisie winced as she tried to sit up, pulling the needle from her arm. As Maisie got up, Annie reappeared at the door. Gareth had stopped crying.

'What are you doing?'

'I need a plaster for this,' Maisie glanced down at her arm. Annie led her through to the kitchen and pulled open every cupboard until she found a first aid box. Annie gently wrapped Maisie's arm and led her back through to the lounge. Sitting down on the sofa, Annie sighed.

'Are you sure you're okay?'

'I'm fine. Just sore. He's a bastard, Annie. I finally realised I was better off without him and he bloody lost it,' Maisie said. 'What are you doing here anyway?'

'Oh, don't worry about that now. A business thing but I'll leave Terry to worry about that.'

Maisie relaxed and felt the enormity of what had just happened to her creep in as she began to cry. Annie hugged her close as Maisie sobbed, the sound seeming to wake the baby again. Annie got up and went to the bedroom.

Maisie Whitelaw watched as Annie Wicks walked into the lounge, holding baby Gareth. The smile on Annie's face gripped Maisie's heart in a way she hadn't felt before. Not once had Rosie ever looked at her like that. She'd never experienced a mother's love before.

'Is he okay?' Maisie asked.

'Seems to be,' Annie replied, sitting down next to her. 'I think he's just hungry.'

'Can you feed him? My arm is so sore.' Maisie glanced down at the bandage Annie had dressed her arm with and a sadness took over. How could she have been so stupid to let Galzo back in? He'd always managed to do it, no matter how he treated her. She'd been clean from heroin since she'd fallen pregnant. He'd wanted her to take it, so he could deem her unfit to look after Gareth. And she was. Always knew that she would be just as incapable as Rosie.

Annie prepared a bottle and fed the baby. He seemed so much more settled with her than he ever had with Maisie.

'What did Galzo say to you, Maisie?' Annie asked, looking up from the baby as he sucked on the teat of the bottle.

'Said he wanted Gareth, he wanted to be a proper dad. He does want the baby but only to use as a weapon against me. Poor wee guy doesn't know what he's been born into.'

With raised brows, Annie looked horrified. 'You have to go to the police, Maisie. You can't let him get away with this. Just look at the state of you.'

Maisie shook her head. 'I can't bring the police to Lee's door. Not now that he's on his feet and away from that shithole, Mainhill. I wouldn't want to put him at risk. Or me. I know the police would take one look at me, see who I am and where I'm from and Galzo would get a warning, if that.'

Annie fell quiet and returned her gaze to Gareth. She was engaged to Terry Reid, so she must have understood that involving the police when you were part of the underworld in any way, even indirectly, wasn't an option.

'Have you got children?' Maisie asked, shifting the subject.

Annie hesitated for a moment. 'I did. Once. Not so long ago actually.'

'What happened?' Maisie shifted on the couch into a more comfortable position. Her ribs ached terribly from the beating earlier, and nausea was setting in as the effects of the heroin began to wear off.

'He died. Sudden infant death syndrome.' Annie didn't raise her head, instead kept her gaze on Gareth. Maisie felt a lump form in her throat.

'Oh my god, Annie. I'm so sorry.'

'You weren't to know.'

'How's Terry about it all?'

Annie raised her head sharply. 'Baby Jack wasn't Terry's. And he doesn't know so don't you say a word, alright? I don't want him knowing. Not yet.'

Maisie nodded and she held Annie's gaze. A silence fell upon them then and Maisie knew in her head what she wanted. A chance to get her life together, get as far away from Mainhill as physically possible. As far from Galzo as she could. She'd had no role model of a mother to base her newfound motherhood on. She had no idea how she would cope, raising a baby when she had a drug problem and no money. Rosie had failed Maisie. She didn't want to keep that cycle going.

'Do you want another baby, Annie?'

'Honestly, it's all I've thought about since Jack was taken away from me. No baby would ever replace Jack. But holding this wee guy now, my heart breaks. You're so lucky to have him Maisie, that's why you need to get yourself sorted so you can take care of him.'

Maisie was already crying and when Annie looked up at her, she was crying too. 'Annie, I want you to take Gareth.'

'What?'

'I want you to go. Tonight. Take him tonight. Be the mum I can't be. You can adopt him, make it legal. But you have to...'

Annie got to her feet. 'Maisie, what are you talking about? I can't just take him with me tonight. What would Lee say? What would Terry say?'

'They don't have to know. I could make out as though Galzo took him when I was off my face. Please, Annie. You're the only hope Gareth has of having a normal life. My parents failed all of us and I can't let that happen to him. Please. Take his things and go. Please Annie.'

Annie appeared to be in shock but Maisie had never felt so heartbreakingly sure about anything in her life. This was the right thing for Gareth. For the first time in her life she wanted to do something selfless.

'Why don't you come with me?' Annie whispered.

'No. I have to get better on my own. You deserve to be a mother, Annie. I don't. I'm only a kid myself and a junkie. He doesn't deserve that.'

Maisie took Annie by the hand and pulled her to the bedroom and started to pack Gareth's things. Bottles, formula milk, clothes, blankets. She could barely see what she was doing through the tears, every muscle and bone ached as she moved. She threw things in the bag quickly and Annie followed her, looking shocked and helpless.

'I have to do this quickly before I change my mind.'

'Maisie you don't have to do this. If you need help, I can be the person who supports you. You don't have to give your baby away. Please, Maisie I know what it feels like to lose the most precious thing in the world. You will regret this.'

'No, I won't Annie. If I keep him, he'll end up in the system before he's fifteen. You've seen what Mainhill is like. I'd regret not giving him up for a better life just because I love him.'

'How are we going to do this? I mean, oh god this is insane, Maisie. You're just going to hand him over and what?'

'Start off the adoption process. I want you to have him.'

Maisie began pushing Annie towards the door of the flat and handed her the bag. 'It's not like I won't see either of you again. We can keep in touch. You can tell me how he's doing.'

'This isn't the kind of decision you can just make at the click of a finger, Maisie. There are things to think about,' Annie said, gripping Maisie's wrist.

'I have to make this decision quickly. Lee will be back soon. It's now or never. If I tell him I want to give him up for adoption he won't let me do it.'

Annie was sobbing with Maisie now as she wrapped an arm around her gently. 'Maisie, I don't know.'

'I do,' Maisie wept as she bent down and kissed her baby boy on the forehead. 'Go. I'll be in touch soon. Just promise me you'll do a much better job of being his mum than I have.'

Annie opened her mouth to speak but couldn't as she sobbed. Turning, she left the flat and Maisie closed the door before rushing through to the kitchen and ripping the bandage off her arm. She shoved it into the bin, piling rubbish on top of it.

Wiping the tears away from her face with the back of her hand, she went through to the lounge and looked out of the window to see Annie's car pulling away from the building and disappearing from sight.

Maisie sat down on the sofa where Annie had found her and glanced down at the needle Galzo had left for her. There was just enough left to take one more hit. But if she overdosed, where would that leave Annie?

Sitting forward, Maisie grabbed the cushion from behind her and placed it over her face before she let out a cry from the depths of her soul. Maisie didn't know it yet, but giving up her baby was the most motherly thing she could have ever done.

Seventy-Three

Present Day

The sun shone outside on the street and Leah sipped at her coffee mug, watching the world go by. People came and went, but she kept her eye on the door. Samuel sat opposite her, playing the latest version of candy crush on his iPhone.

'You okay over there, wee man?' Leah asked.

He raised his eyes briefly from the screen and smiled. 'This is the best present ever. Thanks Mum.'

Smiling, Leah returned her gaze to the door of the café. They'd been sat there for almost twenty minutes before the door opened and she saw her come into the café. Leah got to her feet and waved before moving towards her.

'Hey you,' the woman said and Leah hugged her close.

'How are you?' Leah asked.

'Nervous. But in general terms, I'm good. Just finished my final year of uni and start my probation year as a teacher in a primary school up in Aberdeen,' she said as they sat down at the table.

'Oh that's fantastic news,' Leah said.

'How are you after the trial?'

Leah sighed. 'Getting there, bit by bit. It doesn't get easier. I still see him, every night when I close my eyes.

But now that he's behind bars, I know he can't hurt me anymore.'

They fell silent for a moment and Leah took another sip from her mug. 'But enough about all that. Come on, I want to introduce you to someone.' Leah took her hand and led her to the table where a waitress took Leah's order of two fresh coffees.

Samuel looked up from his phone and sighed. 'Can I have a cake?'

'And a cake, please,' Leah smiled. The waitress nodded and left.

'Samuel, remember I said that I was meeting a friend here today. Well I'd like you to meet her,' Leah said. Samuel looked up at the woman as she sat down across from him.

'Hi,' he said. 'I'm Samuel.'

The woman smiled and Leah saw tears glistening. She swallowed hard and briefly glanced at Leah before returning the introduction.

'Samuel, it's so lovely to *finally* meet you. I'm Maisie.'

Samuel smiled back and got up from the table to choose the cake he wanted from the counter. Leah reached over the table and took hold of Maisie Whitelaw's hand. Emotion caught in Leah's throat when she saw a tear roll down Maisie's cheek.

'I can't believe how much he's grown.'

'I know. He'll be towering over all of us soon,' Leah chuckled.

'Leah. Thank you. I couldn't have asked for a better mum for my son.'

Lea's squeezed Maisie's hand tighter. They both turned to see Samuel tucking into some cake and grinning widely at them.

In all the madness, the years of fear of being found, it all came down to this. In all the decisions and mistakes they'd made, they'd got this one decision right.

A letter from Alex

I have sat down to write this letter to you and can't stop thinking about the year we've had. 2020 has been like something from an apocalypse film. Being stuck in the house from March to August meant I was able to shut myself off from the terrible things that were going on in the world and I focused my time on writing, not one but two books. *The Housewife*, the second book I wrote in lockdown and book five with Hera Books, took just a few months to write and I absolutely loved the process. It took me just a few months to write. In those few months, I created the Mainhill Estate, a crime organisation and a book filled with characters all fighting their own demons. I absolutely loved creating Annie and Leah's stories. And what a world apart they were.

I really enjoy exploring the gangland crime genre and finding out just how far I can push my characters. The Reid Organisation, the Whitelaw family, the Martins and Annie developed into so much more than my initial plans imagined, and I truly hope that you enjoyed reading about the dramas which unfolded within the book.

I want to thank you for coming back for book five. It really is amazing to think that you've enjoyed the previous books and have come back looking for more. If this is your first Alex Kane book, then I hope it has spurred you on to read more.

I'd love to hear your thoughts on *The Housewife* and would thoroughly appreciate it. Alternatively, you can contact me directly. I'd be happy to chat to you about the book. You can contact me via:

www.facebook.com/alexkanewriter
www.twitter.com/AlexKaneWriter
www.instagram.com/alexkanewriter
alexkaneauthor@gmail.com

Once again, I'd like to thank you so much for all the support you've shown me from the day I released my first novel with Hera Books. And thank you for reading *The Housewife*.

Best wishes

Alex Kane

Acknowledgments

As always, I want to start off by thanking Keshini Naidoo and Lindsey Mooney for their hard work at Hera Books. If it wasn't for them, I don't know where I'd be. It has been an honour to watch Hera grow from strength to strength and knowing that I am a part of that is amazing. I want to thank Keshini for her expert editorial skills, her ability to know exactly what I am thinking in line with my stories even when I don't know it myself.

Thank you to Dushi Horti for the little details, as always. And thank you to Andrew, my proof reader.

I want to thank my agent, Jo Bell. Adding you to the team of strong women behind me has only helped me to feel stronger as I aim for my dream of becoming a fulltime writer.

I also want to thank my family, especially my parents and my husband. You always check on me to see how I'm doing when writing, always ask how my books are doing. Chris always brings the tea and biscuits to fuel the story. I'll be forever grateful.

Finally, I want to thank the readers. Again, you have come back for more from me and if it wasn't for you I wouldn't have a writing career. So, thank you so much. You genuinely have no idea how close I am to living my dream and it's because of you.